Birdcage

Victor Canning's first novel *Mr Finchley Discovers His England*, was published in 1934, since when he has been a full-time author, with over thirty novels to his credit. He has also written many short stories and serials which have been published in the principal newspapers and magazines of England and America. Born in Plymouth in 1911, he was a features writer for the *Daily Mail* before World War II, during which he was commissioned in the Royal Artillery. He has worked as a scriptwriter in Hollywood and now lives in Devon.

Also by
Victor Canning in Pan Books

Victor Canning

Birdcage

Pan Books in association with
Heinemann

First published 1978 by William Heinemann Ltd
This edition published 1980 by Pan Books Ltd,
Cavaye Place, London SW10 9PG
in association with William Heinemann Ltd
© Victor Canning 1978
ISBN 0 330 25934 2
Printed and bound in Great Britain by
Hazell Watson & Viney Ltd, Aylesbury, Bucks

And you all know, Security
is Mortals' chiefest enemy.

Shakespeare (*Macbeth*)

chapter one

The bus, because of the unevenness of the road, lurched and swayed so that the old man sitting across the way from Sister Luiza had trouble with his eating. Cradled in a red handkerchief spread over his knees were fish croquettes and a piece of *queijo da serra*. With the flat of an old bone-handled knife he scooped up the runny mountain cheese and carried it to his mouth, holding a croquette under it to catch the drips. From behind him in the crowded bus someone called out to him and laughed. He turned, grinned, and then made a jerky upward thrust of the knife, his old face crinkling with pleasure, and mumbled an answer. The words were mildly lewd, suggestive. They gave her no offence. From long-held habit she shut them from her mind. A transistor radio began to play loudly from the back of the bus and a woman's voice, deep, husky and sensual, complained of a lost love.

She turned her head away and looked out of the window. The road was flanked by a growth of green cork oaks. Against their dark background she saw the reflection of her own face as though in a mirror and the flight of a hoopoe across the crests of the trees. She made no attempt to avoid her own reflection; seeing her own face was no longer a lapse. For her now there was no longer any *mea culpa* to make, no chapter of faults to lay before her confessor. For a little while now she was free to turn back to a personal liberty which she had renounced when she had entered the convent. Three months ago her body had betrayed her. The victory of flesh over spirit had been no sudden triumph. Her own spirit and nature, she knew now, for eight years had slowly worked against the anguish of her longing for the true calm of deep love and holy devotion to the service of the Saviour. Now there was nothing that could move or touch her except an earthly pride strong enough to bring her here in this bus and to serve her for a few more short hours.

The old man reached beneath his seat and lifted a wine skin to his mouth. As he drank his adam's apple pulsed above the brass stud of his collarless shirt neck and a small purple floret of a fading lupin bloom in the band of his shabby black trilby hat shed itself and lodged in his lap on his red handkerchief. A youth with a jacket slung over his shoulder moved past her and stood by the driver who took half a cigarette from behind his ear. The youth lit it for him. His patched blue shirt was stretched tightly across his shoulders and his hips were as slender as a girl's. Sister Luiza dropped her eyes and her fingers smoothed the surface of the letter which rested in the pouch made by her belt across her scapular. Across the way from her the old man belched, and the radio began to play a military march. Sister Luiza watched the road. There had been a time in the distant past when she had known it well and had been happy sitting with her mother in the back of the big Rolls while Giorgio drove, green-liveried with silver buttons, the sun flashing from the polished blackness of his peaked cap, hating the moment soon to come when he would have to turn off the road and take the rough track to the beach with his beloved car, and her mother chattering away, restless as a bird, flourishing her cigarette holder, leaving little trails of blue smoke from the Balkan Soubranie cigarette ... her mother dead now for years.

The bus began to slow down. When it stopped she got up and moved forward. The youth jumped down to the road. They were the only two leaving the bus. She took out the letter and handed it to the bus driver.

'Would you be kind enough to post this for me when you get to Lagos?' She spoke in Portuguese.

'Of course, Sister.' He nodded absently. She spoke his language confidently and without fault, but he knew at once that she had no claim to it by birth. He took the letter and put it on the wind-screen shelf.

'Thank you.'

She got down and stood at the side of the road until the bus had passed on. The young man was already striding away down the road, whistling to himself. He raised a hand to the bus as it passed him. She waited until he was out of sight round a corner. Crossing the road she took a path through low umbrella pines, a path that sloped and twisted gently finally to join the rough road, gullied and worn with winter rains, which Giorgio had hated. The last time she had come down this way was when she had been fifteen, a year before her mother died. Her father had been with them, a rare event.

The sun was low now and the western sky had a brilliant green and blue glow, bold kingfisher colours. Through the trees she now and then caught a glimpse of the sea, calm under the windless evening. For that calmness she was grateful.

She walked on, void of any disturbing emotion, passing along the side of a tile-capped villa wall overhung with swatches of bougainvillaea and trailing geraniums. Some late-flowering wild white irises grew along its foot and the yellow plaster of the wall was daubed with political slogans in red paint. At the bottom of the slope the road swung right, became soft with drifted sand, and ran between a handful of small, poor houses and reed-thatched beach cabins. Outside a wine shop three fishermen sat at a rough table drinking. They watched her go by without curiosity, but a long and low-bodied brown and white nondescript dog with a high curled tail joined her and trotted ahead.

A woman stringing beans under the reed-thatch of a cabin watched her pass, giving her a brief nod as her hands worked automatically at her task. The dog led her away from the houses out on to a stretch of sandy ground. On either side it was furrowed and green with the growths of vegetables and young maize. The circular wall of an irrigation well carried a notice that the water was unfit for drinking. Swallows and swifts flew low over the ground, hawking the flies and gnats. From ahead came the sound of crying gulls. Between the red rocks of the small valley mouth she saw the smooth run of the sand edged with a gentle foam break of an idle sea. It was here that Giorgio had always stopped the Rolls, carried the beach baskets and umbrellas to the sands and had then driven off to return eventually at his bidden hour, Giorgio with his hard, brown impassive mask of a face that never changed expression no matter her mother's uncertain moods.

With the dog still trotting ahead she walked clumsily across the sand. Behind her, far down the long beach, fishing boats were pulled up clear of the water and a few men were working around them. The tide was high, almost at its turn, and she felt that there was a righteousness about this small chance. The tide would take her where she wanted to go. Seeing its calmness the serenity which was in her grew, leaving no room for fears or doubts. As she walked she turned her head to the left, freeing her eyes from the limiting coif and the stiff frame of the guimp about her face, to give herself a full view of the far-reaching waters. She had been taught to swim here by her mother who loved the sea, and here, too, her father had once raised an arm in anger to strike her for spilling a glass of red wine over his white immaculately creased trousers. The blow had never fallen but she could remember even now the fine shake and tremble of his body and raised hand as he had forced control on himself. Released now from the disciplines of charity and forgiveness she could frankly acknowledge that he had never had any great love for her. From her mother, yes . . . love and affection poured out, bright, warm and enveloping, spendthrift and bounteous with her caresses and tenderness.

She moved over a footing of low, bare rocks, around the point of a headland covered with tamarisk bushes, and came to a small cove, still with solitude, the dying shimmer of rising heat from the sun-baked rocks breaking the clarity of sea and beach. Far out where sea and sky met there was no firm break, only a nacreous haze of pale colour like the inside of the sun-dried mussel shells that littered the beach.

She sat down in the shelter of the low cliff. The dog came to her and gave a short bark. When she ignored it the dog turned away to the sea's edge and began to forage along the drift line. She watched it, unmoved by its company. Then, because long-held discipline had no force now, she freed her hidden hands from her habit and idly picked up a small stick, bleached ash-grey by the sea and sun, and took a mild pleasure in the smooth run of the wood under her fingers. The dog came back and curled to sleep on the sand at her feet. The sun died slowly into the sea, the rock shadows lengthened and over the fast-darkening waters the gulls cried with a monotonous melancholy. With the polished stick in her hands, her fingers turning and working over it as though it were the rosary which she carried in the big pocket of her long serge skirt, she sat until full darkness came. The dog still stayed with her. A high thin mist almost shrouded the stars. The sea drew away from her as the tide ran out.

She stood up and slowly began to undress. The dog, expecting true movement, ran to and fro for a while and then came back and whined in disappointment. With a deftness gained over the years she shed her clothing, folding, arranging and laying each item neatly over a flat rock top. The clothes were not hers, they belonged to the Order. Not wishing to know her own nakedness she kept on her undershift and her long coarse woollen stockings. She set her heavy black shoes on top of the pile of garments. Last of all she undid the tight drawstrings of the cap which covered her head, folding it and then tucking it into one of her shoes. For a while the night air, moving over her close-cropped hair, surprised her gently with its cool caresses.

She walked down to the sea's edge and the dog came with her. Without hesitation she waded into the water, only a little aware of the cold as it rose above her thighs. She stopped, feeling the drag of the wet shift growing, and then dropped her hands so that they took the freshness of the sea. Behind her the dog barked and whined, running to and fro along the water's edge. She felt the slow roll of the sea move across her belly and she lowered herself until the lip of a rising swell moved smoothly over her shoulders. She swam out with easy, unhurried breast strokes, the strength of her limbs bearing her up against the drag of her shift and the slack pull of her black stockings. A few hundred yards out she turned and looked back to the shore. Distantly a car's headlights wheeled briefly and low against the sky. To the east a cluster of lights from an hotel and its garden chalets trembled in the night. Above the beach where she had undressed a villa's lighted window was cut by the black shape of an almond tree. From the slow movement of the tree's silhouette across the window she knew that the tide was under her now and, setting her offshore, was taking her steadily westwards. She was content to go with it, content to wait for coldness and fatigue to league with her will. As she turned her face away from the shore she felt the stocking on her left leg slip down to her ankle. Without thinking she reached down and pulled it free from her foot. The tide took her away from the land faster now. A little later she freed herself of the other stocking.

The curly-tailed dog went back to the wine shop and settled on the sandy wooden steps of the terrace. Sitting outside still the three fishermen were drinking the red *vinho de casa* and eating grilled slices of tunny-fish, the *atum di direito* which were now running in shoals along the coast, heading for the Mediterranean to find its river mouths for their spawning. None of them gave a thought to the nun who had passed by. Mosquitoes whined around the naked light bulb that hung from the vine-laced terrace roof. One of the men belched against the sourness of the wine and threw a scrap of tunny-fish to the dog.

A rat foraging the stranded tidal sea-wrack along the shore scented strangeness in the air and turned from the water's edge to find the nun's clothing neatly piled on its rock. It nibbled for a while at the starched edge of the guimp and then went back to the sea as, far to the west, its lights distantly seen, its four engines faintly heard, a TAP Boeing 707 headed for Las Palmas, the Cape Verde Islands and Rio de Janeiro.

As the lights of the Boeing faded into the night Sister Luiza, who had been born Sarah Branton, the daughter of Lieutenant-Colonel John Branton and his wife Jean, and who knew herself to be nearly three months gone with child, felt coldness and exhaustion possessing her to the point where she longed for the charity of oblivion. She raised her arms above her head and let herself sink below the water. She went down deep only to find that the body, the spirit's great betrayer, fights always for survival and lives at war with death. In the brief darkness she found her body traitor to her will and her beating arms and legs brought her back to the surface, retching and choking. She found breath and for a long time hung with slow, feeble strokes of her arms on the strong swell which a freshening breeze had raised.

Richard Farley sat with his feet outstretched, his heels on the edge of the stone kerb of the fireplace. A pile of old pine cones flared with yellow, blue and green flames in the grate, spitting and crackling. He sipped his brandy and found it tepid from the warmth of his hand about the bowl of the glass. He was a man close to his forties, dark-haired and dark-eyed, his face hard and brown, carrying a battered look and close to being ugly. He wore a loose blue linen shirt patched on one shoulder and with two of the front buttons missing. His light-coloured drill trousers bore ancient stains of oil and tar. He was nothing much to look at, knew it and had long ceased to care. He heard Herman Ragge moving about upstairs, heard the sound of running water from the bathroom and then the familiar knock-thump, knock-thump of the villa's ancient cistern filling. He sipped at his brandy and then leaned back in his chair and began to doze, the glass cradled in his hands on his lap. He was awakened by Herman Ragge taking the glass from his hands some time later.

'You were spilling it over your trousers.' Herman went to the sideboard, helped himself to brandy and topped up Farley's glass. Coming back he squatted on a stool by the fire, gave Farley his glass and said, 'Another of your strays?'

Farley lit a cigarette. 'I suppose so. It seems that there's always someone who wants a bed, or a boost or a handout. Like calling to like, maybe. Or perhaps I haven't learnt the trick of saying no to the wrong people. However, I didn't have any option tonight.'

'Why did you call me?'

Farley considered Herman. He was a big, rugged man who could give him ten years in age. He had a lion-tawny head of hair, a great smiling gash of a mouth and he was as safe as a father confessor with any confidences. He played guitar in the band at the Palomares Hotel by night and worked a few hectares of olives and lemons by day. He was a Berlin-trained medical man but had never gone into practice because his guitar and a taste for a carefree life had claimed him. They liked and understood one another.

'I had the feeling she might not want anything official made of it. If I'd called a pukka doctor he would have had to report it. And anyway, Marsox brought the launch in to the beach just below and we carried her up here – and you were handy. The nearest doctor would have been a couple of hours getting out here. How is she?'

'I gave her an injection and a sponge down. Don't worry if she sleeps the clock round.'

'How does a woman dressed like that fall overboard unnoticed? Or was she pushed?'

'How far out were you?'

'Couple of miles – we'd just begun to get into some fish.'

Herman unhooked the stethoscope from around his neck and pushed it into his jacket pocket. 'She could have come off the beach and the tide got under her.'

'It's a bit early in the year for night swimming. And just wearing a shift? And what's she doing with her hair cropped like that?'

Herman grinned. 'You can ask her when she comes to. She's a well-made, good-looking woman. Late twenties, I'd say. Perhaps she just swam out wanting to end things.'

'If she did she changed her mind. She was screaming like a banshee and when I got to her she damned nearly ripped me apart in her panic. Look—' Farley pulled his shirt open to show the deep scratches on his chest. 'I had to hit her hard to quieten her before I could do a thing.'

'You want something for those scratches?'

'No, thanks. I rubbed some stuff in that the Holderns had in their cabinet when I changed.' He breathed deeply. 'I tell you there was a time when I thought we were both going to go under for good, but old Marsox got alongside and fished her aboard, where she just passed out—' he grinned suddenly, 'as near stark naked as didn't matter a damn all among the tunny we'd caught.'

Herman stood up. 'All right, Richard. I'll look in tomorrow evening. But if you want me sooner give me a call.'

'Thanks, Herman.' Farley went with him to the door. 'Did she say anything to you at all?'

'No. But I think she was conscious until I put her under. I'd say she was in a state of shock . . . or maybe just didn't want to have to face anything or anybody for a while. See you tomorrow.'

Farley stood at the door and watched him to his car. The headlights came up and bleached the olive trees and the oleanders with a false frost. He stood there for some time after the car had driven off.

When he went up to bed he looked into her room. Herman had left the door open and a shaded lamp switched on. She was lying in bed with her face to the wall, the covers pulled high over her neck and she was breathing heavily. Marsox's big launch rug in which they had wrapped and carried her lay on the floor by the shuttered window. He went in, picked it up and folded it, feeling its dampness. Over a clothes horse hung the coarse white shift, palely stained with washed-out blood. His blood. When he had got to her she had clamped herself around him like a wild animal, tearing and gripping him and they had gone down together . . .

He went out, taking the rug and the shift with him. He left the lamp on and the door open. In the bathroom he switched on the electric towel rail and hung rug and shift over it. In his own room he left the door open so that he could hear her if she moved about or called in the night, though he doubted she would. Herman would have sedated her heavily. He stripped, put his pyjamas on and said his prayers. He was asleep within ten minutes.

He was up early the next morning. The woman was still sleeping, her position unchanged. While he was having his coffee and toast Maria, the Holderns' old caretaker and house servant, arrived. He told her that there was a guest in the spare room who did not want to be disturbed. When he told her that it was a young woman she showed no surprise. He had often taken over the Holdern villa while they were away on their annual trip to England and she knew that there was nothing like that where he was concerned. Just before Maria left at noon he heard Marsox's motor cycle come into the villa courtyard and the sound of his voice booming in talk with Maria, who was a little deaf. Marsox ran a small fish restaurant with his old mother and also did holiday fishing trips with his launch in the season.

When he came in he gave him a glass of wine. Marsox, who was sixty-odd, scrawny and as hard as a cork oak, had the gentlest of manners, a fine singing voice and had never married because he preferred a running freedom of choice – much to his mother's chagrin because she longed for grandchildren.

Farley said, 'She's sleeping still. Herman came and gave her an injection. We've caught some queer fish – but never one like this.'

Marsox grinned. 'Beautiful fish. I'm going to Faro. You want anything there?'

'No, thanks.'

'You don't do anything about her yet? Tell the police, or something?'

'No.'

'That's right. It's better to wait to see what she says. If you do something for a woman without asking – then it's always the wrong thing.'

After Marsox and then Maria had left – she only worked in the mornings while the Holderns were away – he went upstairs. She was still sleeping, though she had changed her position so that her head was turned to the window and one arm and her shoulder and part of her breast were showing. There was a bruise on the left side of her chin where he had struck her hard to quieten her struggles. As he pulled the bed cover across her nakedness he told himself that he should have looked out one of Helen Holdern's nightdresses for her. When she recovered he would have to tell her to take some of Helen's things; they were much the same size and build and Helen would not mind. As it was he went through to the Holderns' bedroom and found a dressing gown and a pair of slippers which he left in her room by the side of the bed. If she came to while he was working at least she would have some cover if she wanted to move around. He had a cold tunny-fish cutlet and a glass of vino for lunch and then went out to the swimming pool. Part of his arrangement with the Holderns for his accommodation was that he should repaint the swimming pool and the villa's shutters. That was how he liked things. It was good to do something with one's hands, good to stand back and admire the fresh paint or plaster or masonry work. He was working and whistling when Herman's car came through the open wrought-iron gates and up the drive.

Herman sat on the swimming pool wall and said, 'You should take it up professionally. How is she?'

'Sleeping her head off at lunchtime.'

'I'll go and have a look at her. Came over now because I've had a call for a rehearsal at the Palomares this evening. They reopen next week.'

He went into the house, but was there only a very short while. He came back and said, 'She's still sleeping, but normally. Her pulse is all right. She'll be shouting for food and attention soon. I'll look around tomorrow to get the news.'

'What news?'

'Well, what it's all about. Who she is and so on and why she was out there. Don't you want to know?'

'Not really. It can't be a rollicking happy tale, can it? I like jolly stories.'

Herman shook his head, laughing, and threw a pine cone at him and went.

Farley worked on, whistling gently to himself. A lizard, beady-eyed and beautifully bronzed, came out of a wall crack on the pool surround and watched him. The swallows flew low over his head. Two hoopoes called to one another and the first bee-eater he had seen that year came and perched on the pole which carried the telephone line to the villa. Butterflies rested on the bougainvillaea and sunned their wings. God was in His heaven, he thought, but he did not know about the rest.

When Sarah Branton woke the late afternoon sunlight was flooding through the balcony window. From somewhere outside she could hear someone whistling 'Greensleeves'. It had been many years since she had heard the song and she lay relishing the sound which was welcoming her back to life. Her memory was perfectly clear and void of any distress. She had wanted to drown herself and her body had betrayed her ... Sister Luiza was dead, Sarah Branton lived. But the Sarah Branton who lived now was far removed from the Sarah Branton of the convent school, the noviciate years and the final vows. Whatever or whoever she was now time would discover. For the present she was in no hurry to come to any discoveries about herself. A man had come into the sea and fought her panic and rescued her. She was reborn and there slowly began to build in her a warm stir of happiness and gratitude untroubled by any questioning of its source. She was alive and glad to be alive. And this time she could choose her own way of living ... not let herself be manipulated and directed by others ... a puppet with no will of her own, no life until others moved or jerked the strings which gave her the semblance of living.

She got out of bed and in the long bedroom mirror she saw the slim white nakedness of her body for the first time in years. Without any shame or sense of breaking any rules now she eyed herself, remembering the time when her body had been tanned from sunbathing. Briefly she ran a hand over her abdomen which showed no sign of growing fullness yet, touching herself without shame, knowing the beginning of the first of many freedoms to which she had been reborn.

She slipped on the dressing gown, swayed with a moment's passing giddiness and had to sit on the edge of the bed to recover. Then she put on the bedroom slippers and went out on to the small balcony. The full warmth of the sun greeted her as she stood breathing in the resin-scented air. A few sparrows quarrelled and foraged around a handful of bread crusts someone had thrown on to a small strip of lawn which was bordered by lemon trees, the fruit hanging in shining, sunbathed colour against the dark green leaves. Away to the right was a small orchard of almonds, the blossom long gone and beyond them, through a break in a clump of tall pines, she caught a glimpse of the sea. For a moment or two her body trembled with its own memory of the dark moments of terror which had seized her. She looked away from it to her right and, as though to greet her, was met with the sound of fresh whistling and saw a man standing in a swimming pool painting one of the side walls.

She made a move to turn back to the bedroom, but was halted when the man looked up and saw her. He raised a hand in greeting and then climbed out of the pool and walked towards her. He stood below her and said in Portuguese, 'Are you all right?'

Just as other people knew with her she sensed that it was not his native tongue, but she answered him in the same tongue, 'Yes, thank you.' Then, because she knew him from the tangled panic moments of her rescue, she was momentarily betrayed and filled with a sharp coiling of emotion and confusion, she laughed and said, 'You've got blue paint on your face.'

He touched both his cheeks with his finger tips, examined them and said, 'So I have.' This time he spoke in English and his brown ugly face was gullied with a broad grin.

She said in English, 'You were the one, weren't you?'

'Yes. I'm Richard Farley. Are you hungry?'

'Well . . . yes. I think I am. But, I don't really know about anything at the moment.'

'No need to rush things. Would you like something up there or come down?'

'I'd like to come down but I've no clothes.'

'No problem. Second door on the right down the corridor. There's a big wardrobe in there full of stuff. Take what you want. You're about the same build as Helen.'

'Helen?'

'Helen Holdern. She and her husband Jim have gone off to England. I just caretake. Helen won't mind. I'll go and knock something up for you.' He paused for a moment or two, then smiled at her and said hesitantly, offering comfort, 'It's all a bit of a rum do. But don't worry. No need to rush things. We'll get it all sorted out. No matter what it is, you're safe here.'

He turned and walked away around the house. She stood there, trembling from the warmth of his kindness, breathing deep the warm, flower-scented air, and momentarily closed her eyes against the soft press of slow rising tears.

The master bedroom was lofty and elegant with its own bathroom. The floor was covered with pale pink tiles and blue rugs, both colours repeated in the coverings of the twin beds and the long curtains at the windows. It was a feminine room, the still air faintly touched with the fragrance of scent, the dressing table holding a silver-mounted toilet set and cut-glass containers and jars all set out neatly and sparkling in the light from the window. She had a distant memory of her mother's untidy dressing table and with it a much closer remembrance of her own little bedroom cell at the convent, bleak and barely furnished. She picked up a silver-backed hairbrush and ran it over her own short hair and her mouth twisted wryly at its intransigence. Well, time would alter that and there was all of time before her and no hurry to decide how she would use it. For the moment she was free from any claims or routines being put on her. With a calmness which surprised her she went about selecting clothes to wear. After eight years of the same habit her freedom of choice was too fresh an acquisition to stir her. She opened the wardrobe and picked out a plain blue heavy cotton dress with a high collar and a skirt which came well down over her knees. In a dressing-table drawer she found a brassiere which by lengthening its strap was a comfortable fit for her full breasts; breasts – the memory swam back, making her half smile now – which had embarrassed her by their early fullness when she was a schoolgirl. In the same drawer she found brown tights, a small pair of white panties and a short silk underslip. In the bottom of the wardrobe was a row of shoes but as they were all too small for her she settled for a pair of loose *alpargatas*.

She dressed slowly, more and more aware as time and the actions of this new, unexpected life flowed by and possessed her that she was a stranger to any Sarah Branton or Sister Luiza she had ever known, that in her power lay the gift of creating a new personality. The richness of that miracle was too immediate, too heady for her to think about rationally. For the time being she could only stay poised on the crest of present movement and the forced decisions of each passing minute. Hanging partly over the dressing-table mirror was a large white silk square decorated with wavy blue lines. She folded it and wrapped it around her head in a bandeau to mask most of the starkness of her short hair. Then, as she looked at herself in the wardrobe mirror, looked into the eyes of a stranger, saw the discoloration of the bruise on her chin where she had been struck in her panic and remembered the black horror of the night, she felt the strength go from her body and her head began to swim. She sat down on the dressing-table stool, held her head in her hands and could find no will in her to control the violent trembling which possessed her body, could do nothing but sit and let the cold passion in her body exhaust itself.

She had no idea how long she sat there before her body began to quieten as the storm passed. All she knew was that, with a swift lift of relief, she felt a hand touch her shoulder gently and his voice said comfortingly, 'Don't worry about it ... It's sort of delayed shock. Just when you think it's all right, you suddenly remember. I've had it. Smack between the eyes just when you least expect it. Just hang on there for a minute.'

Through the dying turmoil of her mind and body she heard him clatter down the stairs. When he came back he put his hand under her chin and lifted her head. Through the mist of tears in her eyes she saw that his face was still paint-marked; an ugly, brown, comforting face, full of warmth and concern. In that moment she knew the fullness of her debt to him and knew that it must be repaid, had to be repaid, no matter the price asked or secretly assessed by herself.

He put a glass in her hands and said, 'Here, drink this.'

Holding the glass, looking up at him, not wanting to lose the comfort of his face, she shook her head and said, 'It's brandy. I can't.'

With a sudden roughness, he shook her shoulder and said, 'You drink it – or I'll make you. Go on!'

It was then that she gave him a small smile, blinking at him through her tear-confused eyes, knowing that this was the first time that this man, to whom she owed her life, had asked her to do something for him and there was no refusing him, not in this or in anything else he might ask of her. She raised the glass and drank, drank fully, hating the raw touch of the spirit in her mouth and throat, but drinking gladly and silently pledging herself to him, to serve him and to ask nothing from him except the charity of giving her some way of repaying the debt she owed him for her own salvation – no matter whether he had been sent from God or the Devil.

With a sudden chuckle, he said, 'That's it. Down the hatch. And then we'll get some food inside you, and you can tell me the whole sad story.' He eased her to her feet, stood back a little from her and then, giving his sudden puckish grin, said, 'And I'll tell you something – you look a damn sight better in that dress than Helen Holdern ever did.'

There was a small vine-and-rose-covered patio on the far side of the house from the swimming pool. She sat at a glass-topped table and he fussed over her and chatted away easily, leaving no long silences to embarrass her and avoiding any questions about herself. They would come and she would answer them, but he spread an atmosphere of protecting warmth and care about her, a slow caressing and gentling to smooth all emotional disturbance from her.

He was a good cook and there was a neatness and easy deftness in his manner and moves which surprised her from his stocky, craggily built body. His hands were big and short fingered, but they moved without clumsiness or hesitation. Now and again, as he served her and she ate, his dark green-flecked brown eyes would hold hers and his big mouth would stir with the edge of a reassuring smile. He brought her a salad of young lettuce hearts and green peppers and a cheese omelette which she found herself eating with relish. It was with some first small surprise that she found herself reaching without any reservations lingering from the past for the glass of dry white wine which he poured for her.

She said, 'You're a very good cook, and also very kind.'

He shrugged his shoulders, pleased with the compliment and said, 'Well, the first is a sort of professional thing. I used to run a *ristorante* on the coast down here. Went bust though – good cooking isn't all. You've got to have good management with it, and I'm a lousy manager. As for the kindness ... well ... I've been in bad trouble too at times and know the value of a helping hand, a friendly word. Now you take your time and eat and drink. I'm just going to clear up my stuff from the pool.' He nodded to a brass bell on the table. 'Ring that if you want me. Also ...' he hesitated and scrubbed at his chin with a hard, brown hand. 'Well, it occurred to me that there might be someone ... you know, someone who ought to know right away that you're alive and well, and not to worry about you.'

She dropped her eyes from him momentarily, touched the side of the cool wine glass with one finger, not wanting to reveal her sudden emotional stir at his concern. Keeping her eyes from him, she said, 'No. Not for the time being anyway, thank you.'

'Fair enough. Well, don't let the omelette get cold.'

She looked up then, gave him the shadow of a smile but could find no words for him and knew as he gave her a gentle wink before turning away that he was matching her feelings with an instinctive sympathy and understanding.

She heard him whistling as he collected his gear from the swimming pool. She ate and drank, surprised now by the contentment building in her. In the convent you were one among many, all love and emotion directed to the Blessed Saviour, making of each Sister an isolated world. To have this man wink at her with warm compassion, though he knew nothing about her, was like the sudden burst of bird song in winter; a warm, ugly, solid man, bringing back to her all the beauty of the world, rousing in her for the first time in many, many years a sense of her own personality, marking for her with his manner the fact that she was a woman hungry now to dedicate herself to a new devotion ... to the richness of a world which she had once thought was gone from her forever.

He was a long time away from her. When he came back he had changed into a light blue denim jacket and trousers and a white cashmere turtle-necked jersey. The paint was gone from his cheek and his dark hair was damp and glossy from the shower he had taken. She had heard him singing under it while she had sat and watched the sun drop towards a range of low hills to the west. He cleared the stuff away from the table into the kitchen and coming back said, 'The sun's going. We'd better go inside. I've lit the fire.' He pulled the chair back from her as she rose and then lightly took her arm and escorted her into the house, where he settled her into a chair by the fire. Sitting across the fireplace from her he was silent for a while, watching her while he fiddled with the lighting of a pipe. When the tobacco was drawing, he said nothing for a long time, just sat and looked at her with the flames of the fire burnishing one side of his face. Then with a sudden grunt and jerk of his shoulders he sat forward and said, 'It's only just occurred to me that, of course, it's all your business and you may not want to go into it. If so, that's ok. You don't have to say anything. You can borrow some clothes – and money too, if you want – and I'll telephone for a car for you. What I mean is that you don't owe me anything more than, well—' he grinned suddenly, '—than a polite thank you for being in the right place at the right moment and pulling you out of the drink. So just say.'

She shook her head violently. 'No, no. I owe you everything and I want you to know everything ... and, well if it's not awkward, I would be glad to stay here a little while. You see ... I've only just come back into the world and I've been very fortunate because you were there to bring me back, and I know you are a good man and this is a good place and—' She broke off, bereft of words, tears beginning to touch the corners of her eyes.

He laughed quietly and said, 'And I make a fair omelette, and just take it easy, and of course you can stay. Here.' He pulled a clean folded handkerchief from his breast pocket and handed it to her.

Sarah blew her nose and wiped the corners of her eyes. When she would have handed the handkerchief back to him he shook his head. A lock of damp hair fell loosely across his forehead and she suddenly saw him as a boy and as a young man with that spring of unruly hair and she knew again, but this time with the balm of near adoration for him, that she never wanted to leave him for his coming had been directed and her loving servitude fixed for her forever. Whatever he wanted from her he should have, whatever he dreamed of for himself would be her dream and part of her passion would be to provide it for him. Feeling all this, she knew, was far from hysteria, far from a search for comfort for herself. No matter who or what had shaped the design of their lives so that she sat here now, she believed beyond all doubt that it all had been immutably fated.

Straightening herself up, fortified by the removal of all doubts, she smiled briefly at him and said, 'I was a nun ... for eight years. I walked into the sea to drown myself from shame. I'm three months gone with a child. But when it came to the point I couldn't let myself go. I wanted to live and – you gave me back my life.'

He said nothing. He just looked at her blankly for a while. Then he slowly put down his pipe and walked across the room to the pinewood sideboard. She heard the thin notes of glasses touching and the sound of drinks being poured. He came back, a glass of brandy in his hand, and stood above her, palming one hand about the bowl of his glass. Suddenly he smiled and said, 'I was a bit slow. Your hair I mean. I did think of prison, but I was pretty sure they didn't do that these days, not even in this country. But a nun never crossed my mind. What's your name?'

'It was Sister Luiza but before that and now it's Sarah Branton.'

'I prefer Sarah. English or Irish?'

'My father's English. My mother was Irish.'

'I thought I heard it there somewhere.' He lowered himself into his chair and gave her a sudden grin. 'Well now, that's the main part cleared up. Are you sure about the child bit?'

'I've missed three periods.'

'Your mother's dead?'

'Yes.' It was easy to answer now.

'But your father isn't, and what about the convent people?'

'I wrote a letter to the Mother Superior telling her what I was going to do. As for my father, I've been dead to him for a long time. Anyway, he and my mother parted when I was quite young. I've got an aunt living still in this country, but she spends most of her time in America. I really haven't got anyone.'

'What about the man. The child's father?'

'I want to forget him. It was all my fault. He's a doctor who works in the little hospital run by the convent. Sometimes I can't believe that it ever happened. That it was all a dream.'

'Perhaps it was. Anyway, we'll get Herman to look at you. He'll know.'

'Who is Herman?'

'A doctor friend. He tucked you into bed and gave you an injection to make you sleep long.' He was silent for some time, gently biting the edge of his lower lip, and then he asked, 'Would you have been happy to stay on at the convent if this baby thing hadn't cropped up?'

'I don't know.'

He shook his head. 'It's my experience that people who say they don't know are usually really quite certain but don't want to commit themselves. You wanted to get out, didn't you?'

'Yes, I did but all this happened before I'd really made up my mind.'

He gave her his big, crooked smile then and said, 'You know what I think? I think you just want to flop back and let things ride. You can take it from me that walking into the sea doesn't seem to be your style.'

She smiled hesitantly back at him, tightening her lips a little to control the emotion which flooded through her at his soothing kindness and naturalness and then said, 'You make it all seem . . . well, natural and not all that important. I can't tell you what that does for me.'

'Don't try.' He got up and walked to a radio-cassette player that stood on top of a low run of bookshelves. Over his shoulder he said, 'You just stay there and get smoothed out. I've got to go and shut the hens up and put the goats in their shed for the night.'

Behind her she heard the click of the player switch. The room was suddenly and gently touched by the sound of music. She lay back and closed her eyes, feeling the slow caress of violins gently wrap itself about her, knowing with a deep gratitude that some kind fate must be working for her that he should bring her to life with one of her favourite Schubert pieces.

At that moment in his rooms in Cheltenham, Arnold Geddy, the senior partner in the solicitors' firm of Geddy, Parsons and Rank, stood looking down at the late afternoon traffic moving along the Promenade, the light April rain washing the young growth of the trees with a soft gloss that took the reflections of car and shop lights in brilliant ripples of gold and silver. He sighed for a moment with a rare emotion ... forty years a solicitor, and always people, people and their problems. Not a moment of real satisfaction in his professional life such as a man would know if he could take brush and palette and capture on canvas the colour and life he looked down on now. He smiled ruefully, recognizing and touched by his rare moment of romantic excess.

He was a short, plump man, going a little bald and with a smooth face, pale, touched on the cheek bones by fine vein bursts, a face which he could control to a neutral, unmoving passivity to show no signs of his emotions or dreams to others.

The telephone on his desk rang and he reached behind him and picked up the instrument.

'Yes?'

'Mr Geddy, sir – the international exchange are on the line, a personal call for you from Portugal. But they want to know if you will accept the reverse charges. It's from a Father Dominic at Lagos.'

For a moment or two he made no reply. But there was no surprise in him for he knew quite well who Father Dominic was, though he had not spoken to him for years. Then with a partly suppressed sigh he said, 'Yes, tell them I'll take it.'

A little later Father Dominic came on the line and they talked together for about five minutes. Afterwards he got the girl to call Lieutenant-Colonel Branton's house and ask if the Colonel could see him that evening. The girl rang back to say that the Colonel was away fishing in Wales and would not return until late the following afternoon.

As he put the receiver down Mr Geddy shrugged his shoulders. What did it matter? It could wait until tomorrow or next week or next month. The Colonel would be completely unmoved to know that his pregnant nun daughter had drowned herself. But there were others who would not. He picked up the second telephone on his desk which gave him a direct outside line by-passing the switchboard and dialled a London number.

As he waited he sighed, remembering the girl, fair-haired, quiet and shy; and then the mother, all brightness and quicksilver . . . aye, and reckless too, with a greed for the good things of life and with a ruthlessness which had given her all she wanted.

chapter two

Although it was still cold at night she slept with her window partly open and the curtains drawn back. As she lay watching the stars and the black silhouette of a cork oak against the sky there was a tranquillity in her which she had never known before, a deep calm which left no place for anxiety. Everything, she knew, would be resolved with time. Nothing had happened by chance. Everything which had happened to her since leaving the convent – and maybe long before that – had been ordered. The power behind the ordering she did not question. She was simply grateful for it and could have no curiosity whether it was or was not benign. She was logical enough in her thinking to realize that the future might not bring her happiness, but that was not important. She lived now for a purpose, to serve a man as she had once felt called to serve Him. Where she had failed before she had no doubts of any failure in the future if this man gave her the chance. Nobody else might understand her conviction. She had been sent to him because he needed her. That truth was hidden from him now, but he would know it one day.

For the rest of that evening they had sat either side of the fire talking a little but offering no intimacies to one another. Most of the time they were silent, listening to the music he played for her on the cassette. She needed no more than that, taking the music to herself and losing herself in it. Coming up to bed he had suggested she should leave her door open so that she could call to him. She smiled to herself in the darkness, seeing and hearing him. His face for a moment serious, his under lip pushed out, and then his sudden smile as he said, 'Well, you never know. The night's a bad time for reliving things – waking or dreaming. So if you want me just yell. I'll leave my door ajar.' It was at that moment, although she had never known it for herself that she realized what he was being to her; a brother to a sister who was in trouble. She was content with that as she knew she would be content with anything he wanted from her or wanted her to be to him.

Thinking about him she drifted into sleep. When she awoke it was to a morning of strong wind, blowing from a cloudless sky. He brought her breakfast in bed; orange juice, coffee and toast, and a small pot of home-made strawberry jam and another of marmalade, all laid out meticulously on a fresh tray cloth.

Smiling at him, surprised by how relaxed she immediately felt with him, knowing, too, that she was genuinely glad to see him, she said, 'It all looks very professional. I don't see how you could have failed with a restaurant. And this.' She reached out and lifted a small jar from the tray which held a few heads of Spanish bluebells.

He smiled. 'You'd be surprised. I'm an expert at failure. Still, to be true I didn't do too badly when I sold it. Got a fair bit of my money back. Shall I pour the coffee for you?'

'No, thank you. Do you know ...' she hesitated a moment, '... I can't remember the last time I had breakfast in bed.'

'Well, enjoy it now.' He turned away to the door, but when he reached it he stopped and looked back at her and said with a touch of guilt in his voice, 'I've got to tell you something. I hope you're not going to be upset. But I thought it was a wise thing to do.'

'What is it?'

'Well, you said you wrote a letter to your Mother Superior about what you were going to do. She'd have got it either yesterday or this morning. I thought it was a wise thing to let her know you were safe. You know what the police and the authorities are like in this country. And your clothes on the beach and all. Somebody's probably found them by now. So ... well, you must see that it's better they know you're alive so that they get a chance to cover up.' He grinned suddenly. 'Convents don't like scandals. You did say you were pregnant to them?'

'Yes, but no more than that. Not who. And, please – I'm not upset about it. You did the right thing. How did you know the right convent? Oh, yes, of course, I told you last night. But whom did you speak to?'

'The portress I suppose it was. Anyway, I made her write it all down and then read it back to me. I just said that you were all right and safe and so on. I didn't say where you were or who I was, but I did promise that you yourself would telephone some time today. Is that all right?'

For a moment she lowered her head and with the tip of her finger touched one of the bells of a *jacinto dos campos*. She was nothing to this man, he had saved her, taken her in and comforted her, and in everything he did and said there was a kindness and humanity which overpowered her. She looked up and smiled. 'Everything is all right and I don't know how to tell you—'

'Don't try,' he cut her short gruffly. 'Well, enjoy your breakfast.' He went out quickly. But from the top of the stairs he shouted to her, 'When you take your bath don't worry about the tom-tom noises the cistern makes. With any luck I may get round to fixing it for the Holderns before they get back.'

But she scarcely heard him. Her whole being was engulfed by the warmth of him. Her eyes filled with tears and she felt her body begin to shake so that she had to hold the handles of the breakfast tray to steady herself.

*

Herman Ragge came at mid-morning and went up to see Sarah in her bedroom. Farley went out and turned the garden sprinklers on and then went round to the swimming pool to go on with his painting. The window of Sarah's bedroom was closed. Maria came out and began to hang up some washing on the line rigged in the orchard. He heard her talking to the hens and the pegged-out goats which were the idols of the Holderns' eyes. She came back and with her empty laundry basket on her hip stood and looked down at him, black-skirted, a black knitted shawl over her white blouse, her old face as brown and lined as a walnut and a man's black felt hat on her grey hair. There was usually not a lot of talk between them except on small household matters, but now and again she could be disarmingly straightforward and percipient.

Now she said in almost bad-tempered tones, 'Senhor Farley, she comes from the sea. It is not good for her to be in this house. It is not good for you.'

'How do you know she comes from the sea?'

She nodded briefly to the orchard where her washing hung. 'I take her shift this morning and wash. It is stiff from salt water. No other clothes. She wears the Senhora's. When I am in her room making the bed this morning she stands by the window and gives me nothing but a good morning and then her back but already I have seen her eyes.'

'She was probably embarrassed.'

'No. When you ran *Il Gallo* you were good to my man and gave him a job. Now, for this, I tell you. She is a witch. She is not good for you.'

She used the word *bruxa* ... witch, sorceress ... and Farley smiled. Her half-crippled husband had often used the same word about her. Maybe, he hid his smile, it was a matter of professional jealousy. He said, 'Maria, she was in trouble. I can't tell you any more than that. I just did what anyone else would do.'

She shook her head. 'You always do more than anyone else. Don't keep her here. Otherwise there comes trouble – for you. When I go back today I will look for it.'

'Where? In a crystal ball?'

'That is my business. Maybe I tell you about it, and maybe I don't. But anyway it will be good for her to go, and better for you.' She gave a pugnacious jerk of her old head and turned away to the villa.

Farley went on with his painting, smiling to himself, and thinking about her husband, Cesar, who had a withered left arm, a sporadic passion for the bottle and an aged but lively eye for the girls. He had helped around the kitchen and the bar which had given him opportunities for both his passions. Still, with one arm he did more work than many men would have done.

When Herman came down Farley fetched some beer from the house and they sat in the shade of a Judas tree, its blossoming long over.

'Well, how did you get on with her?' Farley asked.

'I don't know. She puzzles me.'

'How?'

'Well, she was polite enough. Shy, too, a bit. But I don't think she wanted to have much to do with me. She thanked me for what I'd done for her and I sensed she thought that was the end of the matter. She was over the hump and there was no more to do except say a nice thank you. I had to persist a bit.'

'Why?' Farley began to pack his pipe slowly.

'Well, you told me she'd said she was pregnant. After all – and I told her this – she'd been in the water a long time, damned near drowned. That's the kind of thing that can muck a pregnancy up. But she said she felt well and unworried, and there was no reason for me to do anything. Just from her manner I knew that the last thing she wanted was me giving her a proper examination. So . . . I just took her temperature, pulse and all that. She's ok. I told her so, and she eased up a bit.' Herman grinned and then drained his glass. 'As a matter of fact I think she was afraid of me as a doctor, not as my charming self – and that if I gave her a thorough examination I might tell her something she didn't want to know.'

'Such as?'

'That she was just convincing herself that she was pregnant when in fact she wasn't.'

'But that would be ridiculous. She missed three periods.'

'Ach! What's that? A woman can go off for months but she doesn't have to be pregnant. At this stage only a proper examination and a urine test could tell. She could just be anaemic.'

'She doesn't damn well look it.' Farley spoke almost sharply. He had the feeling that Herman was hiding something from him, and because of this and their long friendship he said frankly, 'Come on. Cough it up. You don't have to keep anything from me. She looks bonny enough. What is the score with her? You're hinting at something. Let's have it.'

Herman tossed a pebble at a green lizard on the path and gave Farley a sideways look. 'The trouble with you, Richard, is that you always believe what people say. Take them at their word. You've been let down often enough by it but you still don't learn. All right, so I'll give it to you straight. I think your Sarah Branton, or more properly Sister Luiza, is probably a classical example of a common form of female hysteria.'

Farley gave a dry laugh. 'Well, that's a fine statement. What does it mean?'

'It means that where you help lame dogs over stiles without a second thought, a doctor can't help considering the lameness. Is it real or is it faked?'

Farley laughed. 'I'm having a great morning. First Maria tells me she's a *bruxa* and I should get rid of her. And now you say she's just worked up some kind of fantasy for herself – even to the point of chucking herself into the sea!'

'Listen, you idiot. I think Maria in a way is right. She's bewitched herself. I think she wanted to get out of that convent. But her pride wouldn't just let her admit to them that she couldn't take it any longer. There had to be some reason she couldn't ignore. I think on some small incident she built up a whole fantasy for herself. Nuns get crushes on doctors and priests. Somewhere along the line something happened that made her think she'd had intercourse with a doctor and had become pregnant. She believed it so absolutely that her periods stopped. The Lord knows what the details are but the fantasy became real.'

'Even to the point of walking into the sea?'

'You'd be surprised. There's nothing more demanding than a fantasy. She only broke free from it when the moment of drowning came. That's when reality returned – and luckily you were there.' He stood up. 'You like to bet on it?'

Stiffly Farley said, 'I don't bet on that kind of thing. All I know is that she's in trouble, real or imagined. Trouble's trouble, and I don't think being clinical about it helps any.'

'I'm not surprised. But we happen to have different views and a different approach to people. She's had eight years of fantasy being a nun. She creates another to escape from it, the ultimate escape that we're all free to take. That's bad. But worse is why someone so clearly unsuited for the life ever embraced it. It's bad enough to have a fight each day against time and chance without other people brainwashing you or twisting your arm to make you do what you don't really want to do.' He knuckled the side of Farley's face affectionately. 'We friends still?'

'Of course we are, you damned idiot.'

'All right. If you want me – give me a ring. *Bruxa*, eh? That's typical Maria. She feels things without fully understanding them. That's more than a lot of people do.'

'Maybe, but I just don't know. I don't like to think of people screwing themselves up in the way you suggest.'

'Nor I, but they do. However, I don't think your lovely sorceress will take long to come back to normal. Not with a nice, soft-hearted guy like you to bring her back to earth.'

Farley smiled. 'Sometimes, the way you talk – you make me feel that I'm no more than a universal plaster, a cure for all ills, going around slapping myself on people's troubles and making them feel fine again.'

'Not far from the truth. You're a soft touch. Always a bottle of the milk of human kindness in your pocket. You attract the wrong kind of people. The kind who realize at once that they can get anything you have to give. How many drifters along this coast owe you money?'

'Quite a few.'

'And they'll owe it forever.' Herman chuckled. 'You're the one who should withdraw from the world – tuck yourself away in a monastery. Brother Ricardo, safe from spongers and lame dogs.'

'Get away, you ass.'

'All right. Call me if you want me.'

When Herman was gone he sat for a while thinking over the things which had been said. He was not fool enough to deny to himself many of the things Herman had said about him. But what do you do, he thought, about the way you are? Were, are and always would be, he supposed. Anyway, there was little point in thinking about it. He picked up the drinks tray and went into the house.

Sarah stayed in her room until Maria had left, and then she came down to him. He was stretched out on the settee, reading the previous day's *Daily Telegraph* which Maria always brought up with her from the village.

He stood up, smiling, and said, 'Well, how are things?'

She said, 'I used the upstairs telephone and called the convent.'

'How did it go?'

'I spoke to the Mother Superior, but not for very long. I just said I was all right and not coming back. That I was in good hands . . . that I was sorry for all the trouble and so on.'

'Did she ask about the child business?'

'No. She just gave me her blessing and said she would pray for me, and that was that. Oh, except that she said she would let my father know I was safe, and that I should write to him.'

'Will you?'

'No.'

'I think you should.'

She smiled. 'I knew you would think that. Well, perhaps later I will. But I'm telling the truth when I say that I mean nothing to him. He and my mother were more or less separated when I was quite young. Just now and again for appearance sake he would come and spend a few days with us.'

'Well, that's that.' For a moment or two he was silent, remembering Herman's lecture about her and his own too-abundant good nature. Then, moved by a touch of resentment about his own softness, he went on, 'So what are your plans now?'

'Well, I thought perhaps you'd let me make lunch for you. I'd like to be in a kitchen again. I always used to enjoy it. And then . . . well, I would like some clothes of my own to wear. I could put a scarf around my hair this afternoon and we could go and do some shopping . . . say at Albufeira or even Faro. Only I would have to borrow some money from you – only for a while. Until I can arrange things with my aunt.'

He nodded. 'Fine. Let's start with the lunch. The kitchen's all yours. If you can't find anything you want just shout.'

'I'll manage.'

He watched her go and then sat down with his paper and stared at it blankly. His own 'So what are your plans now?' had not been meant for the immediate future, but so what now about the whole business, herself, her future and the child had been in his mind, and he felt that she must have known this and deliberately evaded it. Well, perhaps not. After all, for Christ's sake, she had not got herself really on her feet in the present yet. Plenty of time for the future. He should know that for there had been a time with him when only the present counted, when the past and the future were not to be thought about. *Bruxa* – what an absolute lot of nonsense. She was just a badly shaken woman, probably still obsessed with those awful moments when she had thought she was going to drown. It took a hell of a long time to live that kind of thing down. He should know. Bad memories lived on, lurked always in the mind, waiting to ambush you when you least expected it.

Arnold Geddy drove without haste along the Cheltenham to Cirencester road. It was early evening, a lovely April evening when, he told himself, the beauty of everything hit you suddenly and made your eyes blink on the verge of tears. An early rhododendron was a great flaming beacon of colour. The sudden flood of song of a blackbird was so exquisite that it was almost painful, while a roadside kestrel hovering over the tall grasses, wing tips trembling, seemed fixed not for the moment of kill but for all eternity. Daffodils, grazing sheep, a cloud shadow across a pond starred with milkwort, and away to his right where the land fell sharply away from the Cotswold scarp the distant pearl-grey ghosts of the rising Welsh hills . . . all fixed in the mind, impressed there one would think for ever. But in a few hours one would forget it all. Forgetting the important things was the easiest of things, remembering the unimportant gave no trouble. Not at least to him. Remembering details of a deed drawn up years ago gave him no trouble. Ghastly things he had seen and taken part in during the War came back without trouble, but try as he might he could not remember the face or the frock or the true timbre of the voice of the woman he had walked a night beach with at Positano and made love to in a hotel room on a brief summer leave from his regiment. Maybe that was why he was a good lawyer. He remembered all about the deeds and contracts and conveyances. He smiled, knowing himself so well and this mood induced by the bite of spring. The few war years had been his great escape. He mourned with levity the true Arnold Geddy who had foundered somewhere years ago. *I weep for you, the Walrus said, I deeply sympathize.* He suddenly laughed out loud with happiness, an emotional outburst reserved mostly for moments like this when he was driving and alone. He was glad the woman was alive ... the solemn-faced, good-looking girl with the golden hair; glad that she had escaped. Good luck to her. And glad, too, that he had not been able to see Colonel Branton yesterday to give him false news of her drowning.

John Branton lived on the outskirts of a small village to the west of Cirencester. The house was old and of Cotswold stone. The gardens were large and badly kept and the driveway was full of potholes still filled by yesterday's rain. The house had once been a rectory and the ghosts of the former churchmen who had inhabited it, Geddy thought as he drove up, must be highly disapproving of the life style of its present owner, who would probably die leaving a heavy mortgage on it.

The present Mrs John Branton – the union, it was rumoured, unsanctified by Church or regularized by the State – opened the door for him. She was red-haired, her face still boldly good-looking but loose-skinned, her body – he made no effort to suppress the wayward thought (after all he was a bachelor and owed no ties to any woman, except minimal ones to a lady he managed to visit once or twice a month in London) – a splendid creation for bolstering any man's concupiscence. But Geddy thought, for himself, the butter was spread too thick.

'Arnold! How lovely to see you.' She pushed her face forward to be kissed and faint on her breath he smelt her evening gin.

'Not come to pester dear Johnny with legal or money matters, I hope? God, no – he's in a mood. Four days on the Wye and not a fish.'

'Nothing like that, my dear Dolly.'

'Good. Go right through. He's expecting you.' She gave him a friendly push with a heavily ringed hand to start him across the hall towards the study.

Branton was sitting at his untidy desk hunched over a multiplying fishing reel patiently unravelling a bad tangle of the line. He stood up as Geddy came in and tossed the reel on to a couch untidy with fishing gear.

'Bloody bird's nest. Take me hours to get it out. Well, enough of my troubles. That's only a small one. How are you? Looking damned smug and prosperous as usual. No good offering you a drink if you're driving, is it?'

'No, thank you, John.'

'Well, shan't let it inhibit me.' He waved Geddy to a chair and then went to his sideboard to pour himself whisky. He was a tall man, strong, with a good figure still. His face was long, handsome and ravaged, his blue eyes deep sunk under bushy, greying brows, his near-white hair thinning to show the pinkness of his scalp.

There were times, Geddy thought, when he knew that he positively disliked this man; and there were other times when, because he hated human waste, he felt a deep, warm sympathy, near to affection, rise in him for the Branton that had been and, somewhere along the road, had lost his way. He was as selfish as a pig at a trough – but it had not always been so; and the change had been far from his own doing.

Over his shoulder, he said, 'Well, what brings you out here? God—' he nodded through the window, 'look at that garden! You pay a man a fortune a week, and he spends half his time smoking in the greenhouse. My father had four gardeners and a groom and there wasn't a weed in a bed or a badly turned-out horse.' He turned and smiled, and the ghost of young manhood shadowed him briefly. '*Sic transit gloria* what-have-you. So let's have your little bit of dreariness. Or are you going to break your record and tell me something good?'

'I'm afraid not. It's about Sarah.'

'Sarah?' Branton cocked a bushy eyebrow, puzzled.

'Your daughter Sarah. Or Sister Luiza.'

'Oh ...' Branton sat at his desk, sipped his whisky and said, 'What's she done or undone? Or is it really serious and I have to prepare myself for crocodile tears? Sorrowing father, send a wreath and all that?'

His reaction did not surprise Geddy. He shrugged his shoulders. 'No ... a little more complicated. She got herself pregnant somehow and she's run away from the convent.'

Branton slowly shook his head. 'She's her mother's daughter, isn't she? All right, spell it out for me.'

Precisely Geddy told him of the two telephone calls he had had from Father Dominic. 'She eventually telephoned the Mother Superior and said she was safe and being looked after, but gave no details of where she was. Naturally you had to know.'

Branton shook his head, unmoved. 'Not naturally. By law, I suppose, but not naturally. For a consideration, long since squandered, I gave her mother my name – wedding bells and orange blossom, and a nice big settlement. Damn little of that left now. I'll hand it to her for guts – running away. Pregnant, too. Well ... that's in the blood lines. Her mother would go to bed with anyone if the dividend was right. Even Giorgio. He bought it, you know. Few years ago. Got tanked up too much and drove his employer's Mercedes over the edge of some corniche.' He grinned. 'Probably because he hated the Mercedes. Giorgio was a Rolls-Royce man. Anyway, she's not my problem. Do I sound callous to you?'

'No, you sound as I expected you would. As your lawyer I had a duty to tell you, obviously.'

'Obviously, and thank you, Arnold. Have you let Bellmaster know? She's his girl. He might feel inclined for sentimental reasons to pick up the pieces. Though I doubt it. He's as short on sentiment as I am.'

'I got in touch. But he's abroad. I left a message for him with his confidential secretary.'

Branton drained his glass, thumb-and-fingered his big nose, and slowly shook his head. 'The biggest mistake I ever made was falling for her mother, and doing the big thing. All that Sir Galahad

38

or whatever it is stuff – while all the time they were just bloody well using me. Captain John Branton. There was a lot of talk from Bellmaster about pulling strings. He was in the War House then. Bright, coloured baits being dangled before me. Brigadier, Major-General. He could have worked it, too. But once I was gaffed and landed, I was just left flapping on the bank.'

'You got the settlement. Legally that was all that was promised.' But there was more to it than that, Geddy knew. Bellmaster could have made any promise good. Still could. But a settlement and Lady Jean Oriston were bait enough for a young gunner captain. *O let us be married! too long we have tarried; But what shall we do for a ring?* Bellmaster found one and Branton still wore it in his nose.

'Legally, that sums it up!' Branton got up and went to refill his glass. 'Well, thank you for letting me know. But there's nothing I can do or want to do. Sarah's free, white, and over twenty-one. And as I said, she's her mother's daughter – though she could never hope to be as two-faced a witch as Lady Jean. Sarah must look after herself.' He laughed to himself. 'My God, it's her mother's style, isn't it? Managing to get herself pregnant in a convent! Just up dear Lady Jean's street.' He swung round suddenly, frowning, and his voice harshened. 'But don't get me wrong, Arnold. I loved that bloody woman, even when I knew all about her and she screwed up my life.' He smiled suddenly, his mood changing, a shrug of his shoulders seeming to Geddy to throw off his years so that he saw again the hard-framed, good-looking gunner captain, popular, polo-playing, night clubs, girls, good with his men, efficient and promotion waiting for him until Bellmaster had come along with Lady Jean dancing at his side . . . a slender pink and white and gold fairy dancing tip-toe on a broad rosin-back while Bellmaster cracked the whip in the centre of the ring. But even Bellmaster could not hold her against her will. Bellmaster knew that she could destroy him – had once obliquely confessed it to him and had set him to work without success to find the protection he needed from her.

He drove home under a bright Sirius, a late frost black-icing the road. What would Branton think, he wondered, if he knew that Bellmaster and Lady Jean had also screwed up his life,

respectable Arnold Geddy, Cheltenham solicitor, county council-
lor, and enjoying all the little honours and duties that came with
his position? A moonlight beach in Positano and the next morning a voice over the telephone cutting that idyll short while the
woman lay sleeping on the bed with the early sunlight turning the
sea outside to moving turquoise and amethyst. *The State, in
choosing men to serve it, takes no notice of their opinions. If
they be willing faithfully to serve it, that satisfies.* Yes, but Oliver
Cromwell had been talking about a very different kind of State.
He had been given no opportunity to choose or to express an
opinion. Just a simple order. It had not been until he had leaned
over the sleeping woman to kiss her goodbye that he had discovered she was dead.

Sarah Branton lay in her bed her mind too active still for her to
have any hope of sleep. The day had been too full of long-
forgotten pleasures, of small joys and almost forgotten freedoms
for her to even wish for sleep; a heap of coloured pebbles and
seashells gathered quickly and now to be turned over and looked
at closely so that no detail escaped her. The clothes and other
things she had bought lay now, neatly set out on the velvet couch
by the window. Farley – she was far from yet naming him Richard; the time and mood for that would come – had stopped at
his bank and drawn money for her. To her pleasure but against
her wish that he should go off and have a drink in a café he had
insisted on staying with her and she had not noticed a moment of
boredom or impatience in him for the next two hours. 'All the
shop people know me. You won't be overcharged if I'm with you.
Besides I shall enjoy it.' That he was well-known and well-liked
was clear; and that her presence with him roused curiosity but
not one word out of place told her, too, the respect people had
for him. On the way back they had made a long detour and
stopped at an inland restaurant for an early dinner. The pro-
prietress and her husband had greeted him with cries of pleasure
and boisterous embraces and while they smiled and greeted her
their eyes had swept over her making appraisal but giving her no
hint of whether they approved of her or not. 'I'm a lone wolf.
Now they're wondering who the gorgeous girl is.' He had said

it easily, joking, but for a moment or two the faint start of tears had pricked the back of her eyes. Gorgeous girl. After eight years she had long lost the habit of self-awareness about her looks. Just one of a row of nuns in chapel, arms crossed, heads bent in modesty and worship.

Over the meal he had told her something of himself, always talking lightly, never going into anything in detail, and never using her curiosity about him to return it with any that he held for her. His father had retired from the navy to become a tea-planter in Kenya. Both his father and mother were now dead. He had no brothers or sisters and only a handful of relatives in England. He had gone to school in England, flying back to Africa for holidays and he had done his national service in Kenya. Beyond that he was reticent about what he had done for a living, except that he had travelled a lot, spoke competently three or four languages and had never married and '... never made any money worth speaking of. No ambition, no drive.' Giving her a swift pursing of his lips and that ugly, warm smile.

From somewhere far away a church bell struck three. In the convent now the bell for Lauds would be chiming and, since the order kept strict rule, the nuns would be rising to assemble in chapel. How often had she sinned at the small agony of rising which filled her body. And then castigated herself and her struggle for grace, chanting with the others:

O Lord, our Lord, how wonderful is thy name in all the earth;
Thou who has proclaimed thy glory upon the heavens.
Out of the mouths of babes and sucklings thou has prepared praise
to confuse thy adversaries;
to silence the enemy and the revengeful.

She put down a hand and smoothed her belly through the silk of the new nightdress she had bought. Silk against her skin and sin within her. Tears moved in her eyes but she was lost to know their origin. Self-pity or self-deceit. In the eyes and manner of his doctor friend, Herman, she had read his thoughts and had known that she, too, in the last months had now and then not been stranger to them. Had she, so incredibly innocent of her own body, embraced a dream in order to escape from a reality which she could no longer tolerate? *He* had more than once found excuses for coming into the store-room, hot and stuffy, high under the hospital roof where the bed linen and blankets were kept and of which she had charge ... from design more than accident, she sensed, had touched her hand or moved his body against hers while turning in the small space between the tiered linen and blankets. The room like a furnace with its steam pipes, knowing she was going to faint, as she had done once before from the heat, and then fainting. She forced her mind to hold the memories, scourging herself with them ... coming-to each time with her clothes loosened and free, but refusing to open her eyes while she knew he cradled her head and shoulders and his free hand moved over her skin until she groaned, shook her head and pulled herself up to open her eyes and meet his unmoving face while he said, 'You frightened me. After this second time I'll tell them you mustn't work up here any more.' Then his smile and the seeming confirmation of everything as he touched her cheek gently, smoothing it with the back of his hand. And then the missing periods and the confusion in her mind a slowly growing hell. She sat up suddenly, groaned, and buried her head in her hands, remembering the look on the face of the other doctor, Herman; reading his thoughts because for a while they had been hers, her hope that the passing of each month inexorably stifled.

She got out of bed, pulled Helen Holdern's dressing gown about her and went to the window and opened it. A nightingale greeted her with a great sobbing of song ... a stream of liquid, magic notes, their beauty filling her with swift, unquestionable joy.

At that moment, through her open bedroom door, she heard him half scream and then shout aloud, and go on shouting ... shouting, shouting.

Switching on the light she ran along the corridor to his room. The door was half-open and as she went in he shouted again, a sobbing, wildly passionate flood of hysterical words in some language unknown to her. She went to the bed and sat by him, putting her hand on his shoulder and shaking him and at her touch all sound went from him for a moment. Then, unaware of her presence, he sat up, his head bowed, and while he reached out automatically to switch on his bedside light he muttered, 'Oh, Christ ... Oh, Christ ...'

She shook him gently by the shoulder and he slowly looked up at her, his rugged face deeply shadowed by the oblique fall of the bedside light.

'Are you all right?'

He nodded and dropped his head a little to hide his face and he reached out – she was sure without knowing he did it – and took her hand for a moment or two. Then he looked at her, half-smiled and breathed deeply, bracing himself, and said, 'Was I shouting like a banshee?'

She nodded. 'Was it a bad dream?'

'Sort of. I'm sorry.' He grinned. 'I left my door open so that I could hear if you called in the night. Worked the other way round. Pay no attention. I'm used to it. Been going on for years. You go on back to bed. I'll be all right.' He reached out, held her arm and gave it a friendly shake. 'You go back. I'll read for a while.'

'You're sure?'

'Absolutely.'

She stood up slowly, looking down at him. Her heart in that moment yearned for the chance to do something for him. She wanted to sit beside him, take him into her arms as though he were a child and comfort him, she wanted him with a passion that had nothing to do with her woman's body, to hold him to her and wipe away whatever memories or fears had racked his dreams. Hesitantly she said, 'I could make you some coffee. Or get you a drink.'

He grinned then, tight pressing his thick long lips and puffing them out with held breath. 'No thank you, nurse. I'm ok. Really.'

She went back to her room. The nightingale was still singing but now, almost as though in irritation, an owl called complainingly as well. She lay in bed, propped high against her pillows. In the darkness which melded sea and sky, in the agonizing sanity of knowing she had wanted to live, she had screamed and shouted as he had done. And he had come to her. But this night he, too, had known terror and her presence and touch had drawn him from whatever horror haunted his sleep. There was a pattern, a deliberate shuttling of their destinies, being worked by some power. There was no hysteria in the thought. She *knew* and *believed* that it was all ordained. God or the Devil had drawn them together. It did not matter which. He belonged to her and had claim to all the love and service he might ask from her. Those were the terms written into the deed of her survival through him and as surely as that was so, then as surely the way of her love and service would be shown to her. She lay there and the tears shone in her eyes and her body began to tremble with the power of her desire.

When she awoke to the sunrise and the lusty calling of the cock who squired the hens in their pen she found that in the night she had been given the first sign that she was free from all restraint to serve him, free from any division of her love for him with any other.

At mid-morning Farley walked over to Herman's place. It was about a mile away inland on a slowly rising hill covered with holm and cork oaks. He took a footpath that avoided the roads and whistled gently to himself as he walked. He had left Sarah in her room where she was making some minor alterations to one of the dresses she had bought the day before. It was a cloudless morning, but with a faint touch of cold in the north-west wind coming down from the Monchique hills. The lupins were in bloom and here and there the walls around the cultivated patches were bright with patches of tricoloured convolvulus. Early purple orchids were showing through the pathside grasses. Once across the path ahead of him slid a harmless horse-shoe snake, the sun heightening the purple bloom of its black skin, its yellow spotting blurred to a golden line as it moved rapidly away from him. A woman came down the path, riding a mule side-saddle, and gave him a greeting, a big smile spreading over her walnut skin. Eight years he had been in the country and he knew nearly all of the people around. At a small cabin he stopped and talked to another woman who stood, tall for her race, carrying a plastic container filled with water on her head cushioned by a twist of rag made into a *sogra*. From somewhere distantly came the smell of baking bread.

Herman was hoeing between the rows of young maize with a tape recorder perched on an upturned bucket playing Spanish guitar music. He said, 'I'm glad you've come. Let's go and have a drink.'

They sat under a bamboo-thatched awning and he brought a jug of white wine and a dish of black olives. He filled Farley's glass and said, 'What brings you up here?'

'I felt like the exercise.'

Herman pulled his long nose and smiled. 'And our nun friend – didn't she want a walk?'

'No. She's busy making alterations to some new clothes she's bought.'

'Marsox was up here. Told me you'd been out with her.' Herman flicked an olive pip at a lizard which slid under a clump of mesembryanthemum. 'You advanced her some cash of course.'

'Well . . . she'd got none of her own.'

'Famous last words. The kind of woman you want is one who will take over and manage you and fill your dwindling bank account. I'm right, you know.'

Farley nodded and smiled. 'You're always right, Herman. In fact, I've walked all the way up here just to tell you how right you were. Her woman's thing started during the night. As you said. Just hysteria.'

'She told you?'

'When I took her breakfast. Didn't make a thing of it. Just told me. Sitting up there, blue-eyed and fair-haired like a close-cropped Madonna. Made no fuss about it.'

Herman shrugged his shoulders. 'Well, that's good. But I'm not surprised. There are still plenty of naïve girls about who think they'll conceive if a man kisses them. Well, now she's got nothing to worry about and she's free to travel . . . without any embarrassing luggage.'

'You don't like her – do you?'

'It's not like or dislike. I just have a feeling about her. That she's not good for you. *Bruxa.*'

Farley chuckled. 'You're on Maria's side now.'

'No, I'm not. But I have a feeling about her. There's nothing I'd like better than to see you shack up comfortably with a

45

woman. Even better, get married. But not with this one.'

'That kind of thing never crossed my mind.'

'That's what makes the situation dangerous. She's got to have a very special feeling for you because you saved her life. That would be all right if she'd been out for a night's fishing and fell overboard. You'd get a big thank you of one kind or another then – and that would be the end of it. But this is a woman who's going to put you in the place of everything she's rejected. Eight years a nun and she couldn't take it, never should have tried it. Then she imagines herself – out of some innocuous incident probably – to be pregnant. Even makes her body think so for a while, and herself that the only way to maintain her honour or whatever she would decide to call it is to swim out to sea and drown. But when it comes to the point her real nature, the true woman, surfaces knowing she wants to live. And you give your life ... coming to her over the face of the dark waters. Now she really has got something to hold on to. Something solid and real ... someone she'll convince herself, whether it's true or not, needs her.'

'For God's sake, that's going it a bit. I don't need anyone. Anyway she's got nothing to give me.'

Herman shook his head. 'Then what are you doing up here? You don't come up more than once or twice in a year when the phone's out of order. Why the morning stroll?'

'I don't know.'

'Of course you know. You could have told me about the period thing over the phone, or any time when I was down.'

Farley raised his head and looked squarely at him and then he smiled, a warm, frank smile full of admiration for Herman. 'You're a clever old sod, aren't you? You really should have gone on with doctoring. You've got a flair for diagnosis that could have made you a fortune.'

Herman laughed. 'There's not a fortune or a diagnosis that makes a sound like a guitar. Listen to that—' he nodded at the tape recorder which he had brought from the garden with him and which was still playing. 'That's Zaradin. Every note is golden. So, stop side-stepping and tell me.'

'I had a letter from the Holderns this morning. They're coming back at the end of the week. He wants to play in some golf tournament at Val de Lobo so they're cutting their trip a bit short.'

'No problem. Move in here. You've done it before. You like music and you're a good worker. Anyway, there are half a dozen people who'd take you . . . Ah, I see. I must be better than I thought I was. You told her.'

'Yes. When I took her breakfast up. We had a chat. After all, the Holderns can't be expected to keep her there. I said I would have to look for a new place and – well, what was she going to do?'

'She's got relations or friends somewhere, surely?'

'She's got a father in England but there's no love lost there. She wouldn't go to him. Some old family trouble. She didn't go into it. Her mother's dead, but she's got an aunt who has a villa up in the hills, in the Monchique area.' He shook the little wine in his glass, then swallowed it. 'She wants me to drive her up there.'

'Then do it, and she's off your hands.'

'It isn't as simple as that. Before I could do anything she was along to the Holderns' bedroom and telephoning her aunt. Then she came back and told me that her aunt was over the moon at hearing from her. Apparently she'd heard the news about leaving the convent. And – this is the bit – she'd told the aunt about my being on the loose soon and the old girl, if she is an old girl, I don't know, I didn't ask, insisted that I should stay there for a while. Oh, you know the old gubbins. I'd done so much for her and so on. And she was so damned pleased and excited about it and, I suppose, about being able to do something for me in return that I . . . Well, I said – ok – if that's what she wanted. Anyway,' Farley's chin tightened stubbornly, 'it's a billet for a while. Besides, I've had it here. I thought I'd stay a while for politeness and then move on.'

'Where?'

Farley spread his hands wide. 'Where? Well, I can't go back to Kenya. I thought England, America . . . I don't know. This place is getting as crowded as Blackpool or Cannes.' He reached for the jug and refilled his glass and then with his eyes on Herman, his face still and carved with thought, he went on, his voice edged with the small rasp of bitterness, 'Damn it all, I'm near forty. I haven't done a thing with my life. Not a thing, Herman. And I won't unless I find something soon. All I've got in the world is a few thousand escudos, a car, a few clothes and some fishing tackle. I don't even own a decent book. I put everything into that restaurant and when that went . . . well. So, I thought, move on. Maybe the gods want it that way.' He grinned, his manner changing abruptly. 'The sad story of one, Richard Farley, the eternal but not over-industrious optimist. But just wait for the next instalment. Rags to riches. Oh, Christ, what does it matter anyway?'

Geddy got out of the lift on the third floor of the Savoy Hotel and began to walk the corridors looking for the number of Lord Bellmaster's room. He was long over his irritation at being summoned to London at such short notice. Anyway, he had already made arrangements to improve the not exactly shining hour which he would have to endure with His Lordship by a pleasant divertissement of his own later in the day. Wryly he was thinking that once *they* had ever made use of you, no matter the lapse of years, they had a lien on you for ever and had only to raise a finger to have you come running. Not that they had bothered him much or importantly in the last ten years. Bellmaster, like himself, was no longer active with them, but he was still part of them. No one ever truly left Birdcage until death came.

Turning a corridor corner he came on a small Arab boy, shouting, and pushing a vacuum cleaner (filched, no doubt, from the housekeeper's storeroom) along the carpet, chasing an Arab girl who ran laughing ahead of him wheeling a toy pram. He side-stepped them both as an Arab woman came out of a suite and began to shriek at them, bearing down on them, her head shawl and robes full spread like a dhow before the wind. The ghosts of Edwardians past, Geddy mused, must have long in distress given up haunting these corridors, their eyes blurred with phantom tears for the demise of an empire. A faint smell of *couscous* made the still air piquant. The first couscous he had ever eaten had been in Tunis, a young territorial gunner captain enjoying the wartime escape from his father's Cheltenham office. That was the day when Bellmaster – though not in person – had come into his life and he had been seconded to Intelligence. Bellmaster had arrived after the war when the marriage settlement with Branton had to be made. His choice as a solicitor, he knew, had been no accident. The skeletons in the cupboard must be kept in the family.

There was a DO NOT DISTURB notice outside the door. He knocked and Bellmaster opened it to him, greeting him with a puffy handshake, a big amused stare, and 'My dear Geddy. How nice to see you.' The door closed with the notice still hanging on its knob.

In the sitting room there was no sign of personal belongings or even temporary occupancy. But on the sideboard was a tray holding a bottle of whisky, glasses and – the man's memory gave him no surprise – two bottle of Perrier water. They endeared you – there was no denying that, by their memory of your preferences, though they never drew attention to it.

Bellmaster poured two whiskies and came and sat down across the low table from Geddy. He was a big, well-preserved man who had to be nearer seventy than sixty, dressed in a single-breasted dark suit, platinum watch chain and a shirt whose white front shone like a virgin snow slope over his great chest. His dark hair was silvered but still abundant; a big man, full of appetites and craft, and with a mind and intelligence all under control and all serving his ambition. Geddy had known once what it was. Now he could only guess.

They drank and Bellmaster said, 'Good of you to come. I had your message and I thought we ought to have a talk.' A small avalanche of a smile slid over his face. 'For old time's sake – not yours. But mine and that of other interested parties. Dear Lady Jean – she reaches out after death and sets us dancing. Now tell me about Sarah.'

Geddy very precisely, allowing nothing of his imagination to intrude, told him all he knew. He knew well Sarah's mother's past connection with him personally and professionally, this latter particularly so, otherwise he would never have been called in to deal with the settlement to Colonel Branton on the marriage.

When he had finished Bellmaster said, 'Nobody knows where she is?'

'No. Except, I imagine in Portugal still.'

'This baby business. What do you think of that?'

'Only that her letter said she was pregnant.'

'In a nunnery? How did she manage that? Sounds a bit mediaeval. Still, she's Lady Jean's daughter so it could be true.'

'Lord Bellmaster, that's not what you're concerned about.'

Bellmaster smiled. 'I always liked that about you. You never minded forcing things. No, it's not what I'm concerned about. She's got an aunt out there, hasn't she? Didn't she take over the Villa Lobita?'

'Yes.'

'God, I've got some memories of that place – good, bad and otherwise. I've forgotten the aunt's name.'

'She married an American – but she's widowed now. Mrs Ringel Fanes. Plenty of money. Travels a lot. But I have nothing to do with her affairs. The villa was left to Sarah in her mother's will. Sarah gave it up when she went into the convent. She dispossessed herself of everything.'

Bellmaster smiled. 'If she's anything like Jean she'll probably be asking for it back now. You think she might go to this villa?'

'I don't know.'

Bellmaster frowned. 'Not a question of knowing. What do you *think* was what I asked.'

Geddy recognized the crack of the whip but shrugged his shoulders. 'Someone's looking after her. She made that clear. As for thinking, I think she will be like her mother. She'll fall on her feet. Yes, I suppose, if nothing better turns up, she might go to her aunt.'

Lord Bellmaster rubbed a hand slowly over his big jaw and smiled with an almost boyish pucker of delight. 'Oh, Geddy. You've been out a long time but it's all there still. You're waiting for it, aren't you? But you won't ask the direct question. You were there when the settlement was discussed and you heard what Lady Jean said.'

'I remember clearly. She was rather distraught. She was carrying your child and she had naturally – or optimistically – thought you would marry her and make her Lady Bellmaster. Captain John Branton was a pretty cheap substitute.'

'You've missed a few things out.'

'I didn't want to embarrass you.'

Lord Bellmaster laughed, refilled his own glass and ignored Geddy's, which was no surprise to Geddy because he would have refused anyway and His Lordship knew it so preferred not to waste his time on trivialities. 'Go ahead. Let's see how good your memory is. Or, rather, whether it is still as good as it used to be. The slightest approach to a false pretence was never among *your* crimes.'

Geddy grinned at the modification of a quotation from his beloved Lewis Carroll. He said, knowing full well what Bellmaster wanted from him, 'She threw one of her celebrated scenes. You won't want me to go into the trivia, mostly springing from the Irish side of her bloodlines, my lord. But in essence she said that she would agree to the marriage and the settlement for Branton, that she would still . . . well, be available to you for personal and professional services—'

'Her words were blunter. Thank you for your delicacy.'

'—but that if you ever gave her cause she would destroy you and cause hell where . . .' he hesitated, old habit prevailing even in this room which he knew must be secure, '. . . it would be most unwelcome from an official point of view, and particularly as far as foreign relationships were concerned. But, I presume, my lord, that you didn't send for me either to refresh your memory or to test mine.'

Lord Bellmaster was silent for a while, dabbling a long brown forefinger in his glass to revive the Perrier bubbles. Then he slid from his inside coat pocket a slim gold cigarette case, tapped it on his chin thoughtfully for a moment and then took out a cigarette and lit it. Geddy waited with untroubled patience. Distantly outside the window, from the inner service well of the hotel, came the clatter of refuse cans and a faint, boisterous tangling of cockney voices.

Abruptly Lord Bellmaster said, 'When she said a thing, she meant it. Frankly, too, I did give her cause. Oh, many many years afterwards. But I won't go into that. She died unexpectedly shortly after the final break was made between us. Naturally Birdcage took precautions. All her stuff was vetted.' She was living in Portugal at the time – as much as she lived anywhere. You remember you kindly and confidentially made her will and all her papers lodged with you available.'

'A breach of professional ethics ah ... justified would you say in the national interest?'

'What else would I say.' Bellmaster's voice was suddenly brutal and pugnacious, the bully surfacing, thought Geddy, or more truly a prick of concern for himself and his reputation and his still-pressing ambitions. 'But she was a clever bitch. She'd have known we could and would have done all that at any time if we'd had the slightest reason. And she'd have known that we would do it immediately, anyway, after her death. Who do you think was most active in pushing – and that's the word – Sarah into the life of a religious?'

Geddy made a pretence of considering this, though he well knew the answer, while his mind reconnoitred all the nuances of this interview. Limited though his own career had been in Bellmaster's arcane world he had never been able to deny to himself its fascination and he had quickly come to acquire the habit, and still had it, of looking beyond, above or behind a question to assess its true provenance in the mind of the asker, and knew that often a question was asked when the answer was already known; the questioner merely casting a piece of bread on the waters to see if a fish unexpectedly would rise to it. He said, 'I think it came from both sides. Branton had no time for her, and when they broke up she was mostly with her mother or her aunt. In her fashion I suppose Lady Jean loved her, but she had little time for her either. Short holidays when she was all over her and an exciting companion. I think – quite without any ulterior motive – I mean one which would survive after her death, untimely or otherwise, Lady Jean influenced the girl. She was a romantic. Maybe she wanted the girl to have a life which – with deference to you, my lord – was quite different from her own.'

'To hell with deference, Geddy. You know what I'm driving at. The girl's out. I can hear Jean saying, "You don't have to worry if you find you can't stand it. Leave it. You'll always be provided for. All you have to do is . . ." What?'

'I've no idea, my lord.'

'Do you hold anything on Sarah's behalf now? Bank safety box key? Any documents? Anything at all lodged with you by anyone since Jean's death?'

'Nothing. And frankly I can't see even Lady Jean being so devious or long-sighted enough to hide anything away, and then confiding in her daughter that whatever it was it would be there if she were ever in trouble and wanted to leave a convent which at that time she hadn't even entered.'

'Yes. I'm rather with you. At least, I want to be. What about Colonel Branton?'

Geddy smiled. 'If he had anything – would he be any problem to you?'

'Not the slightest. Accidents happen.'

'Of course, my lord. But as far as I am concerned you've never made the remark.'

Lord Bellmaster stood up. 'All right. We'll do something about finding where the girl is from this side. But if you hear from her – let me know. Sorry to drag you up here from your rural haunts, but I've no doubt you'll enjoy yourself in Cadogan Square before you catch your evening train.'

Without a shadow of surprise, though he had not anticipated that they would still be monitoring him, Geddy said evenly, 'I always find my visits there very pleasant, my lord.'

When Geddy had gone, Lord Bellmaster of Conary sat thinking and unhurriedly finishing his whisky. For a while Geddy lingered in his thoughts. When he, himself, had been far more closely involved in an active life with them they had used the young Geddy. God knew who had spotted his limited but useful flair, but after a few months they had wrapped him up to total commitment with one of the oldest tricks. Laid him wide open as a target, a weak spot for probing so that the girl – even the name came back over the years – Francina Pavi was put on to him. A brief wartime romance, a weekend in Positano where on the second night he was to doctor her nightcap before bedding so that while she lay drugged he could go through her luggage, supposedly to make a list of all names and telephone numbers in her notebook, which they knew was of no importance for it had already been checked. They had already decided that she was not worth the use of any great finesse but was better out of the way because she was serving two sets of masters. If they did not do it most likely the others would quite soon. So, thanks to the unsuspecting Geddy, she died in her sleep, poisoned unknowingly by him and, fifteen minutes after the early morning telephone call, he was being picked up by car on the cliff road to Amalfi. Bellmaster was in London then and yet to meet Geddy. The personnel comment which came through about Geddy simply said – *reaction nine-tenths* – which meant that whatever he felt only the smallest tip of the emotional iceberg showed above water. And the report ran on – *Material wasted in field work; suggest London duties and then re-routing.* Which was turkey gabble for: *Put him to something more suited to his talents and intelligence.* So he had come back to London and to their first meeting and later to more civilized work. It was natural then, knowing his man, that Bellmaster should use him privately years later in peace to draw up the Branton settlement. Jean had liked and trusted him on sight.

Dear Jean, he smiled ruefully, who was quite capable of arranging to strike from beyond the veil. Only a fool would ignore that threat when in a few weeks the choice would be made and he did not care much which it would be, either a premier ambassadorship or a vice-presidency of the Commission of the European Community which meant eventually, by rotation, the Presidency in due time. He had never lacked for money. Power was the true ichor demanded by his vanity.

He left the room after a brief telephone call to the porter's desk. A taxi was waiting for him. He paid it off at the end of the Mall and walked across St James's Park, loitering briefly on the lake bridge to watch a couple of cormorants fishing and a small flight of mallard take off and for a few seconds was back on the lochside at Conary as a sixteen-year-old. The only thing he had passionately wanted in those days was for his drink-sodden father to die so that he could take over title and estates and to bed eighteen-year-old Sheila, the daughter of Angus the ghillie. He had got the latter within three months and the former nine months later. The memory of both never failed to give him a sharp *frisson* of pleasure.

He left the park and strolled up Birdcage Walk. Not far from Wellington Barracks he entered one of the houses overlooking the park.

Late that afternoon Kerslake, sitting in a top-floor room of the same house, was reading a memorandum which had just been handed to him by his secretary, Joan.

It read:

Sarah Branton, daughter of Lady Jean Branton (née Oriston) and Lieutenant-Colonel John Branton. 28. Past eight years, nun, Convent Sacred Heart, Calvira, Algarve, Portugal. Deserted Convent, believed pregnant, April 4th last. Has communicated convent. Whereabouts unknown. Has aunt – Mrs Ringel Fanes, widow – Villa Lobita, near Monchique. Have Lisbon trace and report. No direct contact Sarah Branton. No involvement Portuguese authorities.

Kerslake read it twice. He was comparatively new in the service and none of the names meant anything to him. If there were office files on them and it was intended that he should know something of their background the references would have been given. He was a patient, intelligent young man, who knew his place and, given the chance (which must in the nature of things here eventually come), he meant to improve it considerably. He unlocked his desk drawer and pulled out the Lisbon codes and began to encypher the necessary message.

At that moment Geddy, sitting in his first-class carriage on the Cheltenham train, having an itch on the tip of his nose rubbed it with his right forefinger and smiled at the faint ghost of perfume that still lingered on his skin. Lanvin's *Arpège*. So, they and Bellmaster knew all about that. Well ... let them. Bellmaster had not changed greatly – except that now his ambition showed too much. It would be ironical if Lady Jean should return from the shades deviously (which had been her style) to haunt and destroy him.

chapter three

There was an oil painting of Lady Jean Branton in the wide, cool hallway. She stood at the top of a short flight of steps. At her side geraniums cascaded from a stone urn and among the cracks of the old steps pads of stonecrop grew, their golden blooms complementing the colour of her hair which the artist had painted lightly flowing back from her brow, lifted and streaming in a breeze. The breeze, too, took the soft nacreous stuff of her long flowing dress so that it flared backwards from her, billowing about her arms and sides and clinging boldly to her long slender body. Although only her hands and face were free of covering she seemed to stand poised in a moment of wantonness, more naked than true nakedness could ever be. About her waist was a wide gold belt or girdle, jewelled and intricately worked, with a great clasp formed of two cupids reaching out their chubby, baby-creased arms and fat hands to one another. It was good to look at, but – Farley felt – had something undeniably vulgar and meretricious about it. The likeness in the face to Sarah's was there, but distant. This woman wore her beauty like a challenge. Her smile provoked, the coral lips offered themselves with seduction, while her pale blue eyes carried laughter without kindness and the pose of her body was glorious with arrogance – a beautiful witch, Farley thought, whom most men would have found hard to resist.

He turned away from the painting and went out on to the terrace from which the hillside fell steeply and above the trees the great sweep of country rolled away to the far distant sea. Although it was not over-big the Villa Lobita had been built without thought of cost. There was an outside heated swimming pool, a terraced fall of ornamental gardens to the south, and a driveway which ran in from the west through a grove of carob and fig trees. At the top of the driveway was a small lodge occupied by a married couple who acted as housekeeper and gardener-chauffeur and who lived at the villa all the year round. The villa itself was Moorish in design with all the bedrooms and two bathrooms on the first floor. Each of the bedrooms had its own private terrace. On the ground floor was a long lounge facing south-east to take the morning and escape the afternoon sun, a library-study, a kitchen, and backquarters for Mrs Ringel Fancs' private maid. At the moment these were unoccupied because Mrs Ringel Fanes – who had not used her title after marriage – had left the villa to go to America two days before Farley and Sarah arrived.

Farley was thinking about this as he walked to the swimming pool. When they had driven down the drive to the villa – two days previously – he had sat in his car while Sarah went in to greet her aunt. Distantly through the partly open hall door he had heard her talking, he presumed then, to her aunt, but in fact it was to the housekeeper. A little later Sarah had come out to him with the housekeeper and, in English, had told him that her aunt had had to go off unexpectedly to America but that they were to make themselves at home for as long as they liked. He smiled to himself now at the recollection. He had been sure that Sarah was lying in some way and not even bothering to try to make the lie convincing as many people would have done by attributing the sudden American visit to a sick or dying relative or even unexpected business affairs. He was beginning to understand Sarah now. Once her mind seized on a notion it became real for her. He was sure that because she had wanted him to come to the villa with her, but knew the aunt would not be there, she had maintained the fiction of the aunt's presence in order not to disturb him. Maybe it was some remnant of propriety surviving through her years in the convent which demanded that some element of chaperonage should be offered to him, to get him on the road, and then to be almost casually discarded on arrival. It made no difference to him because he meant to be a bird of passage. She had set him moving and he meant to keep going. This was a staging post which would not hold him long.

When he reached the pool she was just climbing out. She stood on the edge, smiled and raised a hand to him, and then started to towel her hair, which was grown longer now into a boyish crop. She had used the pool twice a day since their arrival and he wondered whether this was to kill any lingering fear or memory of her hours in the water. Of the spare swim suits in the pool house she had chosen a modest one-piece blue one. Standing there he could see that she was built like her mother, large-breasted and slim-hipped, but her face lacked that mocking, laughter-touched awareness of her own beauty and sensuality which belonged to the mother. Modesty still moved strongly in Sarah. She, as she had done before, seeing his eyes on her, turned away and picking up a sleeved bathing wrap put it on.

The housekeeper had left them drinks and glasses on the table under the beach umbrella. Sarah sat down and said, 'What will you have, Richard?'

The *Richard* had crept in first on the drive up from the coast. He said, 'A beer, I think. Thanks ... Sarah.' For himself he found he was reluctant to use her name very often. Why, he wondered – because one should not get too close to a *bruxa* ... in fact, keep one's name hidden?

He sat down and sipped his beer and, since he had been mildly brooding over it all the morning, decided that he should come out into the open with her. As he began to fiddle about preparing himself a pipe, he said, 'I want to talk to you ... frankly, about the way things are between us.'

She laughed nervously. 'Isn't that funny. I was going to be frank with you, too. I don't like ... I mean I've found I can't bear anything but the truth between us.'

He grinned. 'Well, who's going to talk first. Do we toss for it?'

'Is yours very serious?'

'Not particularly. But it's got to be said.'

'Well, mine is. I want to get it off my conscience.'

'Well, then you start.'

'Thank you.' She picked up two drinking straws and absently began to plait them into a ring. 'It's about coming up here. I deceived you. But it was such a little lie that I thought it would be unimportant. But, it's funny, you mean so much to me because of what you've done that I couldn't bear a tiny, even – as I thought – a happy-making lie. I did speak to my aunt on the telephone from the Holderns' villa. And she was very happy for us to come and stay as long as we like. But it so happened that she *was* going off to America that very day – leaving for Lisbon to get a plane to London to fly on from there. In fact, she said, now that I'd left the convent she didn't regard this villa as hers any longer. It used to belong to me did I tell you that?'

'No.'

'I made a gift of it to her when I entered.'

Farley lit his pipe and blew out the match. 'You could have just told me the truth. What difference would it have made?'

'I thought you mightn't come. I mean the two of us being alone here together.'

He laughed. 'You're eight years behind the times ... perhaps more. And anyway I'm not the casual jumping-into-bed type. Did you think that?'

'It's the last thing I thought. In fact the opposite. I thought you might think ... well, think that I would, if we were alone together, be a nuisance to you. I mean I do owe you so much and, of course, I long to repay you. And I shall repay you. I must!'

Farley smiled. 'I think your logic is going a bit astray. Ok I did something for you and you're grateful. So you didn't want to lose sight of me until you could repay me. So you, one way and another, felt that our being here alone would queer the whole pitch? That we should begin to build up a relationship leading to bed and all that?'

As she looked across at him he saw the glint of starting tears in the corners of her blue eyes. Nothing that she had said made any sense. It was self-contradictory ... a feminine tangle of thought and reasoning. As though she read his thoughts, she said with a sniff, 'I don't know what I thought. I got it all mixed up. I was so happy with you, and grateful, that I didn't want to risk anything going wrong. I wanted still to be with you.'

He was silent for a moment or two. He had a real mixed-up number here ... then, remembering all she had been through over the years and recently, he reached out and took her hand, gave it a squeeze momentarily, and said, 'Just forget it all. You told a little white lie which was of no importance and quite unnecessary.'

She slowly sat up very straight in her chair and said in a hoarse, almost harsh voice which marked the sudden emotion in her, 'I wanted you to come here. To this villa which used to be mine. I wanted it because I wanted to repay you. And it could only be done here. I couldn't risk your not coming. And, please, don't ask me to say any more than that at this moment.' She stood up and, pulling her wrap closely about her, went on, 'And please don't tell me what you wanted to say because I can guess what it is. You gave me back my life. You can't deny me the right now to do something for you. I've got to do it and I'm going to do it.' She came round to his side, the tears escaping from her eyes and bent and just touched his forehead with her lips. 'Please ... it's only a small thing to ask. I want to repay you. But it means going to Lisbon first.' She smiled suddenly, ran a finger under her eyes to clear her tears and turned away, saying, 'Now I'll go and make some lunch for us. It's Saturday and Mario and his wife are away in Monchique shopping.'

Alone, Farley reached to help himself to another beer and then changed his mind and poured himself a stiff gin and vermouth. He drank and then sighed. What did it matter, anyway? He was not going anywhere in particular and he was living with free board and lodgings in beautiful surroundings. Anyway, maybe she was right. She did owe him a great deal. Her life. What was the price of a life? He shut his eyes and raising his head let the sun beat against his lids. Perhaps it was time to take a good long look at himself and discard those elements and characteristics which made him too easy-going and good-natured. For years people had taken advantage of his good nature, and he had not minded. It might be interesting and rewarding to make himself over. So, if she felt she owed him something and wanted to make repayment, why should he object? Though, how in God's name she could do anything for him was beyond him. And what the hell was Lisbon all about? Did she have a secret

60

bank account there – never renounced when she had entered the convent?

But that evening, as they sat in the glassed-in small terrace that opened from the southern side of the large living room she came – and this now gave him no surprise, even amused him by her directness and the firm passion that possessed her to clear her debt to him – without any embarrassment back to the subject.

The sun was low in the western sky, its red glow firing the tips of a clump of eucalyptus trees on the slopes below the villa. A stray butterfly had found its way into the sun-room and was resting on a hanging bowl of lobelias. She was wearing a light silk blue dress which she had bought on their shopping expedition, a demure dress, long-skirted and with a row of mother-of-pearl buttons running up its front to a little rolled-over high collar. She had a modesty about her body after eight years of convent life. Knowing this, he seldom went to the swimming pool while she was bathing. Seeing her sip absently at her glass of orange juice, he sensed that she was poised to make some positive approach to him, frowning a little, waiting for the right moment or word to break into the beginning of, if not intimacy, then frankness. Before he could make up his mind whether to help her or not, she suddenly in a rush of words said, 'I want to talk to you about me and, more importantly, about you. Do you mind that?'

Not looking at her, watching the butterfly slowly opening and shutting its wings as it rested on a flower bloom, he said, 'No—' and then looking at her, grinning, he went on, 'You're going to do it anyway, aren't you? I'm beginning to know that look on your face.'

She smiled at him and then quickly lowered her eyes and brushed her hand across the lap of her skirt. 'Let me start with me. It's easier. Maybe I won't put things in order, but I want you to know the main things, things which I knew about or which I was told about.'

He leaned back and listened, seeing the sky over the far land and the sea pass from smoky red to pale gold and green as the earth swallowed the sun. He had to admit after a while that she told her story very well, seldom missing the chronological line and avoiding any too confusing digressions. Perhaps life in a convent with its simple duties and devotions cleared the mind for unencumbered thinking by the rejection of trivialities.

Her mother had married a wealthy army officer who still lived in Gloucestershire. Two years after she was born her mother and father separated, but on amicable terms so that he often came and stayed with them wherever they might be. At first they had seldom settled for long in any one place ... Paris, Florence, Rome, Cairo, Madrid, but their base for all these moves was the Villa Lobita. Mostly she had been left behind with nurse or governess and later had been sent to school in Florence and then to a convent school in Lisbon. Somehow her mind had from an early age always held the idea that she would like to enter a convent.

'I'm sure now that my mother encouraged it because her own life was so worldly. I know that she had lovers, always wealthy, and that she loved the world and all its pleasures – but there must have been a dissatisfaction deep in her heart at her way of life – a way of life which would have been the last she would have chosen for me. From the time I was fourteen onwards she influenced and directed me towards the choice of becoming a religious. It seemed to me that I had lived with the thought of that kind of life so long that there was never any questioning it.'

However, her mother had never lived to see her become a nun. When she was sixteen her mother had fallen suddenly ill at the Villa Lobita and she had been brought down from school in Lisbon to see her.

'To her deathbed, really, I knew when I arrived. Though that was something she would never have admitted to anyone, even to herself. She could shut any unpleasant or unwelcome thought from her mind. Of course, all her life she was very dramatic and excitable, but also discreet and secretive. When I came she didn't talk about herself at all hardly. She was just concerned with me ... chiefly about eventually entering a convent. I had the impression, even as a girl of sixteen, that she might be feeling that she had over-influenced me and that she was trying to give me a chance – if I felt at all doubtful – to change my mind. But when

I made it clear that it was the one thing I wanted she seemed overjoyed. I shouldn't perhaps say this, but knowing what her own life had been like, I got the feeling that, dying, she drew enormous comfort from knowing that her own daughter was going to dedicate herself to God and that that act ... well, somehow, would restore to her a grace which had long been missing. Oh, it's very difficult to say things like that of her ... but it was something like that in her mind. And, because I knew it, I wanted only to please her. And anyway it was also what I wanted for myself. Oh, dear, am I being awfully long-winded and rambling .. ? I do so want to get it right.'

For a moment as her head turned slightly away from him he caught the soft gleam of tears in her eyes. Looking away to the terrace slopes he caught the staccato sound of a burst of song from a warbler in a thicket of oleanders. Quietly he said, 'I'm with you. There's no need to rush.' He looked back at her and found her facing him, dabbing at the corners of her eyes with her handkerchief, and quite irrelevantly the thought came to him that the one thing she had not bought herself on their shopping trip was a handbag.

'Well, I told her that I was absolutely certain about what I intended to do. I can remember her now. She was sitting in a chair by the pool well wrapped up even though it was June. She said to me – I remember it so well, "Absolute certainty at sixteen, like an absolute certainty on the track", she adored racing all her life "often lets you down. So I've got something to say to you which must not be repeated to anyone else unless you do at some time, even after you've become a nun, decide you want to change your life. You know that your Order insists that you renounce all your worldly goods when you enter?" Well, I did, of course, naturally. When she very soon died I inherited this villa and quite a lot of money ...'

She went on explaining, without any emotion now, how she had made over the villa to her aunt, and the rest of her inheritance to her father, not because there were any deep ties between them, but because she thought it right and proper not to wound him by giving it to anyone else. Seeing that she was straying from her line now, he said, 'And what was it that your mother said to you? That's if you want me to know, of course.'

'Oh, yes, Richard – of course I want you to know. That's what it's all about. All this, I mean. You see, I know you haven't got much money. And I know if you had there are lots of things you could do and be successful at doing. You know why I want to do this. We don't have to go into that any more, do we?'

Farley smiled. Her logic and orderly progression of thought were breaking up now, but her confusion and warmth touched him for he knew how deeply she felt about what she wanted to do. As for himself – despite the touch of self-interest he had felt by the swimming pool – he was content to listen to her without commitment. Anyway she had given everything away – so what could she have now to give him? Because he knew she would be pleased at the use of her name, he said, 'Sarah, we don't have to go into me. Not yet, anyway. What did your mother say to you?'

'Something I've really never understood. And when she'd said it I almost got the feeling that she wished she hadn't. Her face was quite changed. She was beautiful, you know. Even in illness. But her face suddenly changed and she looked very, very old and bitter and she said almost in anger something like, "Nobody can foresee the life ahead of them. God and the Devil fight over you day by day and you live in their hands. I just want you to know that, if you ever leave the life of a nun, don't think you'll come out into the world having to ask charity from anyone. You will have taken vows, but I haven't. And what I've done can never be on your conscience. You've only got your aunt and your father. Your father won't lift a finger and your aunt's ten years older than me and could well be dead." And then she told me.'

She was silent for a while. It was darkening outside now and a few stars were beginning to show. Now and again the headlights of a car climbing a slope fingered the sky like a searchlight.

Gently he said, 'Told you what?'

'That I was to go to Lisbon and ask Melina to give me what was mine, and that if I used it wisely it would look after me in luxury for the rest of my life.'

'Sounds a bit Delphic. Who is Melina?'

'She was my mother's personal maid. She married Carlo, the chauffeur we had after Giorgio left. Then they both retired and opened a small hotel at Estoril. So you see—' she stood up, smiling, suddenly gay, 'all we have to do is go there and get whatever it is. It's either got to be money or something worth a lot of money and I want you to have it. You're not going to say no, are you?'

Farley stood up. Just now and again he got the feeling that, from the moment he had heard her scream in the night, he had slid into another dimension, another world where he was wandering full of nostalgia for the commonplace, worn old habitat and day-to-day small events which had kept him comfortable. A pregnant and then a non-pregnant nun. Running away from convents. Manoeuvring him to a luxury villa. The dying talk of a mother who had lived a high and rare old life. This girl, with a woman's body, repeating an arcane deathbed utterance. This girl, this Sarah Branton, leeching on to him, no doubt like the Princess Sabra had to Saint George when he had rescued her from the dragon, and now wanting to give, if not herself, her all to him when all he wanted was to take a nice thank you and ride on. At that moment, unworthy or not, the thought crossed his mind fleetingly that maybe for all her manner she was unhinged, living in a waking dream that had begun when she had been hauled aboard and dropped sprawling naked among the slithering tunny catch on the bottom boards of the launch. The next time he passed it he would look at her mother's portrait. Somewhere there had to be a touch of Irish madness in her eyes which he had overlooked.

He said, 'I'm going to get myself a drink. What about you?'

Not looking at him, she said, 'No thank you. You don't want to come to Lisbon, do you?'

Surprising himself, he said, 'You're quite wrong. I do. But I think you ought to prepare yourself for a disappointment. I mean no disrespect to your mother. But on the point of death ... well, facts and fancies get mixed.'

She turned to him, her face stubborn. 'Not with my mother. And anyway, I can sense how you feel. You want to get away from me. You did what you did and now you don't want to go on being embarrassed by me about it. But I won't embarrass you. I promise you. I just want to do this one thing for you. I know that whatever Melina has will make that possible. Then, when that's done, I shall be happy and you will be free of me ...'

Spurred by the emotion which filled him at the sight of her pleading yet stubborn face, he turned back and, not knowing he was going to do it, he put a hand gently under her chin, bent down and kissed her lightly and said tenderly, 'You be happy. That's what I want. I'm free already. So, now I'll get a drink and some time we'll go to Lisbon.'

'Tomorrow?'

He laughed aloud at the eagerness in her. But as he walked away she called after him, her voice rising with pleasure, 'Tomorrow, say tomorrow!'

Still moving, he answered, 'All right, Miss Sarah Branton. All right – tomorrow.'

Sunday afternoon, and the park was full of unhurried people taking the sun. The stiff beds of tulips were beginning to show their colour. On the lake a swan raised itself high, breasting the sun and, without taking off, thrashed the water with its wings in spring ecstasy. A West Indian with a red cap and white tennis shoes broke bread and fed it to the ducks. A black girl with an arm round the West Indian's waist suddenly pulled him round, away from the ducks and kissed him. Spring, thought Kerslake, was well and truly in the air. If he were in Barnstaple now he would have taken his rod and walked the tidal river bank to fish the free water and that evening driven Margaret out to a pub for a drink and parked for a while in the sand dunes afterwards. No Margaret now. The letters between them had died as he had meant them to die. In this work a man was better off without the distraction of that kind of involvement. That time would come when he had made his mark. In the meanwhile ... well, if you wanted it, you paid for it and forgot it quickly. This was what he had wanted, this room, this work; and the gods, right, out of the blue, had given him his chance when, a detective-sergeant in Barnstaple a few years ago, Quint had come down on a case and they had met and he had impressed Quint – as he had meant to if he could – and so found himself here.

He put his hand on the telephone to call Quint's room, but left it there while he read through again the report which he had just decoded from Lisbon.

Your OX 137. Sarah Branton. Residing Villa Lobita, Monchique – owner Mrs Ringel Fanes now in America, departed three days before arrival Branton. Branton accompanied by, presumed British subject, Richard Farley. No action taken on Farley background. Advise. Light surveillance Branton. Will continue unless advised change.

Kerslake rang Quint who said, 'I'm just going out. Read it.' Over the telephone Kerslake heard Quint's slight asthmatic wheeze and smiled. Asthma could strike at any time and put a man at risk. One day Quint would be shunted out of field work and upwards and the vacuum would be filled and he knew that it would be by him. He read the message slowly and clearly. Quint was silent for a while and then said, 'Tell them to go total on this Farley, but keep the Portugal people out. And you do the same for him this end. There may be something. Why the bloody hell didn't they give an estimated age for him? He could have war or national service. You try this end for that, anyway. All right?'

'Yes, sir.'

He put down the telephone and began to draft a message to Lisbon. Not for a moment did he allow himself any speculation about the interest in Sarah Branton. He would either know or not know in time.

They left the villa after breakfast. He drove well, and fast when he could with safety. He drove, she realized, as he did any task to which he set himself, like painting the Holderns' pool or shutters, giving himself to the work and letting himself be absorbed in it. Respecting this concentration she talked very little. There was no need, anyway, in her for talk because she was happy. There had been many times when she had been driven along this road, first with Giorgio and then later with Melina's husband Carlo Spuggi. If she were alone with Giorgio, then she stayed alone because Giorgio answered when spoken to but was never willing to take part in any time-passing conversation. The road before him and his beloved Rolls-Royce answering to his hands and feet were all he cared for. Driving, he lived in a world of his own which was completely satisfying. It seemed to her that she had never seen Giorgio out of livery or far from the car. Perhaps he had even slept in it at night. She smiled to herself at the fancy. Carlo was quite different. A jay, a magpie, a chatterer given the least encouragement, and fond of hurling abuse or jokes at any mule cart or other car they passed; a short, stocky gorilla of a man who had won the heart of tall, dark, handsome Melina under whose window when her mother was away he would play his guitar to woo her. And also, in fun, because his whole nature was generous and kind, he would sometimes, because he knew she loved guitar music – pause under her own and give her a short serenade before shouting, *bõa noite*. He had even charmed her father on his rare visits, her father who could only barely tolerate Giorgio.

She was content now with Richard's long silences, for they were quite unlike Giorgio's. In her thoughts and often in her talk with him she named him as Richard. He seldom used her name. Just now and again when, she realized, the use was deliberate and well or kindly intended. When she got wrought up – which was something she must try not to do because she realized any disturbance in her made him uncomfortable – he knew exactly the right moment to soothe her and name her ... no longer Sister Luiza but Sarah. Astonishingly, how distant that so-recent life now seemed.

Not long after noon they went through Lisbon and took the coast road to Estoril. The hotel run by Carlo and Melina stood back from the seafront at the top of a public square. When Farley pulled the car up outside she said, 'Do you want to come in?'

He shook his head and began to fish in his pocket for his pipe. 'No, this is your business. I'll sit and enjoy my pipe.'

She went in. The main hall was empty but the dining room, she saw through the glass doors, was full and lunch still being served. The reception desk was empty. She rang the bell and Melina herself came through from the inner office. For a moment or two she faced her with a look of polite inquiry and said, 'Senhorita?' She had thickened a little with the years and hotel living, but she was still handsome and still with a little shadow of dark hairs across her upper lip.

Sarah said quietly, 'Melina – you don't remember me?'

For a moment or two Melina's face was blank. Then suddenly she gasped, clasped her hands to her cheeks, and cried, 'Oooh! No, no! Is it true?'

But even as Sarah nodded, Melina came round the desk and threw her arms about her, hugging and kissing her.

Sarah let the welcome wrap itself about her and felt tears come to her own eyes to match those in Melina's. She was led into the inner office, fussed into a chair, stood back from and looked up and down, and then embraced again. Had she had lunch? She said she had on the road up, knowing that Richard would not want to be dragged in. A glass of porto? No, she did not—.

Then Melina's eyes widened and, her arms dropping loosely to her sides, she said, 'But . . . but the convent. How—?'

More calmly than she would have thought possible Sarah said, 'I have left it for ever. I was not a good nun. But, please, Melina, cara, do not ask me about it. Some time I will come again and see you and tell you all the story.'

Vigorously Melina said, 'There is nothing to tell. I understand. Many times did I say to your mother it was not for you . . . and that, that she should stop you. You do not have to tell me anything. Also, I know why you have come. Wait.'

While she was gone Sarah went to the window and looked out. Richard had driven the car a few yards down the road to gain the shade of an acacia tree. Melina was gone only a few minutes. When she came back she was holding a parcel in her hands against her body. It was wrapped in oiled brown paper and tied with thick string whose knots had been sealed with blue wax.

Melina said, 'Somebody drove you up here?' There was a shrewd protective note in her voice.

'Yes. A man. A true friend. He saved my life when I left the convent. Don't ask me more. Someday I will tell you.'

'I ask you nothing. It is not my business. I am even glad that Carlo is away at Cascais eating with his friends, for he knows nothing of this.' She tapped the parcel. 'For me, it is a parcel your mother gave me to hand to you if one day you should come to me.'

'And if I hadn't come?'

'I must keep it always. Never open it and put in my will that it be burnt in a furnace without being opened. Very strange, but I think your mother knew one day you would come. And here you are. To please me, you will promise to come again when you have your life properly regulated?'

'I promise.'

'Good. I am glad you are no longer a nun.' She smiled slowly. 'There was always too much of your mother in you for that.'

When she got back to the car Farley opened her door for her as though he were her official chauffeur and then went round into his own seat and started the motor. Before moving off he said, 'It's a long drive back, and we shall be late. Would you like to stop to eat on the road?'

'No, thank you, Richard.'

'Fair enough.'

He drove off and she sat at his side with the parcel on her lap. He had obviously seen it, but he had said nothing about it. That was like him. She had the feeling that he was far from accepting her belief that she could repay him. For him – she could be frank with herself now – all her talk was probably being taken as a different form of the hysteria which had driven her into the sea. He humoured her out of his good nature, but he was far from taking her seriously. She pressed her hands against the parcel but its bulk gave no indication of its contents. The agonizing thought went through her that its contents would be useless . . . that maybe her mother's mind was going when she had made all the arrangements with Melina. She sat there remembering how, in those last days before her mother's death, her mind would wander and she would talk strangely. She had a swift picture of her mother distractedly packing a parcel with any bits and pieces that came readily to her hands.

Richard suddenly said, 'Funny thing. Might amuse you. I spent a week in Estoril once. Never really gambled heavily in my life before. But I decided to have a go with the little I had left. I won enough to start that *ristorante* of mine. Easy come, easy go. Eh?'

She put out a hand and touched his arm briefly. She did not know why, but quite irrelevantly his words had lifted the gloom from her.

As they drove out of the square and swung left on to the Lisbon road, a grey dust-covered Volvo which had been parked lower down the square followed them. It was driven by Matthew Gains, a grizzle-haired, long-faced man in his fifties, the son of a Portuguese mother and an English father. Both were dead. His father had worked in an Oporto shipping office and had married the daughter of the house in which he had had lodgings. According to need Gains could pass either as a Portuguese or an Englishman; considerable assets in a mixed life which might have made him successful and rich had it not been for an irrepressible streak of idleness which always seemed to surface when it was least needed. He had learned to accept it with a cheerful tolerance because it had, particularly in this job, encouraged him to foster an imaginative bent which had always been with him and had made of him a persuasive liar when his duties called for too great a show of industry.

He had no biting curiosity about these two. He had driven down to Monchique and found the Villa Lobita. Making his number with the gardener husband of the couple who lived in the cabin at the drive end of the villa had been no trouble for the old man had been full of talk of the *Senhorita* Branton who had once been a nun when he had met him in the local wine shop. On the Saturday evening the man had let slip that the *Senhorita* and her friend were going to Lisbon the next day.

Following them he was easily convinced – he always was when laziness surfaced – that they could be going nowhere else now but back to the villa. The prospect of the long drive had no appeal to him. He had no intention of making it. Not today, anyway. He would see them through Lisbon, over the river and on the road south and then return to his own private pleasures in Lisbon until the next morning. What did it matter? The pay was poor; all the time you worked in the dark; there was no pension, and no one ever queried one of his reports because he was careful not to make any statement of fact which could be verified false and so proved against him. Anyway, if they had had any sense, they would have assigned another man and car for the return drive. The same car behind coming up and going down, even at a discreet distance, could become noticeable. From what he had seen through his glasses of the man he was far from giving the impression of a born fool, and also the kind to get ugly if you stepped on his toes.

Anyway, he knew *them* – throw them a few crumbs and they were happy; stuck-up sods who thought they ran the world while the sun shone out of their backsides. They would be happy with, *Drove up to Estoril. Hotel Globo. Senhorita enters alone. Twenty minutes inside. Comes out. Carrying fair-sized paper parcel. Enters car. Drives off with Senhor Farley.* A lucky man the *Senhor* if the *Senhorita* was favouring him.

He followed the car, whistling thinly through his teeth. Anyway, his instructions had been light contact in the event of movement. What could be lighter than going down comfortably tomorrow?

It was late when they got back to the villa. Fabrina, the house-keeper, had left them a cold supper which Farley welcomed. For herself, Sarah knew that she had gone beyond the need for food that day. As she stood now in the big hallway with the parcel held to her Farley said to her, 'Don't bother about me. I can look after myself.' He looked down from her face to the parcel she held and then smiled at her. 'I can guess how you feel. You want to get upstairs and be alone with it. Yes?'

She nodded, appreciating his tact, and wondering if he realized – perhaps he did, his understanding of her was wide – the slow growth there had been in her of doubt. The parcel had to hold that which would enable her to repay him. But she kept imagining her mother, distraught, not clear in her mind, packing up a random collection of possessions of no importance or worth . . .

She said, 'Yes, I would like that, Richard.'

When he replied she knew that he had read her fears. His big mouth slanted in a lop-sided grin and with a shrug of his shoulders, he said, 'Don't fuss about it. If it turns out to be junk it makes no difference to me. Whatever you may feel there's nothing

you have to repay me, not even the petrol to Lisbon and back.'
He reached out and lightly touched the knuckles of his right hand
against her cheek as though she were a small girl full of imaginary
fears and he a kindly uncle. He turned away to go to the kitchen
and called, 'Goodnight. And sleep well.'

The burden of her emotions brought a mistiness to her eyes
as she turned and began to go up the wide stairs under the large
oil painting of her mother, dark now with the shadows cast by the
single hall light by the front door.

She put all the lights on in her bedroom and sat down at the
little desk in the window alcove. With a pair of small embroidery
scissors and shaking hands she cut the sealed cords around the
parcel and slit through the lines of scotch tape that held the heavy
paper in place. Inside, wrapped in soft white tissue paper, were
two packages. One was long and thin and the other was rectangular and lighter in weight than the former. Loose between the two
packets was a white envelope, unsealed and without any inscrip-
tion on its cover. From inside this, her hands shaking finely, she
drew a sheet of folded writing paper. As she spread it wide on the
desk she saw that it was a piece of the headed note-paper of the
Villa Lobita, and she recognized at once the small, very precise
renaissance script which was her mother's handwriting. The note,
which was dated just over a week before her mother's death, read :

*The contents of this parcel which have been shown to and packed in
the presence of Father Ansoldo of the Capella da Senhora da Pé da
Cruz, Monchique ...*

She had known Father Ansoldo as a young girl and knew too now
from Fabrina that he was long dead.

*... and Senhorita Melina Montes, my personal maid, of this address,
I bequeath absolutely and utterly to use or to dispose of in any way
she wishes to my daughter, Sarah Branton.*

The document was signed by her mother and witnessed by Father
Ansoldo and by Melina, using then her maiden name. Beneath
their subscriptions and, Sarah guessed, not written in the presence
of the witnesses there was a paragraph in her mother's hand which

read: *Sarah, my darling daughter, if ever this comes into your hands, light a candle for me and pray for the redemption of my soul and the forgiveness of my many sins.*

Immediately touched, Sarah slipped forward from her seat to her knees, bowed her head into her hands and prayed, regardless of her own lack of grace, for her mother. It was some time before she felt able to seat herself and pay attention to the two packages before her. Outside it was moonlight now and a fresh breeze was singing through the copse of sweet chestnuts at the side of the drive. This had been her mother's bedroom and many times she must have sat, as she did now, looking out over the moon-washed country. Her mother had loved this place, coming back to it always from her wanderings ... to live simply and, she felt she understood now, to find perhaps a peace and hope which maybe she knew she could never permanently hold.

Slowly she unwrapped the soft paper from the long package. Inside was a narrow, red morocco leather jewel case. She opened it and the soft rays of the desk light fired its contents with sudden sparkling light, the raising of the lid releasing its beauty from long darkness to a liberty and life which brought pure enchantment to her eyes. She knew at once what it was although she had never seen the real thing before. It was the girdle which her mother wore in the oil painting in the hall.

She lifted it out and held it spread between her two hands. The belt was made of large rectangular enamelled gold links set with diamonds and emeralds. The centre clasp, bordered by small sapphires and supported on either side by gold, plump cupids, was a large oval gold enamelled medallion showing Venus risen from the waves. Inscribed on its lower border were the words VIRTUS VINCIT. For some moments she sat just holding it, enchanted by its beauty, feeling its weight drag gently at her fingers, and tipping it a little each way here and there to set the stones catching the soft lamplight. A great joy rose in her, not only from its loveliness, but also from sensing that it must be worth a very great deal of money.

Then her eye was caught by a thin slip of white card which lay in the bottom of the case. She put down the belt and picked up the card. It was covered with her mother's writing, the slightly

74

faded ink matching that of her letter so that she felt sure they were of the same date. The card read:

The girdle of Venus. It was given to me by Lord Bellmaster, many, many years ago and I was painted wearing it by Augustus John. Personally I think it is slightly vulgar and I never used it much. The stones are diamonds, emeralds and sapphires. It has been ascribed to a French jeweller of the seventeenth century called Gilles Legaré, but I was told by more than one expert that were this true Legaré would never have left the centres of each link unadorned by his characteristic jewelled floral motifs. Its valuation in 1948 – two years before your birth – was £30,000. J.B.

On opening the second parcel Sarah found a thick but pliable book, bound in soft and now faded blue suede covers which were held by a small gold clasp. As she opened it a slip of paper slid from the first page on to the desk. Sarah picked it up and, immediately recognizing her mother's writing, smiled to herself. It had been her mother's habit to write and leave notes to servants and friends all over the place; and also to write notes to herself as aides-mémoire; *Take this to Lisbon for repair* – propped against a French ormolu clock on a mantelpiece. Notes left by the telephone – *If Auguste rings remember to tell her about Melina's priceless remark!*

This note read: *My personal diary, intermittently kept, covering a long period of my life, Sarah. I leave the nature of its disposal or use to you. J.B.*

The diary's pages were of very fine paper and the date of the first entry was Sunday, 16 June 1946. The pages were unlined. Her mother's precise renaissance script, much smaller than she normally used, covered the pages in even lines, leaving only the smallest of margins into which Sarah saw, as she riffled a few pages, her mother had put little fine pen drawings of faces, animals, birds, portions of houses and churches and landscapes and other features which she guessed could have some relevance to the diary entry so decorated. Full of relief now at the knowledge that indeed her mother had left her a possession which she could use as the means to repay Richard, she gave little heed to the diary. Leaving the note in it, she closed it and snapped the clasp home. Some time she would read it.

She picked up the golden Venus girdle and let the soft light play across its jewels and enamel. As though to mark the joyous relief in her the now familiar nightingale began to sing from a clump of strawberry trees beyond the swimming pool whose still waters lay like polished silver beneath the growing moon.

chapter four

Quint's room on the first floor overlooked a small courtyard, paved with close-set red bricks, worn and crumbling from the rains and frosts of years. An old plane tree stood in its centre. As Quint read the report Kerslake had drawn up, breathing with a gentle touch of a wheeze, his right hand played with the round ball of a polished alabaster paperweight on his desk. Standing on the other side of the desk – unless you were in for a long session Quint never invited you to sit – Kerslake watched a pair of London pigeons on one of the lower branches of the tree. The cock bird was making a courting display to the rather shabby hen. Faintly he could hear the pouting, bubbling love talk of the male, iridescent breast swollen, head low, tail high. In Barnstaple his father, dead now, had kept pigeons, a lot of racing birds, mostly dark blue chequers, and another loft of fancy birds, West of England tumblers, Birmingham rollers, and a few kits of tipplers, high flying trios which would soar above the town for hours on end, almost lost to sight. One night when he was sixteen someone bestial with jealous rivalry had broken into the fancy birds' loft and wrung all their necks. His father's distress had so moved him that he had set himself to find out and prove who had been responsible. He had, too . . . his first step in detection and towards joining the Force. And his first step, too, towards this room.

Quint gave a faint, rasping sigh and looked up, studying Kerslake's face so long in silence that the young man felt the unease of embarrassment even though it was a well-known mannerism of Quint's. When Quint looked at him like that he felt totally exposed.

Unexpectedly Quint smiled, and equally unexpectedly he said, 'Lord Bellmaster of Conary. Mean anything to you?'

'No, sir.'

'Then it's time it did. He once, many years ago, sat where I'm sitting. And then he got up and went and sat in higher and higher places. Long ago. But he's still us. It'll interest you to meet him. Brief him on all this. If he asks anything of you agree but say you must first check with me.' He tapped the report. 'Let him have all we know.' He picked up the report and slid it into one of his top drawers. 'I'll let you know where and when he'll see you. I like the stuff you've got from the Ministry of Defence and the other people. You're my Barnstaple boy. Keep your nose clean. Be nice to his lordship but between us don't be taken in. He's a first-class snake.'

At five minutes to three that afternoon Kerslake, with rolled umbrella and bowler hat, got out of a taxi close to the Albert Gate in Knightsbridge and walked a few yards down the road to Claremount Mansions. He gave his card to the hall porter and asked for Lord Bellmaster. The porter rang through from his office with the glass door shut. Coming out he gave a little nod of approval and said, 'This way, sir.'

They went up in the lift and when it stopped, the porter pointed down the righthand corridor and said, '36b. Third door down.'

Kerslake moved down the corridor. There was no surprise in him not to hear the lift door close and the hum of its descent. The porter would wait until he had been seen to enter. London was full of politely monitored fortresses like Claremount Mansions. A manservant let him in, took his bowler and umbrella and then led him across the narrow hall, opened a door and stood back for him to pass. 'Just go straight in, sir. His lordship is expecting you.'

The door closed behind him with a faint hiss, a light came on overhead. There was another door a few feet ahead of him, without handle or knob. He pushed it open and went in, knowing that it was going to close sound-proof behind him.

It was a large, light, comfortable room, its great bay window looking out over the park. Above the marble fireplace was a Munnings painting of a hunting scene. A low bookshelf ran along one wall and was partly hidden by a long settee. Without obvious curiosity Kerslake took it all in; a comfortable room, furnished and littered the way the owner wanted it, the way – he wondered – which gave him a feeling of security? Still lifes of game, an unpleasant-looking cock salmon in a glass case, an original Russell Flint of three naked to semi-naked Spanish women grouped in and around a marble pool, and a fox mask over a door which he guessed could lead to the sleeping and dining quarters.

Lord Bellmaster was looking out of the window. In the moment before he turned Kerslake noticed that the dark, silvered hair was thinning to show the freckled skin of his scalp at the back. When he turned the big face and broad shoulders, slim hips and long legs gave the impression of power poised for use. Without the gift and use of power for many years, Kerslake thought, he would probably have gone to slack and flabbiness long ago.

'Kerslake?'

'Yes, my lord.'

'Sit ye down.' A big single-ringed hand jerked towards the settee. 'And "sir" will do.'

'Thank you, sir.' Kerslake sat down, knowing instinctively that in the next few minutes he must find himself either liking or disliking this man. There would be no halfway point.

Going to the empty fireplace, standing square in front of it, Lord Bellmaster said, 'Quint speaks well of you.'

'Thank you, sir.'

The big lips in the large face moved to the beginning of a smile. 'Praise from Quint is like bloody snow in June. What were you when you left Barnstaple?'

'Detective-sergeant, sir.'

'Not sorry to leave the leafy lanes?'

'No sir.'

'Well, what have you got up to date?'

'A fresh Lisbon report. Miss Sarah Branton was driven by the man Farley from the villa to Estoril yesterday. She went into an hotel briefly, twenty minutes about and came out carrying a brown paper parcel, or at least a brownish parcel. They drove straight back to the villa. The hotel is called the Hotel Globo and it is run by a man and his wife. Carlo and Melina Spuggi. Lisbon have nothing on either of them.'

'Lisbon was always a bad office.'

'They're only using light contact, sir.'

Bellmaster suddenly smiled. 'Loyalty noticed. And you can ration the "sirs".'

'Yes, my lord.'

'What about this Richard Farley?'

'Lisbon have nothing on record. As long as we keep it light contact they won't do anything. But since there was no danger of any personal contact he's been checked from this end.'

'By whom? By the way, smoke if you wish.' Bellmaster nodded to a silver box on a nearby low table.

'I don't use them, thank you. He was checked by me on Mr Quint's instructions. I got most of the stuff from the Ministry of Defence. The rest came from old Colonial Office files. I checked Farley for national or war service. He did national service in Kenya. His father was a naval officer, retired as lieutenant-commander after the war and with his wife went to Kenya. I checked the father with Naval Personnel. One of the older staff there remembered him well, knew him personally, and kept up for a time after the war. As a sub-lieutenant he served under Farley's father in destroyers for a time. From just after the war the family farmed in Kenya. The boy, only child – went to school in this country. A small public school, Cranbrook in Kent. All this on his national service record.'

Bellmaster smiled. 'You've been mining away like a busy mole, haven't you? All this in one morning?'

Kerslake gave a little shrug. 'It was all practically under one roof.'

'The father's dead. What about the mother?'

'I was going on to say – they're both dead. They were killed by the Mau-Mau on their farm during the trouble so Farley's father's shipmate told me.'

'Sods. What about the boy, Richard?'

'The father's friend knew him quite well. He did prep school in Kenya. When he came over here to Cranbrook he spent the occasional holiday with him and short leaves. He said – quiet, reserved, pleasant. I didn't overpress him at this stage because I thought it might not be wise. They'll always help so far but if you press then they dig in their toes and ask for an official directive. I didn't have that. But I made it clear that it wasn't just a chummy little coffee chat between us. Service people get very spiky. Especially about old chums.'

'No hint of Farley's later life?'

'Not really, sir. He left Kenya after his parents were killed and worked in South Africa. That's where he was last heard from. He never kept up with his father's friend. That's it, sir.'

Bellmaster rubbed his large chin thoughtfully. 'Well, I'm not grumbling. You've done well.' He turned away to the window and stood looking out.

Kerslake sat and waited. He would have given a lot, he thought, to know what was going through the man's mind. Once he had been a very big gun in Birdcage Walk. Probably still was in a way because no one ever really went away. He was less interested in this Richard Farley. If you let your curiosity run away with you in the early stages then you just muddled up your thinking. By going too far, or even a little way on your own initiative, you could be repaid with kicks. For all he knew he might have done wrong in probing Lieutenant-Commander Farley's young friend in Naval Personnel.

Without turning Bellmaster said casually, 'What did you get in your field division?'

'A-minus, sir.'

'Languages?'

'English only.'

Still without turning Bellmaster gave a light chuckle and said, 'With a not-too-broad Devonshire accent. How did you do on law?'

'A-plus, sir.'

'What's a great fee?' Bellmaster turned, a smile on his large face.

'The holding of a tenant of the Crown.'

'Ever been to Portugal?'

'No, sir.'

'Abroad?'

'France, Germany and Majorca.'

'Like to play a solicitor?'

'Sir?'

'There is a certain legal matter which I want to arrange – now that I've heard what you have to say – with Miss Sarah Branton. Quite a simple one which won't give you any trouble. You'll get a full briefing from me before you go to see her in Portugal, on the legal and the personal side. But just for the moment, as a favour to me, don't say anything about the possibility of your going to Portugal to Quint. I'll fix that when the time comes. No question of disloyalty just no point in jumping the gun, yet. All right?'

'Yes, my lord.'

'Good. That's all. I'll show you out.'

Fifteen minutes after Kerslake had gone, Lord Bellmaster telephoned Geddy at his offices in Cheltenham and told him that he was coming down to Cheltenham the next day and would be obliged if they could meet for lunch. This call made, he then rang Lieutenant-Colonel Branton's house. The Colonel was out and his wife answered. Lord Bellmaster asked her to tell her husband that he would be in the Cirencester area the next day and, unless he received a call to the contrary he would be glad if the Colonel would see him at four o'clock. He put the telephone down without the least doubt that the Colonel would see him for he had used the phrase in the course of his talk – 'on a matter which could prove very welcome to him.'

At that moment Kerslake in Birdcage Walk was just finishing giving an exact account to Quint of everything which had passed between himself and Lord Bellmaster. He might, he had told himself on the way back, be comparatively young at the game, but he knew which side his bread was buttered. He was Quint's man, not Bellmaster's.

As he finished talking, Quint nodded to a leather armchair and said, 'Sit down, Kerslake.'

Kerslake sat down, knowing that the courtesy marked approval not coming censure. Quint got up and in silence went to his cupboard and brought back a whisky bottle and two glasses. Without asking Kerslake whether he wanted a drink, he poured two stiff measures and handed a glass to him, saying, 'It's a bit early in the day for working folk. But I feel virtue – yours – should be rewarded. Or, though I would find it hard to believe, did you know that unknown to Bellmaster we have a permanent tap there?'

'No, sir.'

'You can drop the sir as long as the whisky lasts which shows how mellow at this moment I feel towards you. So he might want you to go to Portugal to see Miss Branton. It'll be interesting when his tapes come in tonight to know what phone calls he will have made after you left.'

Feeling that Quint's mood would allow it, Kerslake asked, 'Why should he ask me to keep this Portugal thing to myself for a while? It seems of little importance.'

'Good question. And if I told you to think it over seriously for fifteen minutes you'd probably come up with the answer. But I'll save you that trouble. He doesn't run this show any longer but he can still call on our services. He's ambitious. He likes power and he likes having people in his pocket. That's where he thinks he's going to put you. If you'd not given me a *full* report of your talk with him, that's where he would have had you now. It's only a small, unimportant thing not mentioning a possible trip abroad. The best that came to his hand at the time. But the next time it could be something important he'd want you to hold back from us, perhaps. If you refused then he'd let us know about your first little lapse and say that he had been testing you then for your loyalty to us. And then you would be out. But you've been a good boy and I'm pleased with you. So, now you get a directive from me officially. Play his game. If he asks you to keep anything to yourself in the future don't make any bones about it. *Yes, my lord. Certainly, your lordship.* And if he asks you to do *anything* – then agree. *But* before you do it check with us.' Quint smiled, sipped his whisky and chuckled. 'He's a big, powerful man in all senses of those words. And he makes no secret of his ambitions. He's after a plum ambassadorship or something equally im- portant. People don't get those jobs if they have any skeletons in their cupboard. Cupboards can be opened by other ambitious people. The best thing to do with a skeleton is to grind the bones to flour and scatter it to the winds. The only thing that can betray you then is the chance that someone sees you sorting out the bones before you start grinding. Confusing? Yes, I suppose it is. Well, don't worry about it. Climb into his pocket when he opens it. We've got an even bigger pocket waiting which has been made to measure for him.' He finished his whisky and Kerslake, catching the signal, finished his and rose.

'Thank you for the drink, sir.'

'You earned it. We've wanted someone in his pocket for a long time. He'll keep everything very official until one day he'll ask for a personal favour, something just between the two of you. He'll say that he'll get you a promotion jump, say head of a section, in return. Which is what you want, of course. And what you'll probably get, but not through him.' He lit a cigarette and coughed as he took the first draw. Wheezily, he went on, 'It's a long way from Barnstaple, isn't it?'

'Yes, sir.'

'But it's the same world ... the same old dirty world of men's desires and greeds. Where do you think the tap is?'

Thrown for a moment, Kerslake looked blank and then rapidly recovered himself. Quint was into one of his oblique moods.

He said, 'Not the fox mask over the door. That would be too obvious. That would go for the mounted salmon, too. One of the picture frames, I'd say.'

'That's right. The one with the luscious Spanish girls, all tits and tummies, a well-known Bellmaster weakness. All right. Off you go. You've been a good lad.'

'Thank you, sir.'

Kerslake went out knowing that subtly his relationship with Quint had changed to his advantage. Head of a section. That normally could have been ten years away. Well ... time would tell. Closing the door behind him he walked down the corridor, whistling thinly between his teeth.

All day Farley had realized that she was excited and, perhaps because of it, avoiding him as much as she could. That morning he had heard her singing to herself in her room. When she had come down she had announced that she was going off for a long walk, that she had lots of things to think over, and did he mind if she went alone? He said *no* and had spent the morning with Mario helping him to sandpaper down and begin to repaint the big wrought iron ornamental gates at the drive entrance, and from Mario he had heard a lot about the days when Lady Jean had been mistress of the villa. Things were always lively and the place usually full of guests. For Mario those had been the great days. Mrs Ringel Fanes was quite unlike her sister. She was seldom at the villa and when she was there was little entertaining. She was a good, serious woman and, although he did not say it, he clearly implied that Lady Jean had not been.

At lunch and before retiring to her room Sarah was full of her walk and how much she had enjoyed it and clearly had no intention yet of saying anything about the parcel she had collected in Estoril.

He smiled to himself as he sat now in the sun room, waiting for her to come down for a drink before dinner. Unbidden by him Fabrina had brought in a few minutes before a bottle of champagne in an ice bucket and set it on the low glass-topped table with the other drinks. Whatever had been in the parcel, he realized, had been pleasing enough to put Sarah in an excited, slightly distant mood. It was not hard for him to guess that she was probably preparing some surprise for him. Well, he was a big boy now and not easily surprised. Knowing her mood all day, he had made no mention of the parcel for fear of spoiling her coming pleasure. Champagne, no less. From the day he had first gone away to school at Cranbrook his father had always produced champagne to speed his journey and also to welcome his return to Kenya ... sitting on the verandah, foals and mares in the paddock, and away to the south across the Masai lands the crest of Kilimanjaro wreathed with clouds ... his mother's laughter, clear, bright joyful sounds as the cork went *pop*! With a sudden tension of his cheek muscles he shut the memory from him before another could fully intrude.

Fifteen minutes later he heard Sarah coming through the big room towards him. Leaning forward, elbows on his knees, he was reading a book and he kept his position, pretending not to hear her, some instinct telling him that this was a moment she had been preparing all day and he must not spoil it. He heard her stop at the entrance to the sun room and on the air there came to him the slight fragrance of some scent.

There was a little pause and then she said, 'Richard.'

He turned and rose slowly to his feet. She stood smiling at him, waiting for his reaction. Her short hair was arranged boyishly and she was wearing a long white gown, sleeveless and cut modestly low at the front. He knew that the villa still held many of her mother's clothes and he guessed that she had spent the afternoon altering the gown for she had told him once that her mother had been taller than she. She looked beautiful and he guessed that she knew full well she did. Pleased with herself she stood now waiting for his pleasure to show. About her waist she wore the belt which her mother had worn when Augustus John had painted the portrait in the hall. Before he could fully move or find ready words he felt his throat contract with sharp emotion. Even with her short hair she was all loveliness, all woman, and there was a brief stir of anger in him to think that she had spent eight years of her life . . .

'Sarah!'

He moved towards her spontaneously, put his hands on her bare arms and, leaning forward, kissed her on the cheek.

'Do I look nice?' she asked as he stepped back, her blue eyes turning away from his in a moment of rising embarrassment.

'You look like a queen. Albeit—' he grinned to chase away her shyness, 'a crop-haired one. When that grows I'll have to shade my eyes to look at you. You look absolutely marvellous and I'd dot anyone on the nose who disagreed. But what's it all in aid of—' he nodded towards the champagne bucket. 'Come on, I don't like mysteries.'

She laughed and came round the table. 'Can't you guess?'

'No, I can't and don't want to. Tell me.'

'This.' She put her hands on the belt she was wearing.

'Not with you yet. But I know it's the one your mother is wearing in the painting. A bit theatrical, isn't it?'

'Theatrical? Oh, Richard! It's not just a costume accessory, nice but of no real value. This is it!' Her voice rose. 'This is what was in the parcel. My mother left it to me and it's genuine and quite old. Look—' She unclasped the belt and held it out towards him. 'It's real gold, real diamonds, sapphires and emeralds. And it's yours. All yours. Take it, please. Oh, please take it! It was worth thirty thousand pounds when mama was given it years and years ago. It must be worth a fortune now. And I want you to have it.'

He took the belt in his hands, feeling at once its weight, and knowing his own confusion. She had this bee in her bonnet about repaying him ... and he had humoured her, driven her to Estoril. But this ... he ran his thumbs gently over the cupids on either side of the clasp, his eyes on the blonde, streaming-haired Venus walking the foam-tipped waves and he had the odd thought that distantly there was a likeness faintly about the face to Sarah. VIRTUS VINCIT. He had enough Latin still for that. As the belt swung from his hands the evening glow from the setting sun struck fire from the precious stones. Sarah must be mad to think he could take it. All that she owed him was a heartfelt thank you. At the most a copper medal as a life-saving award. Smiling at the thought he handed back the belt.

Quietly, he said, 'Put it on. That's where it belongs around, if I may say so, your very slim and beautiful waist. Go on, put it on, and don't give me that stubborn look.'

With a touch of spirit he had not met in her before, she said, 'It's not a stubborn look. It's an angry look and I can tell you, Richard, if you don't take it I'll ... I'll just go out in a boat and throw it into the sea!'

He laughed then and reached for the champagne, saying, 'What I think we both need is a drink. The champagne was your idea so you can't refuse it. And then we'll sit down and talk this thing over. And, for God's sake—' his face was set stubbornly for a moment, 'don't think I'm being over-sensitive or stupid about it. There are some things that just aren't done.'

For a moment or two he knew that she was on the point of arguing strongly with him. For the first time he realized that in her there had to be a wilfulness and power to force things her way once she had set a course for herself. Then, as he sensed her to be poised to argue and insist, he saw the passion which had stilled her face pass quickly from it.

She said quietly, 'Yes, I think you are right, Richard. We must talk it over very quietly and sensibly. It was silly of me to be so dramatic about it all. But it did seem to be the best way ... well, a celebrating kind of way to break it to you. Oh, Richard, you've got to know that I must be allowed somehow to show you my gratitude.'

He laughed. 'Sure. Of course. And you can begin by sitting down like the beautiful queen you are and enjoying your drink with me before dinner and we'll both talk like two very sensible people.' He began to work the wire from the champagne cork and gave her a wink. 'Agreed?'

'Agreed on condition I'm allowed to say one thing first.'

'Fire ahead.'

'I think you're the nicest man I've ever met.'

He shrugged his shoulders, gave her a smile, and then filled their glasses. They drank to one another. Then, as she sat down, she said, 'The last time I had champagne was in this house on my mother's birthday.'

To avoid the subject of the belt, he said, 'Tell me about her. She sounds as though she were a very lively number.'

Lying in bed later, he went back over the evening. She had talked for a long time about her mother. It was clear that she had loved her, but had come to understand clearly what kind of woman she had been which, put at its kindest was not entirely admirable as far as her appetites and morals were concerned. She had had a zest for living which had forced her to ignore many conventions. He got the impression of someone completely amoral, full of charm and wit, and incapable of loving or hating other than whole-heartedly. A woman, he saw, much better to have for than against you. Thinking that now, he wondered how much of that character persisted in Sarah. Stubbornness and a will to have her own way certainly; for she had come back to the belt and her absolute need and determination to use it to make her repayment to him. In the end to defer any decision on his part, he had said that he wanted time to think about it, and also that it might be a good idea to get it valued. He knew a Swiss jeweller who had re- tired to a villa just outside Albufeira. One day he would drive down and get his opinion on it. He had seen at once that this suggestion had given her the feeling that he was coming round to accepting her offer and they had talked no more about the belt. But she had persisted in an oblique way because over dinner she had probed him about his future. What did he want to do? Start another restaurant? *No, thank you. He had had that one.* Go to England and farm? *He had mentioned that once or twice but knew that he would never do it.* Badgered, he had finally dragged up out of the blue an idle memory. *I know a big old farmhouse in the Dordogne. I did think once that it might be fun to buy it, do it up and turn it into a country hotel.* That had kept her happy, wanting to know all about it to the point where he had been forced to invent details to feed her curiosity and enthusiasm. But the simple truth was – and he just could not say so frankly to her – that there was nothing. He was a day-to-day man. Some time something would turn up and he would know it was for him. Then, going up to bed, as he had stood outside her door to say goodnight, she had said without any hesitation or embarrassment, 'I've told you about my father and my mother. I know nothing about yours. Are they alive still?'

For a moment or two he had known that he was just going to say simply that they had both been dead for years and then, finding a sudden and undeniable urge for brutal truth, he had said, 'They are both dead. I came back late from Nairobi one night and found them – slaughtered by the Mau-Mau.'

Hating himself now for his words, he lay, seeing her face, stricken with anguish, and then she had moved to him impulsively and putting her hands on his shoulders had kissed him, saying, 'Oh, Richard ... poor Richard ...' Then she had turned away and gone quickly into her bedroom.

He lay now, wishing he had guarded his tongue. Telling her could only have added to her feeling for him, feeding her desire to repay him. He picked up his bedside book. He knew now that it was going to be one of those nights when he would have to read himself into oblivion. Through his open window came the echoing, rapid *kutuk-kutuk-kutuk* call of a red-necked nightjar. A night-bird had been calling that evening when, walking across the veranda into the living room, he had found them slaughtered on the floor.

*

They were polite to one another, a politeness which was like walking on black ice, knowing that any moment a slip could come to upset the near-hostile relationship between them. Bellmaster despised the man largely he knew because he had found him easy to buy and to use. Also, and he had never been able to rid himself of this, he was jealous of the man, an illogical jealousy rising from the compromise for which he had paid him a handsome settlement. As her legal husband he had known Jean and slept with her. Once a man was in her bed Jean had known no way of being half-hearted. She followed her body's dictates, joyfully abandoning herself to her senses. Even at those times when through his own direction she had obeyed him and he had profited from her ... whoring, why burke the word? ... he had been jealous.

Colonel Branton sat at his untidy desk, his bushy eyebrows lowered over his frowning, openly hostile eyes. He said, giving a flick of insult to his crisp words, 'You're here on business, of course. On no other terms would I open my door to you, Bellmaster.'

Curbing himself Bellmaster said, 'I'm quite happy about the terms. There's no need to state them. We both understand. I want to talk to you about your daughter Sarah.'

'Your daughter – she's nothing to do with me now. At least, I presume she's your daughter. One could never have known with dear Lady Jean.'

Untouched, Bellmaster shrugged his shoulders. 'It's a possibility I always had in mind, but of no importance now. I had lunch with Geddy today—'

'That pooh-bear number. Does he still enjoy living in your pocket?' Branton smiled unexpectedly. 'I'm sorry, I'm digressing. But a little touch of venom I find now and then as comforting as a large Scotch. Yes, Sarah and dear Geddy?'

'He's had a cable from Mrs Ringel Fanes saying that she is making over the Villa Lobita and all its contents to Sarah.'

'Lucky Sarah, it must all be worth quite a fortune. That settles her. So where do I come in?'

'She can't just live in the villa on nothing.'

'Why not? She can take holiday guests. Plenty do. She's got

the villa and as far as I'm concerned she's welcome to the damned place. I could never stand it. Not knowing which man had warmed Jean's bed the night before you arrived. Sorry, if I reminisce.'

Unexpectedly Lord Bellmaster laughed pleasantly, and said, 'Perhaps I've overlooked something in you all these years. Or is it a late development, this sardonic touch?'

'It's more likely to be indigestion from the badly cooked food that slut out there serves up for me. I don't really begin to be at my best until five minutes after six. Sarah – stick to her.'

For a moment or two Bellmaster said nothing. Whatever Branton might say, Sarah was his daughter, a Bellmaster. She had made a fool of herself over this nun caper, but she was his flesh and blood. He had to provide for her and the fact that by doing so he would be able to remove any possible existing threat to his future was a felicitous bonus. He said patiently, 'I will. She's got to have money as well as a place to live. I want you to make an allowance to her.'

Branton laughed. 'Oh, of course. What would suit her? Ten thousand a year? I'll fix it up with my bank. Or would, if they would only let me through the door.'

'I'm not suggesting you foot the bill. I know full well you can't. I shall do that. But, for Sarah's sake, we must keep up appearances, mustn't we? Even now after all these years.'

'Oh, yes, of course we must. Keeping up appearances is very important and damned hard at times when there's nothing left after you've paid something on your bookmaker's account. But I'm with you, Bellmaster. You'll put up the money and Geddy, humming gently to himself, will fix it all up so that it looks as though it's coming from me. Sarah will never know the difference. She's been eight years in limbo and still thinks I'm a wealthy gentleman farmer, hunting, shooting and fishing.' His voice grew suddenly rasping and bitter. 'If I want to hunt these days I have to get a hack from livery. Shooting? I sold my pair of Purdeys six years ago and now use a cheap Spanish job my father would never have allowed in the gun-room. Fishing, you want to hear about that? I fish the Wye still, but it's hotel water and I get it free in return for giving lessons to bloody Birmingham and Manchester money-bags who take their catch home and sell it to a fishmonger. *Sic transit gloria mundi!* And once *someone* told me that if I were a good young officer I'd make major-general. Not told, no. Bloody promised. All right, don't get me wrong. I'm full of paternal good-will. I'll send her an allowance in my name. It's only a small service since the money's not mine. But I must have a price paid for this service which will soothe my wounded pride. That's really why you are here, isn't it?'

'Exactly.'

'Exactly. Yes, that's the precise word.' Branton picked up an ivory paper knife from his desk and beat a little tattoo with it. Then, with an unexpected smile, he went on, 'Exactly how much would you consider an appropriate fee for my services in this matter, if I may phrase it in Geddy's terms?'

Suddenly stung by the man's manner, Bellmaster said, 'I thought a thousand pounds would be generous.'

'A year, of course.' Branton smiled and the paper knife ceased its tattooing.

With a shake of his head, holding down the anger that this man was succeeding in rousing in him, Bellmaster said calmly, 'I'm sorry, Branton. I'm talking in terms of a once and for all payment. A thousand pounds seems very generous to me since you have to do nothing at all. Geddy will arrange everything.'

'Yes, Geddy's a great arranger. I wonder what put the idea of making an allowance to Sarah in your head? Interesting. Still, that's your business. But I certainly won't do it for a thousand. Why—' Branton smiled, 'I might even be putting myself in an illegal position. You could be going to contravene the currency regulations and—'

'Don't be a damn fool!'

'Exactly. I've no intention of being one. I'm afraid you've got to make it far more than a thousand.'

Suddenly anxious to have done with this man and be away, Bellmaster said smoothly, 'Well, knowing your position and for old time's sake, I'll make it two thousand.'

Branton shook his head. 'There are no old time's sakes between us. Just bloody bitter bad times. But you seem to want this arrangement badly, not that I care why, so I'll be generous and take ten thousand, and let me tell you that five of that will go right away to make the hearts of tradesmen, bookies and a bloody bank manager happy.' He leaned back in his chair, whistling thinly between his teeth. In his clear blue eyes was an icy glint of happiness. For the first time in his life he had Bellmaster over a barrel and was enjoying it.

In the end they settled for seven thousand, the cheque signed and handed over there in the room.

As Lord Bellmaster was driven away down the pot-holed drive in his Rolls-Royce he leaned forward and opened the drink cabinet. Nothing but a large brandy could begin to soothe him. For the first time in his life he had found Branton able to rile him, to stir him up to unexpected and impatient anger. And for what? he asked himself bitterly. Probably nothing at all. For all he knew the money for Sarah and Branton was being tipped down the drain just because he was letting a few angry words spat out at him by Jean years ago haunt him. He could see her now in the main bedroom of the villa as she had shouted at him: *You turned my life rotten, and there's nothing I can do about it while I live without destroying myself. But when I'm dead – then I'll come back . . . come back and destroy you!*

The quick brandy was beginning to soothe him, he shook his head wearily. Probably she had meant nothing at all. One of her wild Irish outbursts. But he could risk nothing of his future . . . nothing.

In his study Colonel Branton leaned back in his chair, holding the cheque in his hands. He was mellow with his good fortune and the clear knowledge that old Bellmaster must be losing his grip to allow himself to be riled so easily. What maggot was eating him, he wondered? Not that he cared. There was a faint tap on the door and his wife came in with a tray.

'I've brought your tea, love.'

Folding the cheque without haste and putting it into his inside pocket he smiled pleasantly. 'Thanks, my old dear.'

'How was his lordship?'

'Nice enough. Just an old-times'-sake chat as he happened to be up this way. By the by, I meant to tell you, I've got to go up to town for a few days. Why don't you pop over and stay with that sister of yours?'

'Oh, that would be nice. I haven't seen Vi for ages.'

'Fine. Have a good old girls' natter. I'll be staying at the club.'

Watching her pour his tea, chattering away without expecting an answer, he thought . . . nice, a real comfortable handful, knew all the tricks. But she was no filly any longer. Even at his age a man needed that now and again. Young flesh. Now, if only it had been seventy instead of seven thousand he'd have put her out to grass permanently and been free to look around . . . *Eheu fugaces!*

Two pigeons, but not the same ones, were in the plane tree. Quint had a solitary sprig of winter jasmine in his buttonhole. It was a clear, brisk sunny morning. He was breathing easily and his face was touched with a rare crease of a smile worked there by an inner glow of well-being. Looking up from the papers on his desk he killed the smile. Kerslake's eyes turned from the window to Quint's face.

Quint said pleasantly, 'You like seeing them there, don't you?'

'Yes, sir. My father used to breed them.'

'I know but that wouldn't surprise you would it?'

'No, sir.'

'You've got an appointment at three o'clock today. A Mr Arnold Geddy of Geddy, Parsons and Rank, solicitors, The Avenue, Cheltenham. Know Cheltenham?'

'No, sir.'

'It isn't what it was. Mr Geddy will brief you. Tomorrow morning, ten – Lord Bellmaster will see you. He will further brief you for Portugal – the Villa Lobita. You'll leave the following day. TAP to Lisbon. Car down to Monchique. Get the latest briefing, if any from the Lisbon office. Make your own hotel arrangements according to the lie of the ground. On no account stay at the villa if invited. When your business is done take three days' holiday. Genuine. You have a free rein from us. You understand that, of course?'

'Of course, sir.'

Quint was silent for a while, keeping his eyes on Kerslake and then with a nod of his head as he resolved some inner doubts, he said, 'You'd better know. Geddy – a long time ago – was here. Wartime only. Not much good on the ground but an excellent seat-polisher. He wouldn't mention this, of course but I thought you'd like to see that some of us finish up happy. Well, that's it. Run away and start pretending you're a very junior partner in a prosperous provincial firm of solicitors. Make a nice change.'

'Yes, sir.'

'And, of course, if Bellmaster gives you a different briefing from mine – and he knows what I'm going to give you – and asks you to keep it under your hat then do as he says. We want him to think that you're corruptible.'

'Yes, sir.'

'Which all men are, of course. And don't say "Yes, sir" to that.'

'No, sir.'

Quint looked briefly out of the window. 'Your birds have gone. Honeymoon flight perhaps. All right. Off you go to the last haven of all retiring service people.'

The next morning at ten o'clock Kerslake went to see Lord Bellmaster at Claremount Mansions. He was in his dressing gown, bathed and shaved, taking his breakfast of coffee and toast. Kerslake accepted a cup of coffee where he would normally have refused. Without any positive instruction from Quint now, but knowing that he had to shade himself to the role which Bellmaster could have in mind for him, he felt it could do no harm to show the smallest edge of pleasure at the possible birth of a private understanding between them, a slight flicker of self-interest and ambition. To his surprise he soon sensed that Bellmaster was proceeding as though it were now a matter of course that they had a purely private understanding, that he would fit snugly into Bellmaster's pocket and Bellmaster would look after him.

'What did you make of dear old Geddy?'

'A very pleasant man, sir.'

'And very able. Of course, he told you that in fact the settlement for Miss Branton was really coming from me?'

'Yes, sir.'

'But not why?' Bellmaster refilled his cup with half coffee and half cream.

'No, sir.'

'Well, at Birdcage Walk it's no secret to some. She's my daughter. The marriage to Colonel Branton was one of convenience – with a large consideration to him, of course. Long since squandered. I had to pay him to agree to this arrangement now. A useless fellow. I can tell you that just to get his consent to the settlement in his name has cost me some thousands. Know why I'm talking frankly to you like this?'

Kerslake studied the Russell Flint painting for a few moments, his face, he hoped, giving the impression of careful thought ... some hesitation on the brink of self-interest, if that were possible. But the plain fact was that he already knew his reply and was thinking to himself that one of the women on the poolside had breasts which were just like Margaret's ... he saw her lying back on the sand dunes, her bikini bra loose in one hand.

He said slowly, to show that he needed to pick his words carefully, that he wanted no offence to shadow the understanding which was to grow between them, 'I understand that when you were at Birdcage her mother was – though not officially – of considerable help to you there for many years.'

Bellmaster laughed. 'Until her death. I can tell you. She was pure Borgia, solid *cinquecento*. Also the kind of woman who, if you crossed her, never forgot and never forgave and would find a way of striking back – alive or dead. There isn't any man living who doesn't have some part of his past make him vulnerable. So now you know why I'm talking like this to you.'

'Frankly no, my lord.' All right, Kerslake thought; he might be giving a good performance of a lightly hooked fish, but there was no sense in coming too easily to the net.

'A little less than frankly, I think. But let it go. The game must have some rules. The truth is she could still be a danger to me and not one that Birdcage might consider they need show too much concern over. They have their interests and I have mine. The advantage is mine because I have a foot in two worlds. Theirs and the openly political world. Do I have to say more?'

'No, sir. I read the political gossip columns. But you know my only loyalty is to Birdcage. That's the only career I want, too.'

'And so it shall be. But even if you sit at the top at Birdcage you have a string round your waist which is pulled – or can be – from higher up. You've got nothing to fear if you do me a small personal service and it becomes known after the fact.'

'My brief, sir, is to take my instructions from you in this matter.'

'But to report everything to them?'

'Naturally, sir.'

'Then there's no problem. You send your reports fully and frankly. Anything I ask you to do you do, and then eventually – a word which is capable of many interpretations – let them know about it. You agree?'

'Yes, sir. Except in one instance where I *must* get prior authorization from Birdcage before I act.'

Showing no surprise, Lord Bellmaster pushed his coffee cup away, leaned back in his chair and slowly lit a cigarette. He sat gently fingering the chasing of his gold case and then with a laugh said, 'My dear Kerslake, did you really think you were going swimming in such deep waters? There's nothing like that about this. This by no stretch of imagination could come to an elimination exercise. There's no possibility of putting anyone to the sword. At the most this would come to a burning of the book or books.' Standing up and moving to the fireplace, he tightened the belt about his dressing gown. 'I just want to know exactly what was in that parcel which Sarah Branton collected from the Hotel Globo at Estoril. And knowing that ... well, it's conceivable that I might want to have possession of all or part of the contents. That's your brief. Find out and let me know immediately. Before you leave I'll give you three telephone numbers – one or other will always find me, no matter what time of day. As a matter of interest, how have you been on elimination?'

'I've never been assigned so far, sir.'

'Well, if you live long enough you will. And I can tell you – the first time you won't like it. But, for God's sake, put the idea from your head so far as this matter is concerned.'

'Yes, sir.' Kerslake was tempted to add thank you, but refrained. He would come to an elimination one day and there was something to be said for sooner rather than later.

'Good. So let's get this clear. You go down there and you find out about the parcel. I don't have to brief you on that. If there was anything in the shape or form of letters or a diary or diaries get them. Naturally you'll cover yourself on that. I don't care how. But get them and let me have them. The odds are I shan't want to keep anything you find. But if I do – well, that's our secret and I shall see you get the kind of reward you want. Birdcage need never know that you discovered anything. So you see, the whole thing is a simple exercise and I'm not asking you to step far out of line. Anyway, it's quite possible that I'm letting old fears get to me.' He began to move away towards the window. 'I don't have to tell you that most men who get to the top have scandals ... dark periods in their lives ... which they don't want brought into the light. There've been times when I wish I'd stuck to Castle Conary and just looked after myself and mine own. But there it is, either God or the Devil gets to you. Pity that the prospectus of the first isn't as attractively laid out as that of the second.' He turned abruptly, smiling. 'Well, there it is, young Kerslake. I'm only asking you possibly to step a little out of line for me. A little concession, shall we say, to your future prospects.'

'Yes, my lord.'

'A pleasant trip tomorrow. You'll like the villa. I've had some mixed moments there.'

When Kerslake reported back to Quint he heard him out without interruption, smiling, and then said, 'He'll make a good ambassador, won't he? You don't know whether you're coming or going, do you?'

'His line is a bit hard to follow, sir.' The evening light was throwing long shadows over the courtyard and through the slightly open window came the low, throaty grumble of London traffic.

'He meant it to be. One moment you think he's asking you to do nothing out of line. The next you think you're agreeing to play some game – disloyal – with him ... on a promise of future fast promotion. Oh, dear, oh, dear! What a man. Yes, he'd make an excellent ambassador or whatever else it is he's got his eye on but the trouble is some people want him as far away from what is popularly called "the corridors of power" as possible. Fortunately for him he's still useful to us at times and fortunately for us he's flawed because he always overlooks something. When you get to the Lisbon office tomorrow pick up a camera. If there is a diary or diaries, you photograph every page and detail before you call him. Dear Lady Jean, she's really got under his skin from beyond the veil. He must have done a lot of things for other people than ourselves. All right. Off you go and *bon voyage.*'

chapter five

Farley drove leisurely, the sunshine roof pushed back, enjoying the morning air. Beside him on the other seat, wrapped in a newspaper held with rubber bands, was the golden girdle in its long case. He had thought that Sarah would want to come for the drive, but she had preferred to stay at the villa. Perhaps she had felt that it would be good for him to be on his own so that he could think things over. Maybe she was right. He really did have to come to some positive decision about the girdle. Taking it to François Norbert for a valuation was only a delaying tactic. There was a touch of stubborn fanaticism almost in her determination to help him. He grinned. Something to put him back on his feet again. The point she missed was that he had never been off his feet. He was the way he was, always had been and was quite content to carry on being so. The *ristorante* thing had been a bolt out of the blue, a one-off diversion which had arisen simply because an impulse to play the tables – which form of activity had no real appeal for him – had proved profitable and then Herman had talked him into opening *Il Gallo*. What she did not seem to understand was that by making this big thing about helping him she was not going to repay any debt – she owed him nothing – but moving to put him under an unwanted obligation to her. He had saved her life. Fine. Finish. But now she wanted him to make her happy by accepting a gift out of all proportion to the service which time and chance and his own natural responses had thrust on him. Well, perhaps it was right what they said about women. Once their emotions were stirred logic went out of the window. Usually the bedroom window, too. Happily, for all her affection, she had shown no signs of that. Well, the only solution he could think of for the moment was to spin things out and hope that something would turn up to free him from ... what? Not her importunities. No, rather this schoolgirl almost passion to see him as a hero, her saviour, and to mark her gratitude by turning lady bountiful – ignoring the obvious fact that he was no bounty-hunter.

He overtook a mule cart, heavily loaded with cork oak bark strips from an early cutting. An old man was driving, a transistor radio playing at his side, and two women walked behind herding a couple of goats. He smiled to himself. There was a lot to be said for keeping women in their proper place.

The Norbert villa was a few miles to the east of Albufeira and stood on high ground overlooking the not-far-distant sea. It was surrounded by trees except on the seaward side. Flanking the short drive were two long strips of carefully tended lawn of which François was very proud. He managed lawns and shrubs while his wife, Elise, had charge of the flower beds. François, French-Swiss had retired from his business in Zurich early because of a weak chest which had made him settle in Portugal to avoid cold winters. Elise, much younger than François, was German-Swiss, blonde, plump and a magnificent *Hausfrau*. After he had made his greetings she disappeared into the kitchen region of the villa and although it was only mid-morning he caught the aroma of sardines being grilled and knew that soon a dish would be put between himself and François where they sat under a plumbago-laced terrace overlooking the lawns, a carafe of dry white wine already on the table. François was gentle and genial, and ate like a horse and never put on weight – Elise's ambition for him, to which she dedicated herself without stint or despair.

After they had made their greetings and lifted their glasses to one another, François nodded to the newspaper-wrapped parcel on the table. 'That's it?'

'Yes. It was left to a friend of mine by her mother. I told her you might kindly give us some idea of its value.'

99

François smiled. 'For you, anything. Let us see. You permit?'

When Farley nodded, François began to unwrap the case. He did it without hurry, folding the newspaper neatly before he opened the case. He lifted the belt out and ran it slowly through his hands, link by link, his long face untouched by any expression. From his pocket he produced a jeweller's optic and gave the girdle a closer inspection and then finally laid it carefully back in the case, and said, 'It is a most beautiful piece of work. Beautiful. You know its history?'

'Well, I understand it was given to my friend's mother as a birthday present, or something like that. It's supposed to have been made by someone called Legaré donkey's years ago.'

'I might question Legaré. How long has your friend had it?'

'She's only recently acquired it. According to the mother it was valued around thirty thousand pounds in nineteen-forty-eight.'

'This friend, is she an old friend of yours?'

'No.'

François smiled. 'Beautiful?'

'Yes, I suppose so.'

'She needs money badly – quickly?'

'I don't think so. She just wants some idea, François. Could be for insurance purposes. I said you were the man.'

'Indeed I am. But to do the job properly I need some time. Say three or four days. Modern jewellery is easy. Old stuff ... the craftsmanship and the history ... well, one must be very careful. You would be happy to leave it with me?'

'Of course. It's good of you to offer to do it.'

'No trouble. And now as you know from many visits at this hour, there is no escaping the grilled sardines of Elise.'

The charcoal-grilled fresh sardines were brought in and white wine was poured. They sat eating them, holding them by head and tail and nibbling away down one side and then the other to leave head-and-tailed skeletons which, Farley thought, had he been with Marsox or Herman they would have put between two pieces of bread to press and then discard leaving the flavoured bread to eat with the last of the wine as the true people of this country did.

François walked with him to his car and, as Farley sat waiting to drive off, he said, 'There is talk that you have rescued a beautiful girl from the sea and taken her off to live with you in the mountains. For myself I do not care if you are living with a mermaid so long as you are happy. But I promised Elise to ask. Life is very even here – a little gossip cheers her up.'

Farley laughed. 'Something like that. But I am not living with her.'

'But you like her?'

'Yes.'

'She is the one of the gold belt?'

'Yes.'

'She will wish to sell it eventually?'

'I imagine so. Could you handle that?'

François gave a little shrug of his shoulders. 'Well ... I am retired, but not so retired that I would not oblige a beautiful lady. I will think about it. It is a most interesting piece.'

As Farley drove off François stood watching him, tweaking absently at the tip of his long nose. Then he turned and walked slowly back to the veranda. His wife was standing by the table looking at the belt in its case.

She said, 'It is a most beautiful thing, François. He wishes you to sell it for his friend?'

'Possibly.'

'It will make a lot of money?'

François shook his head. 'Some – but only a fleabite compared with what it would bring if it were genuine. It is only a very fine copy of the real thing. It is not gold and none of the stones are genuine but even so the workmanship is magnificent and there is only one man who could have done it.'

'But François, you should have told *Senhor* Farley!'

'Do you make a friend unhappy right away? While he drinks your wine and the morning is so beautiful? Bad news can always wait. Besides, *ma chère*, I would like to find out a few things about it first.' He smiled and rubbing the back of his hand against her plump cheek went on, 'Also he is not sleeping with her.'

'Then it is a pity. It is time he found someone.'

*

The letter had come just after Richard had left to go to see François Norbert. It had a Cheltenham postmark and was franked on the envelope *Private and Confidential*. Sitting over her morning coffee Sarah read it for the third time. She vaguely remembered Arnold Geddy. He was her father's solicitor and also had sometimes acted for her mother. A nice man, mild and kind. He had come out to the villa after her mother's death to settle her affairs. Once or twice before that, too, he had been to the villa, always to see her mother. She smiled to herself as memory came back to her. Pooh Bear . . . that's what her mother had called him. Not to his face, of course. The happiness in her made her giggle. Now Richard would not have to fuss about her circumstances, would have no excuse to avoid taking a gift from her.

The letter was written on Mr Geddy's private deckle-edged paper and in his own handwriting.

My dear Miss Branton,
I hope perhaps that I need not recall myself to your memory. But in the legal profession it is unwise to assume too much. I am your father's solicitor and at times acted for your mother and for yourself. I have, of course, through your father heard of the recent events which have led to your being in residence at the Villa Lobita. In the light of this change in your circumstances I have received certain instructions from your father, and from your aunt, Mrs Ringel Fanes, to take legal steps to provide for your future. I will not go into these in any detail in this letter, but will say that they are generous and, I hope, will be welcomed by you.

As a Mr Edward Kerslake, a junior partner in our firm, is by happy chance leaving to take a short holiday in Portugal, I have taken the liberty of directing him to call on you so that he can explain the situation to you and put in train the legal formalities which must follow from the instructions of your father and Mrs Ringel Fanes. On arrival in Lisbon he will telephone you to make an appointment to come and see you. I cannot give you an exact date for his arrival in Lisbon since he is flying first to Paris to conduct some business there for a client. But he should be in Lisbon within two or three days of your receipt of this letter.

Finally perhaps, after all these years, you will permit me a warmer note? If at any time you should need personal or professional advice

*I would hope that, as your mother often did, you would not hesitate
to write or telephone me.
My kindest regards,
    Yours sincerely,
        Arnold Geddy*

Taking the letter with her she went up to her bedroom and put
it on the desk by the window. As she did so she saw the blue-
suede-bound diary lying on the blotter where she had left it. Her
mind tranquil with happiness that she now had an even stronger
argument to make Richard accept a generous gift from her, she
picked up the diary and saw for the first time that it carried in
gold lettering on its spine the words *Dialogues of the Soul and
Body – Saint Catharine of Genoa.* She smiled to herself. How like
her mother mildly to protect herself against her own carelessness.
She often had left her personal letters, papers and her jewels scat-
tered carelessly around. Few people seeing the title would be
tempted to open the book. She opened it now at random and read
the first neatly scripted paragraph, the ink now faded to the soft
brown colour of autumn oak leaves, translating easily to herself
from the French in which her mother had made the entry:

*Bellmaster came back in a thoroughly vile mood. His horse, Bold
Greek, fell three fences from home in the Gold Cup and had to be
destroyed. I am glad I was not there – not that I ever intended to be,
Cheltenham in March has no appeal for me. We dined at the Savoy
with Polidor, and his little wet black olives of eyes were on me all
the time. Dear, dear . . . I hope Bellmaster doesn't want to ask him to
join us on the* Lion de Mer . . .

Her eyes moving at random to the opposite page, she read:

*Charming letter from Bo-bo Branton at Larkhill, enclosing a little
love poem which rhymes but doesn't scan. But he's a dear, sweet man.
Up to his knees in mud. Wants me to go down for some special guest
night mess dinner. Shan't – the military* en masse *bring me out in
pimples. I like him by himself but with his brother officers he quite
changes. Leading me around like a high-stepping filly in the ring, and
as near as damn saying aloud,* Look what I've got. *Only he hasn't.*

Smiling to herself Sarah closed the book. She could see and hear
her mother, bright, brittle and outspoken. Some time she would

settle down and read the diary. That clearly would be no dis-respect to her mother. Clearly she had left it to her so that, if she wished, she could read it.

At that moment she heard the sound of Richard's car coming up the drive. She turned eagerly to go down to meet him. But as she reached the bedroom door, realizing she had the diary in her hand, she paused briefly. To the right of the door was a small set of hanging bookshelves, almost full with hard and paperbacked books. She pushed the diary in amongst the books on the middle of the three shelves and hurried on down.

She reached the hallway as Richard Farley came in through the door. She went up to him, put her hands on his arms and asked eagerly, 'Well, what did he say? Tell me! Tell me!'

He grinned. 'Whoah, you'll have me flat on my back. First I want a drink. Come on.' He took her by the arm and began to walk her towards the sun terrace.

'Oh, Richard, how can you keep me in suspense!'

'All right. Calm down. He's going to value it. To do it pro-perly will take a few days. And he said it was a beautiful piece of work. And I've got a raging thirst from the grilled sardines his wife cooked for us.'

'And I've got news for you. Look – a letter that came from England just after you left. Now there won't be any question of an argument between us.' She handed him the letter which she had received from Geddy. 'Oh, I'm so happy, I can't tell you.'

Holding the letter in his hand, not looking at it, his eyes on her, he said without thought, 'You really do go up in the air, don't you? It beats me how you stuck that convent as long as you did.'

Her face changed abruptly. She could understand why he had spoken so and it was no fault of his that his words had brought a swift pang of misery to her and, for the first time, even though she knew it would quickly pass, a sense of shame at her failure to be what she had wanted for herself. No amount of self-justification could alter the bald facts of her own weakness.

Farley, seeing the change in her, leaned forward, kissed her briefly on the cheek and then said comfortingly, 'Sorry. I spoke out of turn. It was very clumsy of me.'

She shook her head, feeling tears coming to her eyes and said, 'You go on and read the letter. I'll get some ice from Fabrina.'

Kerslake was met at the airport and driven to the Lisbon office. Jansen, who was the Lisbon section head, gave him a pleasant greeting. Aside from being pleasant, grey-haired and portly, Jansen was bored, and had been for many years. He longed for London and Birdcage Walk but knew that he would be in Lisbon until he retired in a few years' time to a modest OBE and a comfortable pension. For up and coming young Birdcage men he had no envy. Seven out of ten would end much as he was going to end. After the usual gossipy chat and Kerslake had politely declined a drink, Jansen said, 'As you know, we've broken off light contact on orders from London. I've got the man who was working it in here now. Thought you might like a chat with him. He's yours, too, if you need him.'

'What's he like?'

'His name is Gains. English father, local mother. He's a good bloke when he works, but he can be effing lazy. He's too fond of the two major pleasures of life. Good company, though.'

'I'd like a word or two with him.'

'Whenever you are ready. We've booked a room for you down there. Hotel just outside Monchique and about five kilometres from the villa. And we've a car for you, and an hotel here for tonight. You're a Quint man, aren't you?'

'Yes, I am.'

'He's all right. I came in ... donkey's years ago, under Warboys. He'll live and serve for ever. They just put in new parts when he needs them.' He laughed and was unsurprised when Kerslake remained unmoved, no smile, no slightest frown. 'Lèse majesté – not enough of it around, I think. But opinions differ. No joking on Her Majesty's Service.'

'I started as a bobby on a beat. I never saw a great deal to smile about.' Kerslake suddenly smiled. 'But then perhaps I wasn't looking in the right places. Does this Gains have a car here?'

'Yes.'

'Then I'd like him to drive me to my hotel. I can chat with him there.'

Jansen chuckled and wagged his head. 'Very wise. I've been debating whether I'd keep the tap in the interview room on. Now happily I don't have to make the decision. I'll take you along and introduce you.'

Ten minutes later, in Gains' car, Kerslake turned to him and said, 'Before we get to the hotel find a quiet place where we can park and talk.'

'Yes, sir.'

A little later Gains turned into an unmade road and parked under a row of trees opposite a building site where a block of flats was being built. There was no surprise in Gains. He had served too long not to know all the types. He could read this one. Wouldn't have trusted his own mother. Still, at least you knew where you were with this type. They didn't always work by the book if it got in their way.

Kerslake said, 'Smoke if you want to.'

'Thank you, sir.' Gains began to fumble for his cigarettes.

Kerslake let the first trail of cigarette smoke eddy past him and then said, 'How many times have you been in the Villa Lobita?'

Gains, surprised, said, 'I don't understand, sir. My orders were light contact.'

'I know your orders. But I asked how many times have you been in the villa?'

With a shrug of his shoulders Gains said, 'Twice, sir. The first time I couldn't avoid it. There's an oldish couple in the lodge and I used to chat up the man – Mario. One afternoon when the villa lot went out for a car drive he insisted on taking me round. Only the ground floor.'

'Describe it.'

Gains did in detail and Kerslake was impressed. His observations and his memory served him well. When he had finished Kerslake said, 'And the second time?'

Gains stared up at the scaffolding on the new flats.

'Well, sir, I thought it might come in handy some time – like now, perhaps if I saw the upper floor. After all, if a thing is going to grow and other people are coming in on it ...

well, the more you can tell them the better. Don't you agree, sir?'

'No, I don't. But since it has happened I want to know about it. The upper floor?'

'Mario let slip that the two of them were going out to dinner one night. So when they did and Mario and his old lady were in their lodge place I went in. One of the villa keys is always left under a small flower trough on the top of the steps, right-hand side.'

As Gains went on with a description of the upper floor Kerslake watched a young woman walk past the flats. She was carrying a bundle of washing on her head and walked awkwardly on high platform shoes. A plasterer working late on the building shouted something to her and she made him a brief, insulting gesture. Two sparrows dust-bathed in the road at the far end of which he could catch a small glimpse of the sea. Suddenly he had a rare moment of tiredness and depression. People were disgusting and that included himself ... snooping about bedrooms, probing into the smallest and most intimate details of others' lives.

Interrupting Gains, he asked, 'Did you see a safe anywhere?'

'No, sir.'

'It's hidden behind a three-shelved wall bookcase in one of the bedrooms.'

'Ay, yes sir. I remember the case. It's on the left as you go into her bedroom.'

'Are they sleeping together?'

'No sign of it, sir. After all ...' Gains hesitated.

'All what?'

'Well, she's not long out of a convent, is she, sir?'

'What about him?'

'Quiet, pleasant enough chap, he seems. He's been around the Algarve for a long time. Well known and liked I gathered. But I had no brief to go into him.'

'Or the villa.'

'That was different, sir. I hope you agree?'

'Let's say I'm not going to bawl you out for doing it.'

'Thank you, sir. I always think that a little discreet initiative ... well, some people understand and others don't. Do you want me to come down with you tomorrow, sir?'

'No.'

Gains held down a smile and a sigh of relief, and said, '*Senhor Jansen* has put me at your disposal. I can be down in a few hours when you want me . . if you should want me, that is, sir.'

'We'll see. What kind of look did you get of the parcel which Miss Branton collected from the Hotel Globo?'

'Not too good.'

'Well, give me some idea.'

Gains threw his cigarette end away and frowned with pretended concentration of thought. They always liked something to go on so why not let them have it. 'Well, sir, she was sort of cradling it in her arms. I'd say longish—' he spread his hands apart to indicate the length, 'rather than squarish. And not all that thick.'

'I see. Do you know the hotel they booked me into down there?'

'Yes, sir. You'll be comfortable there.'

Kerslake was silent for a while. Birdcage had put a stop on any enquires at the Hotel Globo. A wrong word or the raising of a moment's unease might cause trouble. Discretion in that direction had been left to him. Knowing his man now, he finally said to Gains, 'I want to know who runs the Hotel Globo and their past history. But I don't want you to go near the place and I don't want the Lisbon office to know anything about it. You'll get a London bonus direct. Think you can manage it?'

Gains, flattered by the confidence and the prospect of a bonus payment, disguised his pleasure with a thoughtful frown and then said, 'I think it could be managed, sir.'

'Good. If you can get it by tomorrow and phone me in the evening I'd be very happy.'

'I'll do my best, sir.' Why not. Making other people happy was a good Christian thing to do particularly if you did yourself good at the same time. Odd, too. He had thought he was going to dislike this man with his uptight style, but he liked him. He was the kind who could eat two *Senhor* Jensens for breakfast and still be hungry.

'Very well. Now let's get to this hotel.'

The only thing, he was beginning to think, was quietly to disappear. The trouble was that it would take a little time to organize and to decide where to go. He would have to stay until this solicitor had made his visit and gone. Charging off before that would put her in a state. And, anyway, he had to work out where the hell he should go and also the money side of it. He had a little money left, and he had his hands and a few simple skills. He should be able to make out. He smiled ruefully to himself as he lay back in bed, his open book resting on the covers. Maybe there was a virtue in the situation. He had been in Portugal long enough. But where to go? Jesus, the whole thing had started a long time ago. South Africa and a Kimberley mining office. Eighteen months tea-planting in Ceylon. Then England for a spell ... farming in Kent, hops and apples, and then three years as a travel courier. Languages had always come easy to him through his mother – she was the only woman he had ever known who could speak Kikuyu idiomatically and accurately instead of the Kiswahili which most people used. He shut the thought of his mother from him. What the devil was he going to do? Perhaps, anyway, he was being too independent ... sensitive ... about the whole thing? Why not just take whatever she would want to give him? In a way he had earned it. Oh, Christ, he thought, here you go again Farley. You can never weigh the pros and cons of a situation or problem, make a decision and stick to it. She was dead set that he should be rewarded, and even more determined now that she knew her father was going to make a permanent provision for her. Still, what the devil would he do if he had money? There was nothing he wanted to do – literally. No ambition, no life dream. In fact, he had for some time realized that he had been secretly pleased when the *ristorante* had failed. It had been hard and interesting work, but it had also carried responsibility for other people and the ghastly compulsion of things having to be done when they had to be done. All that talk about a place in the Dordogne ... just an evasion. Once, just once, he had known that the only thing he had wanted was Kenya ... to go in with his father, take the farm and work it up ... Oh, Christ, what did it matter? Perhaps the real answer was to sit on your tail and just wait for things to happen. That's what he had been doing before she arrived. The simple answer was to go back to it ... move in with Herman for a while. No, that would not do. She would come chasing after him, wanting to get her so-called debt to him off her conscience. Pity he was not like so many of the men he knew around here who never missed a chance of four legs in a bed if a pretty girl were willing. But the years had proved to him that he had long ago become a eunuch. Perhaps if he had taken himself to a head-shrinker he could have been cured. Impossible. The gekko on the wall un-moving ... the night bird calling ... and the two of them on the floor, naked and bloody ... and the added shock of hearing his own primitive scream of rage and horror.

Angrily he picked up his book and turned on his side to get the bedside light on its pages. He read until his eyes were sore and heavy and then, the book falling from his hand, the light still on, he fell asleep.

When he awoke he was sitting up, leaning forward with his hands over his eyes and groaning and knowing clearly what had happened. Sarah in a dressing gown was perched on the side of the bed with one arm around his shoulders. He said nothing for a while as he recovered. Then he took his hands from his face and looked at her. Her face was drawn with the misery of her com-passion.

She said, 'I heard you shouting and screaming. Is it some bad dream?'

Hating her being there, seeing his weakness, he said sharply, 'Not some but the bad dream!'

'Oh, Richard, can I get you a drink or do something?'

'Oh, for God's sake leave me alone.'

With a sudden firmness and authority, she said, 'That's the last thing I'm going to do. I came to you the first time I heard you. I've heard you once since then and ... I didn't come. But this time I had to. What is it you dream? Perhaps if you told me it would go away for good. I would pray for it to go. I would do anything to help you ... do anything to comfort you.'

Feeling the warmth of her hand on his shoulder, seeing her stricken face, he shook his head. 'There's nothing you can do.'

Almost bullying him with her emotion she said, 'But there is. There must be. I'm not just anyone. Have you forgotten that I screamed in the night – just as you screamed – and you came to me? Now tell me. I don't care how horrible it is just so long as it helps you.'

He stayed silent, waiting to be sure of himself. Well, why not? He had never told anyone else. Perhaps she was the one. Perhaps this was what she really could do for him to make him a return for saving her. Oh, Christ ... what screwy thinking. As though anything, anyone could help. But even as the thoughts ran through him, he heard himself saying bitterly, not caring for any hurt he might give her, 'Well, why not? You're the nearest I've ever let myself get to anyone to do with religion since it happened. God is everywhere they say. But don't you believe it!'

'He sent you to me when I needed you.'

'Oh, yes. But there are plenty of other nights when He shuts His eyes to the world. Plenty. And I'll tell you about one of them ...'

So in a steady, flat voice he told her about the night in Kenya and how the eighteen-year-old Richard Farley had come driving home from the cinema in Nairobi to find his mother and father killed by the Mau-Mau ... both of them stripped, naked on the floor, his mother violated, and his father emasculated. And Sarah listened, saying nothing, the pressure of her arm and hand across his shoulders unvarying.

'... sometimes I dream of it and wake shouting and sweating. Sometimes I wake, just shouting, without any memory of the dream. But I know it was there. And you'd think that would be enough, wouldn't you? But it isn't. Ever since then, not even when I used to drink to help, there's been nothing. The moment I get close to a woman ... nothing ... I'm standing back there, seeing them, seeing her.' He turned to her and smiled suddenly and slowly put the knuckles of his right hand against her soft cheek and caressed her momentarily. 'So there it is, Sarah. The next time you hear me shouting you'll know there's nothing to be done. Just turn over and go to sleep. Now, back to your room with you.'

Sarah rose to her feet. 'I'm glad you told me. Very glad that I'm the first one. Although I am in no state of grace I shall pray to God for you and He will understand.'

'Why bother. He'll probably be sleeping.'

Sarah smiled. 'You do not offend me by saying that. And I am sure you do not offend Him. Now go to sleep.'

Kerslake drove down from Lisbon the next morning, taking with him a camera from the Lisbon office. He went straight to his hotel and booked in and then, later in the afternoon, drove himself around the neighbourhood and into Monchique to familiarize himself with the area. On his way back to the hotel he stopped on the road just north of the Villa Lobita, climbed a stony, pine-covered hill and had a good look at the place through his glasses. Just before a late dinner he had a telephone call from Gains who told him that the Hotel Globo was run by Melina and Carlo Spuggi who had once worked for Lady Jean Branton as maid and chauffeur. The information had not been difficult to get, Gains explained. Carlo Spuggi's name was on the hotel signboard in its front garden named as the proprietor. A few minutes' chat with an old woman selling lottery tickets at a kiosk at the bottom of the square – he had pretended to be looking for a reasonable hotel to stay – had brought up the Hotel Globo and Carlo who always bought his lottery tickets from the woman and was fond of talking about the old days when he had driven a Rolls-Royce for Lady Jean Branton. After he had rung off Kerslake wondered if Lord Bellmaster knew that the Hotel Globo was run by the erstwhile chauffeur and maid. Probably not, he decided, otherwise there could have been no reason not to tell him.

After dinner and coffee Kerslake telephoned the Villa Lobita. Sarah Branton answered the call. After he had introduced himself Kerslake explained that he had only just arrived from Lisbon but had not been able to call her from there because there was a fault on the line. He made an appointment to call and see her the following morning at half-past ten. In the privacy of his hotel room from which he was telephoning he allowed himself the indulgence of a slight smile at the fresh note of eagerness in her voice. The telephone call made, he had a bath and went to bed and began to read Thomas Hardy's *The Return of the Native* which he had bought in paperback at the airport and fell asleep before he was more than halfway across Egdon Heath.

The next morning he drove slowly down to the villa to arrive precisely at the allotted time. He was now a junior partner in the firm of Geddy, Parsons and Rank, solicitors. Making no concession to the climate, he wore a sober dark-blue suit, a dark trilby and carried a brief case. The woman servant Fabrina answered the door to him and showed him into a small study off the hall, most of whose contents he knew already from Gains' description. He waited without curiosity for his first sight of Sarah Branton, the runaway nun and thorn maybe in the side of Lord Bellmaster. Of the two his interest was more closely concentrated on Lord Bellmaster. Instinct told him that, although she was Bellmaster's daughter, the settlement through Colonel Branton must have sprung from more than genuine paternal concern. Three thousand a year was quite a nice sum but in it there had to be a considerable element of self-interest on his lordship's part ... an element which, too, was there purely because Bellmaster – not certain of any real threat to his ambitions – had decided to leave nothing to chance. When a man like Bellmaster set his sights really high he had to be the last type to overlook the workings of time and chance. The ghost of Lady Jean still walked, threatening perhaps or perhaps not, but anyway there would be no comfort for Bellmaster until the ghost was laid.

Sarah Branton came in, fresh and cool, wearing a plain white linen dress, her feet in open sandals. A pleasant, lovely handful of woman, he thought; nothing over-affected or hesitant in her manner, though there was a suggestion somewhere – not of the past nun – but of what? A junior mistress at a girls' school who would find marriage long before she began to think of a head-mistress-ship.

He introduced himself with a little touch of pomposity he felt he owed to the part he was playing, and refused her offer of coffee.

She said, 'It's a long way for you to come, Mr Kerslake.'

He smiled. 'Not at all, Miss Branton. Business and pleasure. Always a happy mixture ... certainly so in the present circumstances. I was due a holiday so Mr Geddy suggested the combination.'

'It's your first visit to Portugal?'

'Yes. And I'm sure I'm going to like it. Now if you will permit, shall we come to the business in hand and I should say that I think you will be very pleased about it. You realize, of course, that I am fully aware of ... well, shall we say, your past history.'

'I'd imagined so. Yes. But I must say I am surprised that my father should be concerned with me. I must tell you frankly that we never did really get on with one another.'

Opening his brief case Kerslake gave her what he considered an appropriately restrained smile and a little indulgent nod of his head. 'Your father is getting on in age. Men change, Miss Branton. Shall we say that this visit of mine comes because of a change of heart ... a desire to make amends for the past? Whatever the reason, however, let me say that I am happy to be the bearer of good tidings. Now—' a touch of briskness inflected his voice, 'let me explain things to you.'

He laid out his papers on the small table before him, the documents concerning the transfer of ownership of the villa to her from her aunt, and the details of the financial settlement from her father, and also the necessary application form for her to complete so that the arrangements could be made for the issue of a passport for her. *Perhaps while I am here you would be good enough to have the necessary photographs taken? The rest we will do and then send the passport on to you.*

She sat, docile and attentive. More schoolgirl now than a schoolmistress. He liked her against his will because there was always danger in liking people met in his true business. But sometimes it could not be helped. A man or woman came through to you, and then you just hoped that things would stay normal. Not that it ultimately mattered because you knew that sentiment was an easily crushed growth.

When she learnt the amount of her father's settlement she was pleased. 'Oh, that's very generous of him. But I could manage on less than that if it puts him at all under any strain. I always understood that things had not gone very well for him.'

'You need have no fear, Miss Branton. Your father can well afford it.' He smiled, feeling a Geddy-like pomposity inhabit him. 'Fathers have a habit of crying poverty. Shall we say, in some cases, as a form of protection against the importunities of the young. No, no, your father is well able to afford the money.'

'I shall write to him.'

'Of course.' Kerslake pulled a typed list from his papers, and went on, 'There is one small matter which concerns your aunt, Mrs Ringel Fanes. She cabled us a list of items which are of personal and sentimental value to her which – while she doesn't wish to have them at the moment – she would like to retain for herself. I am afraid – rather like a broker's man – I shall have to go round with you and satisfy myself that they are all here. And I have a duplicate list to leave with you.'

Mrs Ringel Fanes had, in fact, sent a list to Mr Geddy by cable from America and Quint on reading it after his return from Cheltenham had cocked his head up at him, grinned and said, 'A serendipity. You'll know where the safe is and, with luck, where the key is kept.' He had not known what serendipity had meant and had looked it up.

The list was short and they went round the house together, checking first the items on the ground floor. Before they went upstairs Kerslake consulted the list and said, 'There's an item here. *Two bundles of letters from my late husband. Either in my bedroom safe or bottom drawer of bureau in bedroom window.* Perhaps Miss Branton, if the safe key is kept down here you might get it?'

'Oh, there's no need for that, Mr Kerslake. The key is in the bedroom bureau with a little label on it. The safe is in the bedroom behind some bookshelves. My mother used to keep her jewels in it.'

'I see. Well, shall we go up?'

They went up to the bedroom. There were no letters in the bottom drawer of the bureau. Sarah took the key and then showed him how the bookshelves swung away from the wall. The letters were in the safe. Before they left the room she put the key back in the bureau. There had been nothing else in the safe.

They checked three other items on the top floor. One of them was listed *Geisha Girl with Umbrella by Ishikawa Toyonobu. Three-colour print. Hashirakake c. 1760. Hanging in main spare bedroom.*

When they entered the bedroom Kerslake saw at once that it was occupied. A suitcase stood at the side of the wardrobe. A worn shirt and a pair of pyjamas were draped over the back of a chair and the bed was unmade.

Sarah said, 'I'm sorry about the room. Fabrina hasn't got up here yet. I've a very dear friend of mine staying with me. This must be the print.' She walked to the stone fireplace over which was hanging the Toyonobu print. As he looked at the print – which said little to him – Kerslake wondered about the dear friend. Without doubt Richard Farley. Probably knowing he was coming he had taken himself off for a walk somewhere. From her manner and her ease in the room if nothing else he felt certain that there was nothing between them. Sarah Branton was no girl who jumped easily in and out of beds. He liked her.

Together they went through the rest of the items on the list. As they came down the wide stairs together Kerslake stopped on the lowest turn of the stairs and looked at the painting of Lady Jean. Geddy had mentioned it to him and since for the time being he was wearing the mantle of a family solicitor he played his part.

He said, 'A lovely painting. Your mother was a very beautiful woman, Miss Branton.'

'Yes, she was. It's by Augustus John, you know.'

'Is it? Then it is very valuable.'

'I suppose so.'

Kerslake shook his head indulgently at her. 'There is no suppose, Miss Branton. It *is* valuable. And this brings us to the final point concerning my visit. The villa and all almost of its contents belong to you. Mrs Ringel Fanes' insurance cover expires in two months. Thereafter insurance is your responsibility. Mr Geddy will be very happy to deal with that for you through a Lisbon agent. You can be covered in sterling or Portuguese currency. I'm afraid this will eventually mean making a fresh list of all the villa's contents and any jewellery you have.'

Sarah shook her head and gave a small laugh. 'I'm afraid you're forgetting my recent past, Mr Kerslake. I gave up all worldly possessions eight years ago. I own nothing in the way of jewellery – Oh, wait. I'd forgotten.'

'Yes, Miss Branton?' Kerslake was quietly enjoying the patient guise of a solicitor.

'I'm thinking about the girdle. This one in the picture. It's quite valuable – though to tell you the truth my mother never liked it very much. She thought it was too showy. But then ... No, there's no need to insure it because I've already as good as given it away.'

Kerslake chuckled gently and said with quiet forbearance, relishing his own smooth change of mood, 'Forgive me, Miss Branton, but perhaps you could make things clearer for me. You gave up everything when you went into the convent. There's been only a comparatively short time since you ... shall we say decided otherwise about your vocation in life. How is it then—?'

Sarah laughed. 'But that's the point, Mr Kerslake. My mother was a very understanding and wise woman. She foresaw that I might one day ... well, regret my choice. She told me that if I ever did she was leaving with her maid something which would help me to get started in life again. That I should go to Melina – she married our chauffeur and they run a hotel in Lisbon – and she would have something for me. It's really quite romantic. So recently I did. And it was the girdle. But you see there's no need to worry about it because I am giving it to Mr Farley.'

'Mr Farley?'

'Yes.' Sarah's mouth set briefly in stubborn line. 'You see when I came out of the convent he saved my life. I don't wish to say more than that.'

'Of course. That's the gentleman who is staying here?'

'Yes.'

Not for one moment was Kerslake tempted to step out of his role as solicitor and ask an uncharacteristic question. Melina Spuggi had held the girdle for her for years. What else perhaps had she been holding? If there had been anything else it was a fair bet that it was still in this villa. Lord Bellmaster's words

117

came back to him. *If there was anything in the shape or form of letters or a diary or diaries – get them.* He smiled at Sarah and said warmly, 'You're a very generous woman, Miss Branton.' He looked again at the painting, and added. 'Your mother was a very beautiful woman. I can tell you—' he gave her a little smile of confidence, 'that our Mr Geddy, a confirmed bachelor, quite lost his heart to her.'

'Oh, everyone loved her, Mr Kerslake. Everyone.'

'I'm sure. I'm sure. Now, if we might go into the study again there are still one or two small points to arrange. For instance, you must decide where you wish to open a bank account into which the settlement can be paid and a few other rather fiddly details like that.'

Half an hour later he left the villa, having allowed himself to be persuaded to take a glass of sherry with her; while drinking it, he had seen a man pass the window who, he guessed, was Richard Farley. As he drove away he knew that he had to devise a way of having at least an hour to himself in the villa some time soon. Not a very difficult thing to arrange.

That evening he telephoned the villa and asked Miss Branton if she and, of course, her house guest, Mr Farley, would care to have dinner with him the following evening at his hotel to celebrate the fact that happily – as her mother had once done – she was now giving Geddy, Parson and Rank the honour of becoming one of their esteemed clients? Sarah after a few moments away from the telephone came back and said that they would both be delighted to come. Given the right circumstances it was one of the simplest tricks in the book. He put down the telephone receiver, lay back on his bed, stared at the ceiling for a while to marshal his material and then picked up the telephone and put in a call to Lord Bellmaster.

Lord Bellmaster refilled his brandy glass at the sideboard. He had just got back from Downing Street and a private meeting between himself, the Prime Minister and the Foreign Secretary when the man Kerslake had called. He was less concerned with Kerslake's report at the moment than with his Downing Street meeting. The expected secret lobbying was going on. Plenty of people had the usual good cases for others or themselves to make, but he could read the PM shrewdly now. The man was no fool, but he was secretly vain. If you had been born in Brixham with a café proprietor for a father and had the arse of your breeches hanging out most of your school life ... well, you might make a public virtue out of this, but a maggot worried away inside you. The PM loved his visits to the Conary estates – though, God help us, he was the most dangerous shot in the world. And with a wife who was dowdily and methodistically uninterested in the pleasures of the bedroom, the poor devil revelled in the house-party freedom of Castle Conary. The Foreign Secretary ... a different cup of tea ... Eton and Christ Church turned Socialist, not to rid himself of the family millions, but to shrive his already dried-up soul with constant masochism ... but even he had a price, though he had not made it clear yet ... something or other for the bright one of his two sons? An editorship eventually. Could be done. What could not be done for people if you had power and money, newspapers and wide industrial interests? God knows, he had millions now to play with and play he would to indulge his own fancy. After all he had been doing that all his life. Why stop now? Like losing your sight or becoming impotent. Though God knows he had not always been so well-breeched. Without anyone knowing he had been right down to almost rock-bottom – in his own terms, of course – once.

He drank and then suddenly chuckled out loud. That bloody girdle thing. Fancy that turning up. Jean had never known but she had saved his life financially, and from that moment he had never looked back. Kerslake ... now there was a chap who, if you could get him away from Birdcage, you could train. The first-class men, brilliant, but with the hidden flaw which made them vulnerable. Oh, yes he had a nose for picking them. Just as a kestrel could catch the turn of a leaf from a foraging beetle two hundred feet below so, he guessed, Kerslake could catch the flicker of a thought in the blink of a man's eye and read it. A knack? Telepathy? Mind reading? Useful man. If there were diaries he would find them. She'd always denied she kept one. Aye, a denial with a smile. But what a woman. Packed with nitroglycerine. Don't upset. He laughed aloud and realized that first the PM's and now his own brandy was getting to him. What was it? Claret for boys ... port for men, but he who aspires to be a hero must drink brandy. Perhaps in wartime. But not in the political dog fight. One more, and he was for bed. The girdle of Venus. Where the devil had he had that copy made? No matter. When he had first given it to her he had made her strip to the buff and wear it for him. *Virtus Vincit*. Like hell it did.

chapter six

Kerslake had asked Sarah and Richard to have dinner with him at eight o'clock. They left the villa at half-past seven and Kerslake, who had parked his car down a side road off the one which they had to take and then walked across country to the slope above the villa, watched them go through his fieldglasses. Keeping in the cover of trees and shrubs he walked down to the front of the villa. The two servants were safely in their lodge at the drive entrance.

He took the key from under the stone trough, unlocked the door, put the key back in its hiding place, and then went in letting the door lock itself on the automatic catch. Women, he smiled ruefully, remembering Margaret, were great ones for forgetting things. If they came back he would hear the car and have plenty of time to make his way out through a rear window. In the hall he picked up the telephone and called his hotel to give a message to the receptionist. He was expecting a *Senhorita* Branton and a *Senhor* Farley to dinner – would they please present them with his apologies and tell them that he would be a little late because he had been held up on the road from Faro with a puncture? In the meantime they were his guests and would the hotel please serve them with any drinks they wished to have.

There were only two rooms he wished to search in detail, Sarah's and the man Farley's. He did Sarah's first. He took the key from the bureau and opened the safe. It held only the letters from Mrs Ringel Fanes' husband. Closing it and swinging the bookcase back he ran his hand along the back side of the three rows of books and then his eye carefully over the books themselves. They were mostly paperbacks, some religious works, and some hard-covered book club editions.

He next searched the bureau in the window. In one of a series of ivory-knobbed little drawers mounted at the back of the bureau he found the note from Lady Jean Branton, witnessed by Father Ansoldo and the maid, Melina, leaving the contents of a parcel – containing, he guessed, the Venus girdle – to Sarah. With it was the card giving information about the belt, stating that it had been given to her by Lord Bellmaster. If it had been worth thirty thousand pounds in 1948, he thought, God knew what it was worth now. Lord Bellmaster had been a generous lover ... but then, the man had millions. But for all his money and power, he thought, he had no way of ridding his mind of the maggot of fear which worked there.

Methodically, efficiently, and quickly he went through the bedroom. This was no training course exercise now with Quint in the sidelines watching and appraising. Everything he saw and touched he would remember. On a small table by a side window was a scatter of needles, cotton, threads and scissors and a summer dress with the skirt hem tacked-up in preparation for shortening it. Sarah was obviously making over some of her mother's or her aunt's clothes. He stood in the doorway for a moment before leaving the room. The conviction was hard in him that Sarah had had nothing to hide. She was simple-minded and would have used the safe had there been anything she wanted to keep private. Safes were for secrets.

He went along to Farley's room. All his possessions would go easily into the shabby suitcase. On his bedside table was an old copy of *Country Life* and a battered copy of D. H. Lawrence's *The White Peacock*. Farley was clearly a man who travelled light. The last stub in his cheque book, which he found in the back pocket of an old pair of blue canvas trousers, showed that he had two thousand seven hundred and sixty escudos in his current account still. Probably nothing on deposit. Well, that would all change when he had the Venus girdle to sell. He had the feeling though that money meant little to Farley. He knew the type. Day to day was as far as it looked. Well, if that was what suited you, it suited you and, by God, thousands were getting away with it these days.

Leaving Farley's room he went quickly through all the others on the same floor and then made a quick foray through the downstairs rooms. Walking back to his car he unexpectedly had a sudden uneasy feeling, remembering a stricture of Quint's. *If people know they have something to hide, and they hide it – then there's no problem. Given time you can find it. The real trouble comes when people have something which it never occurs to them to hide. They leave it right under your nose and you don't see it.* Lady Jean Branton now, there was a type quite different from her daughter – if she had had dirt on Bellmaster, a diary, she would have ... No. Now he knew what was happening. It was the same feeling he had used to get in the training sessions; that moment before he turned to face Quint, smooth-faced, to say *Clean.* The moment of harrowing doubt because so much depended on your word.

He got into his car, locked his camera in the dash-pocket and drove off.

They had a pleasant dinner. He slipped easily back into his solicitor role, and he found he liked Farley. The man was easy and natural and, after a few drinks, an amusing talker. Before they left, and while Sarah had gone to the powder room, Farley said to him, 'I wanted a word with you alone.'

'Yes.'

'This is between ourselves, but as her solicitor you should know. When she left the convent she tried to drown herself. She had a crazy notion – quite wrong – that she was going to have a baby. I saved her life. I won't go into the details. But I think you should know, too, that she wants to repay me by giving me this Venus belt. She's got it firmly in her mind. But I don't want it. I wish to God if you got a chance you could ... well, make her see sense about it.'

'She has mentioned it to me. But in the circumstances you can see that there's nothing I can do. You did her a great service. She's got a generous nature and she's well provided for now by her father.' Kerslake smiled dryly. 'I think you've just got to accept or, if you really feel so strongly, quietly disappear before she gets the chance to hand it over to you.'

'Maybe you're right. But I've a dirty idea she might come charging after me.'

'The world's a big place.'

Farley laughed. 'I just wonder if it's big enough.'

'I'm sorry. I appreciate your position, but there's nothing I can do. It must rest between you. May I say, too, that I respect your attitude. Also I'd like to say that I think your being with her over this period must have been a great help to her.'

When they had gone Kerslake went up to his room and put in a call to Lord Bellmaster and then a call to Birdcage, leaving a report for Quint detailing his actions and the substance of his talk with Lord Bellmaster, who had made no attempt to disguise his relief at learning no signs of a diary had been found.

Two days later Farley went down to see François Norbert, whose wife, Elise, had telephoned the previous afternoon while Farley had been out and left a message with Sarah that her husband had made the valuation on the girdle of Venus. He would have asked Sarah to come with him, but that morning the solicitor, Kerslake, was seeing her to collect various documents and complete his business with her.

He drove down slowly to the coast. The crunch, he thought, was coming. Once he was back at the villa with the belt he would have to make a decision and he knew what his decision must be. He could not take the girdle. It was a pity really because he knew it meant he must leave the villa. After a few days in a place he always began to feel at home and reluctant to move on. But move on now he must and – he saw this clearly – he would not be able to make an open departure. He would have to move away while she was out and leave a farewell note for her. For a while he wondered idly whether his real objection did not rest in a now long-acquired reluctance to accept any responsibility or commitment for anyone but himself. He did not want the responsibility of having a lot of money and the commitment which would be urged by Sarah to do something with it to improve ... what?

His station in life, his future prospects? There was a tenacity of concern for other people and a continuing interest in the welfare of those to whom she gave affection and friendship which would make her hard to shake off. She had all the makings of a managing, driving woman – perhaps some character echo from her mother which in anyone less attractive and naive would quickly become intolerable. He did not want to be managed or organized. Never had. And there were plenty more like him in the Algarve. Lotus-eaters. Well, why not? It was a life style which harmed nobody.

François was sitting on the terrace reading a two-day-old copy of *The Times*, a carafe of white wine and two glasses waiting on the table. The lawn sprinklers were on, the sunlight lacing their sprays with rainbow arcs and a pair of golden orioles were bathing in a grassy puddle of water.

François greeted him warmly and poured wine for them, saying, 'I have an apology from Elise. She has gone to Faro shopping so there are no grilled sardines. Then I have another apology – to be so long with this business of the girdle. But I wanted to write to a friend of mine for some information which I thought you might like to have.' He reached down to the empty chair at his side and picked up the long red case. He raised the lid, leaving it open, but made no move to take the golden belt from it.

'Well, what is the verdict, François?'

François shrugged his shoulders. 'A very interesting one. But perhaps not such a happy one for your friend.'

'Why not?'

'Not so fast. I begin at the beginning and we take it step by step.'

At that moment, not knowing how he knew – except that he knew François' mannerisms so well – he sensed that the news was not going to be good. Bluntly he said, 'No, let's start the other way round. It's a fake, isn't it? That's why Elise is not here.'

François ran a finger down the cleft of his chin and then nodded. 'Yes, a fake. But it is really too hard a word. It is the most beautiful piece of replica work I have ever seen. In its own right it would be worth two or three thousand pounds. This disappoints you – for your friend, I mean?'

'For my friend, yes. But happily she is not short of money.'

'Then that is something. You wish me, naturally, to tell you about its history?'

'Naturally.' Farley drank a little of his wine. He felt suddenly at ease and unburdened and knew himself unconcerned at Sarah's coming disappointment. That he could face and then move on to his own freedom. Selfish, maybe. But much better than stealing away in the night and leaving her with a genuine gift which he did not want.

François said, 'I wrote to this friend of mine in Paris who is a world authority on antique jewellery, also an adviser to the Musée de Cluny, the Rijksmuseum in Amsterdam and dozens of others, as well as being in the business himself. You understand, Richard, that these so very eminent experts live in a closed world where they know everything and everyone connected with antique jewellery. Oh, yes ... they know, far, far beyond me.' He paused, his eyes fixed curiously on Farley. 'You want that I go into all the details of this, or just a very broad history? From your face, I think not too long, eh?'

'It's a fake. That's the main thing. But, yes, I'd like to know generally.'

'Then I will keep it short.' He reached for the carafe and topped up their glasses with wine.

Farley sat, watching a green lizard on the terrace wall, as François talked. The genuine girdle had been bought in 1948 from an old French family by an English millionaire, a Lord Bellmaster. In 1950 Lord Bellmaster had had the fake girdle made by an Italian jeweller who specialized in the very highest class replicas.

'... a necessary art, you know, Richard, for the genuine things are always at risk. At these great banquets, you know, the ladies do not always wear the real thing.'

In 1951 Lord Bellmaster had sold the genuine girdle privately to a German industrialist who on his death had left it to the

Kunsthistorisches Museum, Vienna, where it still was.

When François finished, Farley said, 'Do you know anything about this Lord Bellmaster?'

'No. Except he is still alive. So my Paris friend wrote me. This will all be unhappy news for your friend?'

'Yes ... yes, I think it will. Not because of the money, but because it isn't genuine.'

'You can tell her that the real girdle in Vienna was made by a pupil of Gilles Legaré long after Legaré's death. But this replica, sadly, though beautifully done is ... alas ... worth very little compared to the value of the real thing. I am sorry to give you such disappointing news.'

'Well, there it is. But anyway, François, it was good of you to take all the trouble. I wonder why Lord Bellmaster had a copy made.'

François chuckled. 'Rich men are careful with their money. That way they become rich. You give your mistress the real thing and then at a good moment you have a copy made which goes back to her and she never knows the difference. To sell the real thing then is easy since it is so often done privately to collectors without publicity. So it is a cheap way to please an expensive mistress.'

When Farley left François he drove up to Herman's little holding. Bad news could wait, and he shut from his mind the thought of the time when he would have to tell Sarah the truth. In some ways he saw that the blow to her would be greater than his refusal of the girdle had it been genuine. As he got out of the car and waved to Herman who was hoeing down his maize rows there came into his mind the sharp memory of the night when he had heard her screams coming from the darkness. The ways of the Lord could be severe and beyond human comprehending. Maybe, but it was – without any power in him to stop it – now beginning to hit him hard that he should have had a moment of selfish unconcern about her reaction. She was, he knew, going to be desolated and there would be nothing he could do to comfort her ... Hell, hell.

Herman came up to him grinning, wiping sweat with the back

of his hand from his forehead, and said cheerfully, 'And how is life at the Villa Lobita?'

Farley grinned. 'My days there are numbered.'

'And then – you go where?'

'Don't know.'

'Your philosophy is a simple and fatalistic one – even selfish.'

'Sure.'

'Involvement to you is like putting a wild bird into a cage. I met the Alvarez couple last night at the Palomares Hotel. They are off to Bermuda for two months soon and were asking after you. You could move over there.'

'Maybe I'll give them a ring.' The Alvarez villa was at the eastern end of the Algarve, between Faro and Tavira, where Sarah was unlikely ever to trace him.

'Good. You stay now to eat something with me?'

'I'd be delighted.' He was in no hurry to get back to the Villa Lobita.

Lord Bellmaster and Quint were having lunch at Lord Bellmaster's club in St James's. They had a secluded table at the far end of the dining room in a window recess overlooking a small paved courtyard which the sunlight touched briefly once a day. Its centre was dominated by a bronze statue of a bewigged statesman of the eighteenth century, his shoulders snowed with the droppings of pigeons and sparrows. They had talked mild generalities through lunch and now they were taking their coffee and port at their table and the room was fast emptying. In a few moments Quint knew that Bellmaster would come to the point – if there were one – of this rare invitation.

At that moment, almost as though he had read his mind, Bellmaster said, 'Your boy, Kerslake.'

Quint sipped his port and said, 'A promising young man. Everything before him – as once you and I had.' He could see that Bellmaster was relaxed.

'And still have. He's done a good job for me down in Portugal. I wanted to thank you for the loan of his services.'

'He's still got a lot to learn, my lord.'

'Time settles that. I was thinking that if this ... ah, little ambition of mine becomes a reality you might care to second him to me, and he would be useful to you too. You always like to have someone in at the back door of an embassy.'

'It's a thought.' But what lay behind it, he wondered, since Bellmaster knew as well as he did that anyway they would have someone going in through the back door. But the answer was immediately clear. Bellmaster picking up a new creature of his own just as he had picked up Lady Jean.

Bluntly, as though he had read Quint's thoughts, Bellmaster said, 'They were good and useful days for all concerned when Lady Jean and I were together. But a woman's uses are limited to ... well, let us say to appropriately feminine spheres.'

Knowing he could take the liberty for old times' sake and favours still to come, Quint asked, 'Are you still leading the field in the Washington stakes, sir?'

Bellmaster laughed. 'Dear Quint – you always did know when to pitch the unexpected fast one. My dear chap, there is a protocol about answering that kind of question.'

'Protocol, yes.' Quint coughed a little as Bellmaster's cigar smoke reached him. 'Well, one can always tell between old comrades when it can be dropped. As you did when you asked if you could have a collar and chain on Kerslake. But, to be blunt in a warm-hearted way, if you don't answer my question I think protocol would prevent me from making any promises about Kerslake.' He smiled. 'After all one has to think very carefully about detaching a promising young man for ... well, extramural duties. He still has a lot to learn.'

Bellmaster ran a big hand over his ample jaw and gave a grunt and then grinned. 'My dear Quint, does knowing six or eight weeks in advance about Washington mean that much?'

'Knowing anything in advance at Birdcage presumes an advantage. The next Pope, the next Chairman of the Council of Ministers of the Union of Soviet Socialist Republics. You may never want to use the advantage, but it's comforting to have it in hand. Anyway, I think we could find you someone better suited than Kerslake. As I said, he has a lot to learn. Take a simple thing like elimination. Some of our brightest hopes have fallen down there. Nobody is wholly ours until that fence has been jumped. Which is an appropriate metaphor to bring us back to the Washington stakes.'

Bellmaster, enjoying above a small touch of irritation the courteous duelling, said, 'For all I know you may not want *me* there.'

'Equally, we may *very* much want you there, but would like to have the advantage of prior knowledge. Time in hand is a valuable commodity. I don't know – from my lowly position, of course – that this is so. There are many imponderables dealt with on a higher floor than mine at Birdcage. I'm just a snapper up of unconsidered – no offence is meant – trifles.'

Bellmaster laughed. 'You're a damned deep wily dog and always have been.'

'And you're in very good form, my lord. And I know why, of course.'

'You'd be a damned fool – no offence meant – if you didn't. Lady Jean outran or outlived her usefulness to me and to Birdcage. There could have been a lot of skeletons locked up in some cupboard waiting to come rattling out, I thought. So I wanted to be sure.'

'And when the cupboard was opened it was bare, except for a nice piece of jewellery. A happy ending. So that just leaves us with Washington – yes, or no? And Kerslake – yes, or no?'

Bellmaster finished his port. The early afternoon sun slid a yellow shaft of light over the face of the statesman in the court-yard. Quint fingered a loose bread-roll crumb on the tablecloth.

Bellmaster quietly said, 'Washington, yes. No announcement for another six weeks.'

Quint sucked his lips gently, savouring privately his triumph, and then said, 'Kerslake, yes. In six weeks' time.'

Bellmaster chuckled slowly. 'You're a fox. You came prepared to bargain.'

Quint nodded. 'As did you, my lord. I presume we are both happy?'

'Naturally. So I can presume that Kerslake is now more or less my man? At the end of the stipulated period, that is.'

'Yes, of course.' But as he spoke Quint knew that the five- or six-week period was one which Bellmaster – if pressed – would ignore. Would, if needs be, persuade or coerce Kerslake into service with him by fair words or foul. Anyway, all that was of little importance. Bellmaster was going to Washington. So he happily thought. But Bellmaster was the last person Birdcage wanted to have in Washington. It was pleasant to have five or six weeks in hand to work with. It was a pity that Lady Jean had not left her daughter an incriminating diary record which would have had Bellmaster eating out of their hand and available always for missions far more suitable to his quite disreputable talents. The irony was, he knew, that Bellmaster had reached the age and style now when he wanted an impeccable position. How could the man be so guileless as to think that his sins could be shrived from him? Had he been content always to acknowledge Birdcage as his one master they would have been behind him for Washington. But though the hard proof had evaded them (galled them – particularly on the top floor) the plain inferrable facts were that he had worked for others and must have more than once betrayed Birdcage. For a big man, physically and mentally, he had a light touch and an ally who almost to the end of her life had been besotted and enchanted by him. Had he married Lady Jean there would have never been any danger for him. But he had married American money and the dear lady had conveniently broken her neck hunting in the Cotswolds five years later. There were times when Quint knew himself to be uncharitable enough to wonder whether the noble lord had not somehow arranged that, too. She had given him a lusty, healthy pair of sons to safeguard the Conary pedigree and had left him her millions. All he wanted. Yes . . . he could well have disembarrassed himself of her . . . tidied up a loose end. Dear, dear, he sighed to himself as Bellmaster passed the port decanter, it had to be admitted that – quite uniquely almost in its history – Birdcage had been used by one of its own. That was a thorn in the side which never ceased festering. What a pity about Lady Jean. An indiscreet diary could have put him in their net, docile to being collared and chained and dancing to any tune they decided to call.

*

Impatience was building up in Sarah. It was six o'clock and she was in her bedroom, already changed for the evening. For the last three hours she had been waiting to hear the sound of his car coming down the drive. She had told herself many times to be patient. He had probably stopped to have lunch with the Norberts and afterwards ... well, he had plenty of friends he might have called to see. But patience, she felt now, was a virtue which her convent life had exhausted. It really was too bad of him not to understand that she would be longing to know the value of the girdle ... longing to start talking in earnest of the things he could do, the new life he could choose. Oh, she wanted so much for him, but above all to see him come out of his happy-go-lucky existence and immerse himself in some venture, some meaningful way of life, for which his character and all his abilities fitted him ...

She turned away from the window from which she had been watching the turn of the drive and walked restlessly across the room. Catching sight of herself in a mirror she stopped. Part of her mind noted that her hair had grown now so that it could excite no comment, and the sight of herself in a shortish dress, arms and legs bare and sunbrowned, now gave no faintest goad to her conscience. For a moment or two she allowed herself to acknowledge that she was a woman, more than good-looking ... allowed herself to give free if quickly passing indulgence to a glimpse of the future ... marriage, a man to love her and be loved. A blush rose to her cheeks and ashamed her.

She swung away from the mirror. She must be patient and set her mind on something until Richard came. Find a book and sit calmly down and read. Close her mind to the outside world and the moment of his arrival. Yes, she would read. Be calm. Not act like a schoolgirl without control of her emotions.

She went to the wall bookcase and began to look through the titles. They meant nothing to her. Books never had. Her mother, now, had read voraciously ... all night, she knew, sometimes. Her eye was caught by the blue suede binding of her mother's diary. That was it. She would sit quietly and controlled and read her mother's diary until Richard came.

The diary in hand she went to the window bureau and sat down where she could see and hear the car when it came. She opened the book at random (sometime she really would sit down in a calmer mood and read it through properly) and began to read:

Bo-bo has bought this broken-down place in the ghastly Cotswolds. His family had it once – the side that went into the Church, I think – and I'm surprised the Branton line didn't become extinct through pneumonia. One thing I'm insisting on is complete re-plumbing. At the moment it is primitive – not exactly a shed at the end of the garden – but you have to pump the handle of each loo as though you were at work on bilges and if you turn on a tap the water comes creeping through like old W.S.'s schoolboy unwillingly to school. No central heating, of course. Bo-bo very brisk about this which doesn't surprise me. Army types are always so bloody brisk and hearty about discomfort and cold. Makes a man of you – which is what I don't want to be . . .

I got Alistair Queen up to see what he could do about redecorating the place. Bo-bo insisted on calling him Queenie which didn't go down well and BB said over his dead body would anything be done to his study. It was papered in his great-grandfather's time. All pheasant and fur and fish with leprous splotches where pictures have been moved. I shall go back to the villa until it is all done.

After dinner Bellmaster rang. The verdict was accidental death. I suppose I should feel sorry about Polidor, but I really can't. He was an odious man. And I'm not sorry that Bellmaster is selling the Lion de Mer.

At this moment Sarah heard the sound of the car coming down the drive. Immediately her suppressed excitement and impatience welled up strongly in her and, closing the diary, she jumped up and hurried from the room.

He came up the front steps as she opened the door to him, the jewel case tucked under his right arm. She moved to him, holding him by the arms and said, 'Oh, you have been an age, Richard! I've been biting my nails. What did he say? What did he say?'

Farley put out a hand and held her by one shoulder. 'Whoa! Calm it now! Calm it!'

'But I want to know. I must know now!'

'You'll know. But first I want a drink.' He moved her into the hall. 'I'm sorry I'm late. But I had lunch with Herman – you remember Herman, don't you?'

'Yes, of course I do.'

'Well, and after that I had to go and see Marsox and clear up some things with him.' He began to lead her across the hall. 'And then on the way back I had trouble with the petrol feed to the carburettor.'

'Oh, I don't care all about that. You're here now and I want to know.' She almost pulled him into the sun room. 'You sit down and I'll make your drink while you tell me.'

'All right. A beer. I'm thirsty.'

He sat down and put the jewel case on the table before him. Sarah opened a can and poured the beer for him. For a moment her eyes caught his above the glass and there was something in his look, in his whole bearing, which suddenly disturbed her and made her hands tremble. She handed him the glass and sat down opposite him and said spontaneously, 'Something's wrong. You're not happy, are you?'

He put the glass down untouched and said, 'No, I'm not. But that's not the point. It's your happiness that concerns me.' Almost pleadingly he went on quickly, 'Sarah, my dear, you're not going to like this and I hate having to tell you but the Venus girdle ... well, it's only a replica. It's worth nothing, compared to the value of the real thing ...'

She heard him through the shock growing in her, a coldness which slowly possessed her and for a few moments inhibited all thought. She sat down slowly as though any sudden movement would disorganize her body with a clumsiness which would spread to her emotions. She had known fear once and had screamed. Now she knew bitter disappointment and knew she had to school herself to deny it a wild display. She knew now why he had been late coming back. He had dreaded this moment – not because of his own feelings, but for the blow it would give her ... the shattering of all her dreams of helping him. Now she, too, must school herself to curb any outburst to spare him the sight of her naked despair. She had wanted to do so much for him.

Now, denied that joy, she must spare him the sight of her true distress.

Flatly, she said, 'Just tell me, Richard, all that your friend said. It's all right. You've said the worst and I'm not going to—' she forced a small smile, 'to be emotional.'

He put out a hand and held the fingers of her right hand briefly. 'That's my girl. I know you wanted to do something for me. And even if I thought it was unnecessary. I only wish I'd been able to come back now and give you good news because . . . well, I can't bear to see you unhappy and—'

'Richard. Just tell me.'

'Yes. You're right. Let's get it out of the way.'

She sat and listened to him as he gave her the story of the Venus girdle which he had had from François. Oddly, as she heard him, she found a little ease in a growth of a feeling, not anger, more contempt, for Lord Bellmaster, who so clearly had cheated and deceived her mother. She had known him, not well, but from time to time in this villa. With the later growth of maturity in her she had – though she seldom allowed herself the pain of dwelling on it – realized that her mother had been his mistress and had remained so after her marriage. How could a man of so much wealth have cherished it to the point of deceiving her mother? Free now from any bars to uncharitable thoughts she found herself hoping that the greed in his sin would one day be punished. Sinner herself she might be, and in giving way to her weakness of resolution after so many years she knew that true grace would always be denied her . . . but, at least, in her sin she had harmed no one but herself . . . and had wanted so much . . . so much . . . to show her thankfulness to Richard that she still lived. For a moment she felt the first prick of tears in her eyes, and closed them to deny the sight to Richard. When she knew they had been conquered she opened her eyes as his hand came out and took hers, and saw his square, almost ugly, brown face deep-creased with a wry smile.

'That's it, old girl. There's nothing to be done, and I don't think we should sit glooming around here brooding on it. There's a little restaurant in Monchique. On the way back I booked a table there and that's where we are going, and we're going to forget all about the Venus girdle and Lord Bellmaster. And don't fuss about me.' He stood up and she rose with him. 'Something will turn up.'

'Oh, Richard . . .'

She moved to him and he put an arm around her shoulders, holding her against him. 'Come on, now. Go and get your best bib and tucker on. They do a marvellous lobster *flambé* with *aguardente de medronho* . . .'

She enjoyed the evening, abandoning herself to it because she wanted to escape all thought of her disappointment, feverishly almost acting out the role of a new personality . . . the happy, contented Sarah she would have been if all had gone well. She took more wine than was her custom and, after the meal, they danced together and, though it had been years since she had done, she found that in a short while her natural sense of rhythm surfaced. After a time she found that, where she had been determined to be gay and show no signs of her setback, there slowly faded from her any need for pretence. Neither of them talked of tomorrow or the future. This evening was enough, time and decisions were smothered. Tomorrow was too distant to throw any shadow over her.

They drove back with the car radio playing and when they went upstairs to bed they paused at the head of the stairs before she turned to go to her own room. He put his hands on her shoulders and gave her his big, clumsy smile, then bent forward and kissed her cheek.

'There now. Sleep well. And don't worry about all the tomorrows. I never have. Things have a way of sorting themselves out.'

'Yes, of course.' She took his right hand and kissed the back of his fingers briefly. 'I shall be all right.'

She lay in bed with the curtains undrawn, the room grey and shadowed by the starlight, and in a short while, though she fought it, she felt all the euphoria of the evening, all her resolution and spirit, slowly being swamped by the onset of the misery she had been determined to keep deeply contained within herself. The evening, she realized starkly, had been no cure . . . only an anaesthetic, misery-killing and now fast wearing off. She sat up suddenly and, while she despised herself for her weakness, leaning forward, her hands to her face, began to sob, fighting to hold down her emotion, to stifle her childish anguish and disappointment. Her sobbing grew and passed the point where she could neither control her body's response to her misery nor raise any defence of pride to castigate herself to shame for her weakness and so surmount it. Sobbing aloud, she was flooded with self-pity and distorted thoughts. She had no one, belonged to no world ... everything she tried to create for herself and others was always doomed. Richard would go and she would sit alone here in this villa like a lost soul ... better, yes, better if he had never heard her screams.

At the abject nadir of her emotion she realized that Richard was sitting on the bed at her side, his arm around her shoulders holding her comfortingly, his lips close to her tear-wet cheek and his voice soothing her. She turned and clung to him, the strength and hardness of his body balm to the softness and weakness of her own, the comfort of his caresses waking a new passion in her for the stilling of her unnameable hunger and misery ...

When she awoke it was morning. Sunlight claimed the room. Outside the sound of quarrelling sparrows came from the drive. Distantly she heard a goat's bell jingle flatly. She lay without moving, feeling the warmth of his bare arm under her neck. Without turning she knew that he was awake. She had no thought or feeling which she wanted words to mark. Her mind and body were one, translated by a bliss which enwrapped her and was not to be questioned or marred by speech. Slowly he moved and she felt the turn of his arm under her neck as he raised himself a little and looked down at her face, smiling. She smiled back at him and then his lips came down to hers and claimed them gently, and his big hands moved on her, repossessing and waking her flesh again to his. And this time he was all tenderness, gentling and cherishing her, as they both moved to celebrate their passage to true liberation, to a true gifting between them.

It was raining outside, hard, heavy rain with no wind, and bringing out a flowering of coloured umbrellas from the lunch-going women which rivalled the wet, enamelled blooms of the precisely patterned flower beds in the park. Arnold Geddy watched them from where he sat in the window seat of Kerslake's small office and thought with mild delight of Cadogan Square later.

On the desk before Kerslake were the various documents which he had brought back from Miss Branton in Portugal and which conveniently Geddy had come to collect.

Kerslake said, 'By the way, one small point occurred to me. I did, of course, tell Miss Branton that any communications to your office should be addressed to you. But it is conceivable that she might telephone Cheltenham and ask for me. One never knows when something odd like that might ... well, cause embarrassment. She could ask for me and your telephone operator might be dumb about it. *No Mr Kerslake here, madam.* I give myself a black mark for not having thought of it and covered it while in Portugal.'

Geddy smiled. Bright young man. As he had once been. You can't think of everything. That power was given to no man. Nice chap. He, himself, had overlooked the point, but there was no need to reveal that. *Curtsey while you're thinking what to say. It saves time.* He cleared his throat unnecessarily, nodded wisely and then said, 'It occurred to me, Mr Kerslake. My switchboard girls have instructions that any calls for Mr Kerslake should be put through to me.'

'That was very percipient of you, Mr Geddy. My thanks.'

'Habit, my dear boy. Although you've never mentioned it – and quite rightly – you must know that I once worked here. Sat where you do now as a matter of fact. Happily, though you may not agree, my engagement was only of a temporary nature.'

Kerslake smiled. 'Yes, I did know it. Were you under Quint then?'

'Oh, dear me, no. This was wartime. Quint was doing a spell in Washington. No, I worked for Polidor, a charming Greek, well, perhaps not charming to men, but certainly to women. It was, as a matter of fact, one among many of his assets.'

'I've never heard of him.'

'My dear Kerslake ... there are lots of people who have worked here that a lot of people who work here now have never heard of. Anyway, poor Polidor is long dead. I must add since "*the slightest approach to a false pretence was never among my crimes"* that I personally never cared for him. Now tell me a little more about this Richard Farley. Generally speaking, I mean. Not officially.'

Kerslake gave him the general facts known about Farley and his background, and finished, 'I only met him once for any length of time and that was when they came to my hotel to dinner. I liked him, but I wouldn't say he was a type ever to make his mark at anything. One of the waiters at my hotel had once worked for him – when he ran a small restaurant on the coast, he told me. He was a good employer but a bad business man, gave his chums too much credit and found eventually that the tradesmen and suppliers withdrew theirs. A happy-go-lucky drifter, perhaps. But not, according to the waiter, with any interest in women.'

'Queer?'

'No. Just not interested. You're thinking about Miss Branton?'

Geddy shook his head. 'No. She's fresh out of the egg as you might say. But she's the daughter of Lady Jean and if she's only got half her mother's nature—' he smiled gently, 'and the other half equally endowed with a strong streak of self-concern then she's well protected.'

'And well-endowed. An allowance from her father, a good one. And now she's picked up from her mother—' Kerslake tapped the documents on his desk which Geddy would take away, 'this very valuable gold belt thing. Though she did say she didn't want it insured because she was going to give it to Farley for saving her life.'

'Indeed.' Geddy hesitated, remembering the Duchess's precept, *If everybody minded their own business – the world would go round a deal faster than it does.* And then decided that he could allow himself the vanity of telling a Birdcage man something which he clearly did not know. He said, 'I doubt that it would do this Farley man any good. It's a nice piece worth a few hundreds, I suppose. But it's a replica – though Lady Jean never knew that. Lord Bellmaster, who gave her the original, had it made and then just changed them over when he was going through a very difficult financial phase many years ago. I know because—' he was enjoying the stillness of Kerslake's eyes and face, 'as his solicitor in the matter I negotiated the sale of the original quietly for him to a German, now dead, who, I think, left it to some continental museum.'

'Did you ever tell Birdcage this?'

'Why no. My connection had long been broken. I'm back in and here now, you know,' he said with gentle humorous ruefulness, 'only because I have been re-coopted, shall we say, without the option. But since I don't like Bellmaster I thought it was a little unconsidered trifle you might find amusing. But I've no doubt that on some higher floor they know.'

When Geddy had gone Kerslake walked to the window. The lake in the park was lead-coloured and white-pocked with the assault of the heavy rain. He was grateful to Geddy, but he realized now why his had only been a passing assignment to Birdcage – there was too much of the old woman and gossip in him.

As he stood there the door opened behind him and Quint came in, wearing his hat and a raincoat. He said cheerfully, 'I love rain. It clears the air and eases my old bellows. The office car will be round in a few minutes. As you've been a good, tidy boy I've decided to take you to lunch at Scott's. How was dear Geddy? Still quoting Lewis Carroll?'

'That's what it was?'

'That's what it always is. He once told me that this place should be called Crocodile, not Birdcage. *And welcomes little fishes in with gently smiling jaws.*'

'Big fishes, too, sir.'

'Aye – there are no size limits or off seasons.'

Moving to get his own hat and coat from the stand by the door as he saw the office car draw up outside and glad to have momentary cover for his own doubt about speaking, he said, 'He came clean to me about once working here. With someone called Polidor, he said.'

'Did he now? Yes, that's right he did work with ... well, more precisely, under Polidor. Nobody ever worked with Polidor. Either above or below.' Quint paused, watching Kerslake put on his coat. Then with a dry grunt said, 'Come to think of it ... yes, it might be a good exercise for you. I'll give you a chit for his confidential file after lunch. Read it through and give me your thoughts about it.' He beamed. 'He's long dead, you know. Tragic accident. Oh, very. Well, come along.' He put a fatherly hand on Kerslake's arm and steered him through the doorway. Kerslake, allowing himself to be ushered out, his face hidden, smiled happily. It was the first time he had ever been promised a reading of the confidential file of any past or present member of Birdcage and he knew it to be – because he knew his Quint – not just a rewarding titbit but an act of far from momentary impulse on Quint's part. Random impulses with Quint were as rare as water in a desert.

Farley, in his pyjamas and dressing gown, gave the partly open door of the bedroom a bunt with his backside and went in carrying the breakfast tray. Sarah was sitting up in bed, a short silk bedjacket slipped over her shoulders.

He said, grinning, 'Breakfast, Senhorita. And good morning again.' He set the tray before her and gave her a brief kiss. He poured coffee for them both and carrying his cup went to the window and sat down at the bureau.

Sarah said, 'Richard – shut the door. Fabrina.'

Going to the door and closing it, he said, 'Don't worry about her. She already knows.'

'How can you tell?'

'You really want to know?'

'Yes, and don't you want anything to eat?'

'No. Just coffee. She knows because you can't keep love out of the eyes. Mine and yours. And she's no fool. There is a world of difference between a bed which has really been slept in and one which has just been rumpled about to make it look as though it *had* been slept in. And anyway, if you want to make it really all right – then all you have to do is to tell her we're going to be married. There isn't a country in the world where lovers don't jump the gun.'

'You're very coarse.'

'I know, it's because I'm happy. You'll have to get used to it.'

'Are we really going to be married?'

'Not if you've got a better idea.'

'Of course I haven't.'

'Well, then that's settled. Did you want something flowerier in the way of a proposal?'

'No, you idiot. It's just what I wanted. Oh, Richard – I can't believe it.'

'No, you should always be truthful. Of course you can believe it. No half measures. If I paint a pool I paint the whole of it. And so on. Do you want us to talk seriously about this or shall we just enjoy our breakfast and looking at one another?'

'I could look at you forever. Do you think I'll have a baby?'.

He laughed. 'What makes you think you won't the way we're carrying on?'

'You're being coarse again.'

'All right, I'll be practical. You realize that I'm marrying you partly for your money, don't you? All I have in the world is about two thousand escudos, a few clothes and a car that's long since seen its best days.'

'We shall manage. I've got this villa, and there's the allowance from my father ... and we could raise some money by selling the Venus girdle.'

'While I just loaf around? Oh, no, that won't do.'

'What do we do then?'

'I don't know. I'll have to think about it.' He was silent for a while, knowing that they had not been idle words, phrases to shelve real thought about the future. There was no wish in him to question or analyse what had happened between them. Time and chance had brought them to a discovery of one another. Each moment since then he had felt the growth of his love for her and hers for him. It was not in his nature to question what had happened to him and to her. All that mattered was their shared gratitude for the laying of ghosts on his side and hers. She sat now, looking at him, the same woman, but a different woman. And he was still Farley, but a different Farley. Some evolutionary jump of emotion, spurred by their needs, had changed them, and there it was – they had a new unexpected happiness. She was full woman and he was full man now. A true flowering. Ripeness was all. There was no virtue in pulling it to pieces just to see how it had grown and why it ticked. That way there was always a danger of not getting the thing back together again.

As though she had, through some recently acquired powers of telepathy, caught his thoughts Sarah said, 'There's no need to rush to any decisions. We've all the time in the world to organize ourselves and our life.'

'That's right.' He smiled. 'Let's just go on floating together three feet off the ground for a while. When we touch down we can be very practical.'

'Even so, Richard. I'd like to write and tell my father about it. He's the only family I've got and – no matter about the past – he's been good to me now.'

Sitting slewed round sideways to the bureau he reached out to one of its pigeon-holes and said, 'Would you like some writing paper to do it now?'

'Idiot! But I will do it today some time. It is the right thing to do, isn't it?'

'Of course . . .' He turned from her a little so that she could not see the whole of his face. Without anguish now, the ghosts so recently laid, he thought how much pleasure it would have given *them* had they been alive to get a letter from him. His mother would have adored Sarah . . . and his father at some time would have said, *If you ever treat her badly I'll flay the hide off you.* Embarrassed a little, still hiding his face, he let his fingers fidget with a book that lay on the desk and his eyes caught the title along its spine – *Dialogues of the Soul and Body – Saint Catharine of Genoa.*

He picked it up and turning to her went on, 'This sounds pretty heavy stuff for you to be reading.'

She laughed. 'Far from it. It's my mother's diary. It came from Estoril with the belt. The title was her way of protecting it in case she left it lying around, I suppose. She loved little deceptions like that.'

'Did she now? She sounds a very interesting woman, your mother. You must tell me all about her some time.'

'Of course, I will, but why don't you read the diary? You'll get a much better picture than I can give.'

'What? I couldn't read someone else's diary.'

Sarah laughed. 'Oh, Richard, you did sound so pompous then.

Of course you can read it if you want to. It's mine, anyway. She left it to me and what's mine is now yours.'

'Well, perhaps some time.' He put the diary back on the bureau and then slewed round and faced Sarah fully. He watched her as she buttered a piece of toast and spread it with peach conserve. The warmth of his love for her flooded through him. Unlike him she was a hearty breakfast eater; and a beautiful girl . . . woman now, full-breasted, passionate . . . dear God, what a waste of years she had known. There had to be something wrong with that whole business . . . how could God want people to kennel them- selves away from the world? He shook his thoughts from him, and said lightly, 'Your peach jam is dripping all over the place. I don't like sleeping in sticky sheets.'

She laughed. 'Don't worry. I'll change them. Come here and give me a kiss and I'll give you some more coffee.'

He went over to her as she put her toast on the tray and wiped her mouth with a napkin. He picked up the tray and put it on the floor and then slid into bed beside her.

'Richard, you can't! Oh, Richard!'

'Sarah . . . darling, Sarah . . .'

Colonel Branton, his back to Geddy, stood at the window look- ing down at the Promenade. The new leaf on the trees lifted on the slight breeze, sunlight running over it like water. May was soon coming in. Everything was stirring and increasing . . . lambs, crops . . . the young girls . . . aye, and the older girls . . . the young men and the miserable old men like himself. He smiled to him- self.

He said, 'I had to be in Cheltenham so I thought I'd call in and show it to you. Not wasting much time, is she? Eight years in a convent . . . a few weeks out and she's in love and is going to marry. She must have a touch of the old Eve her mother had in plenty. Know this chap?'

Geddy looked up from Sarah's letter which he had just finished reading. 'I know of him. One of my staff went down there to settle up business and met him briefly. He says he's a nice type, but not over ambitious. His father was regular Navy, finished up lieu- tenant-commander.'

'That's something.'

'Also, he happens to be the one who pulled her out of the sea.'

'That so? Then the thing's as plain as the nose on your face. What could more impress a dewy-eyed innocent like Sarah? They're both coming over some time soon to see me. Wants to do the job properly, I suppose. Ask for her hand . . . old-fashioned stuff, but I go along with it. Quite touched in fact. I've often thought that when she was young Lady Jean quietly turned her against me. God knows why. I suppose you'd better let Bellmaster know?'

'Yes, of course.'

Branton smiled. 'Perhaps he'll make a marriage settlement . . . through me, of course.'

'I hardly think so.'

'Neither do I. Odd chap, Bellmaster. Can't really get to the bottom of him. I could never really understand why he didn't marry Lady Jean himself. He didn't really have to marry that American pork-pie-or-whatever-it-was heiress for her money. He was loaded himself. Unless he knew that he'd be taking on too much with Lady Jean. Too much of a handful for marital bliss. My God, she was a woman and a half where men were concerned.' Branton moved to the table and picked up the letter. 'Do you want to make a copy of this?'

'No, thank you. But I'm glad you let me see it. I hope she's going to be very happy and shall write and tell her so.'

'You do that, Geddy old man. Nice family-solicitor gesture.' He laughed. 'Nice family solicitor . . . sound, solid and respectable. I'll bet you've had to clear up some nasty messes in your time.'

Without any sign of the irritation he felt Geddy replied quietly, 'Well . . . so have the Army haven't they?'

'Not only clear 'em up. But get themselves into them. I've seen more damned fools promoted over first-class chaps than I care to think about. Well, I've got to go and pick up my succubus from her hairdresser's. Women . . . God bless me I love 'em, but it takes a damned good pair of hands to manage some of 'em. Got to admit it, though. I never was up to Lady Jean – God rest her Irish soul.'

When Branton had gone Geddy lit himself a rare cigarette. For some reason which eluded him Branton had irritated him today. Where normally he usually felt more sympathy for him than he showed, today he had come close to disliking him. So the girl was going to get married. Well, if the man were right, it would be the best thing in the world for her. It came to him then that that was why maybe Branton had been using a particularly nasty though polite manner. Yes, of course. And he should have had the wit to recognize it at once. Why shouldn't he be full of bitter regret? Bellmaster – with himself to dot the i's and cross the t's – had mucked up his life. The one thing in the world he would have liked to have had was a son or daughter of his own truly to love and cherish. He'd have been a good father, too. Poor Branton, he'd sold himself for money and the promise of preferred promotion. How like Bellmaster to have cheated him over the one promise which had meant the more to him.

He reached for his private telephone and dialled the Birdcage number. There was no reason why he should report to them but old habits recently revived spurred him on. After he had spoken to Kerslake he would get in touch with Lord Bellmaster. He did not, though, imagine that Lord Bellmaster would be very concerned with the news.

Kerslake was reading the Polidor file when Geddy telephoned. After he had finished speaking with Geddy he wrote a short memorandum for Quint to bring him up to date. Information was information and one never knew when it might turn out to be useful. Farley was all right, he felt. No ball of fire but not a scrounger. Given the circumstances the odds had always been that they might form some relationship. The chap was fundamentally sound and decent. Bit idle perhaps. Nice woman, too. Not his type, though. Margaret was his type, small, dark and full of life. Just now and then, though only briefly and with little conviction, he wondered whether Birdcage was worth all the sacrifice a man had to make. He could have gone high in the police force eventually ... a nice house ... kids ... Margaret ...

He turned back to the Polidor file to finish it. It terminated with a brief obituary.

145

*Died – death from drowning – during Cowes Week while guest
aboard Lord Bellmaster's yacht,* Lion de Mer. *Shore-going
motor-boat capsized in bad weather. Lord Bellmaster at helm, with
Lady Jean Branton and Polidor aboard. Both Lady Jean and
Bellmaster strong swimmers. Polidor – non-swimmer, no life jacket.
Body recovered from sea off Selsey Bill a week later. Scalp fractured
presumably by blow from some contact with boat's structure during
accident. Lord Bellmaster gave evidence during inquest. Lady Jean's
evidence, owing to illness, was given in sworn affidavit. Accidental
death. FSO*

And that was interesting. Maybe it was the reason why Quint had
given his permission to read the file. FSO File Still Open. The
Coroner's cut-and-dried *accidental death* was one thing. But a
Birdcage diktat of FSO was something quite different.

chapter seven

Farley was at a loose end. Sarah's allowance had started to come
through from her father into the bank which she had nominated
in Faro. Also from her solicitor she had received her passport.
And today she had gone off shopping for clothes which she
needed for their trip to England – since they had both decided
that before they could get married they should go and see her
father. Might even – and he had no objection, because what did
time or place mean so long as they were married? – be married
over there. But because she knew that he would be bored hanging
around while she did her shopping she had said that she could
take Mario and Fabrina with her – as a treat – and Mario could
drive his car. Well, there was one thing, if Mario were the worst
driver in the world he could not do much harm to his old car.

At ten o'clock in the morning he sat on the sun terrace sipping
a beer, wondering what he should do. Idleness sat uneasily on
him. Drive and ambition he might lack but he felt lost with
nothing to do. Love and marriage, the happiness which he knew
now with her ... they were all there to colour the future. But in

himself he had felt growing the thrust of a need to have something positive to own and cherish which would give him a truer pride in himself and, he supposed, turn him from a satisfied idler into a man with a wife and, he hoped, children to come, who would have the dignity of being a true provider. What was it he had told her once? About a place in the Dordogne which he would turn into an hotel. Pipe dream, then. But not necessarily now. They could do it between them. Neither of them was closely tied by need or sentiment to this country. Well, they were going to drive to England. They could go up through the Dordogne and maybe find a place. Wouldn't have the full capital to buy. But a fair bit and then he could really get his teeth into it. And this time, no more regarding it as a refuge, a joke thing like *Il Gallo*. Raise a mortgage to get it. And then hard work. No credit to chums. By yourself you didn't care. *Amanha* had been good enough then. But from now on it had to be *hoje*. A wife and kids. God, that was a new one for him, but he was already looking ahead to it. Perhaps it was as well that bloody Venus girdle had been a phoney. No help, no pennies from heaven. What you got for yourself was the only kind of real thing to have. What a sod that Bellmaster had been ... probably still was. Might take some time before they could find a place and move. Meanwhile there was this villa. Selling it would help; he had not thought of that. Why should he? He was not used to having assets. One thing he couldn't be was a kept man.

He got up. Take a walk around the place. Mrs Ringel Fanes had neglected it a bit. Could find himself plenty of jobs to do.

He went round the lower part of the house now with a different eye. The paintwork in the kitchen and the servants' quarters had gone badly. Some wall tiling was loose, a tap dripped needing a new washer; there were a score of small things. Cracked window panes. All things Mario should have kept in order but had not because – with a mistress away so often – who cared?

At the foot of the stairs he paused and looked at the Augustus John painting. The likeness of daughter to mother was there, but with a difference. Sarah, her feet on the ground now, was fast showing a solid, practical nature. Lady Jean floated, seeming scarcely to touch the stone steps, buoyed up by her own ebullience and some ethereal spirit in her ... a wild one, he guessed. Perhaps not exactly trailing clouds of glory but certainly never lacking admirers and lovers, he already knew. She'd take a fence and deep ditch without a thought of broken collar bone or neck, and if she had had scruples they could never have been born of conscience, he felt. For a moment or two he had a passing curiosity about her lover Lord Bellmaster. She would have given him a hell of a time had she ever discovered his cheating over the golden girdle. Was the one she wore in the painting the real or the replica, he wondered. Mother and daughter so much alike to look at and a whole shift of genetics between them. Not that he found that odd. He and his father looked much alike, but his father had been far, far more of a man than he would ever be. He shut his eyes for a moment ... glad for the peace which was with him now when he thought of his parents. Sarah had given him that.

He went up and looked around the top floor – doing now what he had so often done in the villas of friends to whom he wanted to repay kindness with service to them; but knowing now that he had a sharper interest in the improvements he could make. In a few weeks he could give the villa a face-lift and raise its value for when the time came to sell it. Dordogne. Well, why not? A gladness grew in him. A married man, a family man, a business man, something to work for. Exit Richard Farley, footloose and free; enter Richard Farley, breadwinner and, without doubt, in the fullness of time family man.

He entered Sarah's bedroom. One of the window frames had warped with the weather and needed easing. The tiling on the floor near the door had bulged slightly and wanted taking up and resetting. All over the villa a host of small things now leapt to the eye and remedying them would keep him busy. He sat down at the bureau, pulled a sheet of paper from a pigeon-hole and carefully made a list of all the things he had noted around the villa. *Method* ... his father's favourite word. The list completed he sat back and lit one of his occasional cigarettes and let the peace of the happiness he had known and, pray God, would know for always, in this room envelop him. Wrapped in his growing bliss, he ran his fingers idly over the blue suede cover of the book entitled *Dialogues of the Soul and Body – Saint Catharine of Genoa* which still lay on the bureau top. Slowly becoming aware of the book he picked it up. Lady Jean's diary. What, he wondered, had made her choose that title to camouflage it from idle eyes? Though, as a matter of fact, he acknowledged, there was an aptness in the words. Soul and Body – the complete human being. He grinned to himself, sure now that it had been no idle choice of the woman who floated down the stone steps, the eternal Eve, wearing the girdle of Venus. *Virtus Vincit.* He wondered. Thank the Lord anyway, Sarah – he had more and more discovered – had no illusions about her mother and her lovers. From twelve to sixteen what son or daughter did not begin to know their parents as they really were?

He slipped the brass catch free and opened the diary, riffling the thin, closely written pages at random. A small pen and ink drawing in a margin caught his eyes. A woman in riding habit, sitting side-saddle, was taking a stone wall jump. It was beautifully done, with a telling economy of line. Augustus John would have been proud of her. He turned the pages and found other drawings. A middle-aged man in evening clothes, sprawled in a club chair, a glass in one hand and a cigar in the other, the face a satanic caricature, a devil's tail curling from under him to the floor. Under the sketch, the ink long faded, were the initials L.B. Well, he was with that one all right. Another of three small birds sitting on a branch with a lean cat eyeing them. Another of a tall woman in evening dress, wearing a tiara, holding a fan in one hand and in the other a dog lead which was attached to a midget-sized man wearing court dress and breeches and a ducal crown on his head, and subscribed *Ella D walking His Grace.* Sometimes the drawings obtruded into the text space to show that they had been done before Lady Jean made her entry. One of these was of a steam yacht with the name *Lion de Mer* surrounded by a crowd of bum boats. As he turned the pages two slips of paper fell to the floor.

He retrieved them. The first read:

The contents of this parcel which have been shown to and packed in the presence of Father Ansoldo of the Capella da Senhora da Pé da Cruz, Monchique, and Senhorita Melina Montes, my personal maid, of this address, I bequeath absolutely and utterly to use or to dispose of in any way she wishes to my daughter, Sarah Branton.

Under their three signatures was a note:

Sarah, my darling daughter, if ever this comes into your hands, light a candle for me and pray for the redemption of my soul and the forgiveness of my many sins.

On the other piece of paper was written, *My personal diary, intermittently kept, covering a long period of my life, Sarah. I leave the nature of its disposal or use to you. J.B.*

For a moment or two as he slipped the notes back between the pages Farley had a strong feeling of disquiet. Sarah had given him permission to read the diary. Yet, somehow, he felt that the only person who could grant that dispensation was Lady Jean herself. But then, in a sense, she had because she had left the diary entirely at Sarah's disposal. Even so, a strong sense of probity filled him with diffidence. The diary still resting open on his knees, he looked at it undecided. What point was there in reading it? He had Sarah, loved her, and was beginning to discover a new life with her. A phrase or sentence glanced already here and there on the neatly written pages had signalled to him that Lady Jean had written frankly and indiscreetly – so much so that he knew that he had subliminally already been making up his mind not to read it. Only the sharp, terse line drawings had captured him and made him turn the pages. The dead should have their privacy respected. But if Lady Jean had wished this – why on earth had she left the diary to Sarah? Because she had something to say and wished Sarah to know it? Sarah was his responsibility now and the truth, half-guessed or already known by her about her mother, was surely enough?

Looking down at the open pages before him he saw what he had already briefly noted; sometimes Lady Jean abandoned making her entries in English and wrote in French or Italian. A paragraph written in French caught his eye.

Bellmaster a toujours fait se qu'il a voulu faire pour sa propre tranquillité d'esprit. Il a fini par me prendre au piège, et par faire de moi sa complice pour l'assassinat.

For some time he sat staring at the entry hardly able to believe his eyes. How could any woman have been so rash as to put such words on paper and even more words for she went on to incriminate herself by describing the details of the murder of a man called Polidor? She had to have been mad. Then the conviction was suddenly sure in him that there had been no fear in Lady Jean that she could write so indiscreetly in the diary; during her life it must have rested in some secure place. No woman either could have written so frankly without a strong motive and this was not hard to guess. There had to have been a wild desire for revenge on Bellmaster should she ever predecease him. Though God alone knew how she could ever have thought that it would happen through Sarah. She must have been unhinged. No: more likely a gambler. Taking a long chance, hoping to give the Fates an unexpected hold which would ensnare Bellmaster – always hoping that there would be in Sarah some of the nature which was so abundant in her so that she might from pity for her mother move against Bellmaster in some way.

He closed the diary savagely and stood up. He was never going to let Sarah read it. If he had to lie he would. He would destroy it ... make all the excuses in the world for its loss. He went to his bedroom and locked the diary in his suitcase. It would be safe there until he decided how to get rid of it. That bastard Bellmaster! First he cheats her mother and then Sarah over the girdle of Venus and then could have come back from her mother's past to plague her. Staring out of his bedroom window he began to swear quietly to himself.

Quint walked in with a file under his arm, gave Kerslake a brief good morning, and stood for a moment at the window before turning and settling himself into a well-worn leather armchair and putting his legs up on the window seat. His severe profile was sharply outlined against the pale blue of the May sky. He said without emphasis, 'I thought it was time to tell you that if Lord Bellmaster gets the Washington place you'll be going with him – under his personal direction.'

'Thank you, sir.'

'For what?' Quint's tone was suddenly sharp and Kerslake

from past experience recognized that he was angry.

'For telling me, sir. I've never been to America and—'

'And, for our part—' Quint interrupted him brusquely, 'I'd like you to know that so far as we are concerned we'd like to make it possible that you never do. With Bellmaster, that is. And further that we'd even more like it to be that Bellmaster never goes but it looks as though we're not going to be able to stop him. Just for a time, when the Lady Jean stuff cropped up, I thought the gods were going to be kind and we'd get something to stop him.'

'Yes, sir.'

'What do you mean *Yes, sir*?'

Stung, Kerslake for the first time ever allowed his resentment to surface. 'I mean, sir, that although I have no facts to go on – I'm sure that Lord Bellmaster's loyalty to Birdcage was and still is divided. And more that you've never been able to prove anything. I've read the Polidor file. He killed Polidor. Polidor was a Birdcage man, solid – that's my bet. And he was on the point of having enough against Bellmaster to finish him.'

'Yes, well …' Quint sounded a little mollified. 'That wasn't hard to come by. They murdered him. Now, my clever little Devonshire dumpling, tell me why.'

'It's purely a fancy thing that came to me – the only reasonable projection.'

'Let's hear this reasonable projection. If you lack facts there's nothing wrong with theory or even a little fiction. Just tell me the story of Lord Bellmaster as you see it.'

'Well, sir, his most active period here was during the War and just after. He must have been a thoroughly competent, useful man. But, possibly for his own reasons, say money, but more likely some ego thing … power, twisted pride or even contempt for this place—'

'That's been known, for sure.'

'—he just started playing a double or even triple game. He could have started for the money and when he had it he went on for the sheer excitement. Ego gratification.'

'That's a hell of a phrase. He went on because that was his nature. And he's still going on, and will do at Washington.

That's why we don't want him there but you can't just go to a Prime Minister who's in his pocket for many favours received and present him with a fairy story. Facts. That's what second-class minds want before they act. So he killed Polidor. Take it from there again.'

'Polidor must have got something positive on him. But Polidor didn't know that Lord Bellmaster knew this, and his lordship wasted no time. He smacked him over the head with a . . .'

Quint smiled for the first time. 'Belaying pin would fit the fiction, no?'

'. . . and then capsized the shore-going dinghy. Easily done. I checked the Met Office for that day in their records. Force Seven south-west wind, gusting strongly. Heavy swell.'

'Did you, now? Clever boy.' Suddenly Quint was all good humour. 'And dear Lady Jean?'

'She'd been in Lord Bellmaster's pocket for years. They both knew enough about one another to realize that any break in the partnership would destroy them both. They both liked living. When he cracked Polidor over the head there was nothing she could do without laying her own head on the block. She'd been his creature for too many years. Once she'd supported his story of an accidental death she was even more in his hands. The trouble now is – with her dead – he wants to be a pillar of society and respectability. Genuinely. Wants the past dead. That's why he got in a tizzy about possible diaries or what-have-you turning up.'

'Not so. He'll still go on. It's like being an alcoholic. No cure. If he does get Washington you stay warm in his pocket and do your damnedest to nail him. Do anything for him, we'll indemnify you.' Quint sighed loudly. 'But . . . above all we don't want him there.'

'Isn't there a simple answer to that, sir?'

'Of course there is. But it's too crude, and against the Bird-cage ethic for a man of his stature and prolonged peccancies. A quick death is no punishment. Birdcage wants him to suffer . . . long and publicly and with the utmost humiliation. Now you know that you serve very jealous gods here. He's one of the very,

very few in our history who has used us instead of vice-versa. We need the pure balm of a public downfall as a panacea to our wounded pride. That surprise you?'

'No, sir.'

'Good. Well, now I have some news for you. Warboys and I have talked it over. From now on Bellmaster is your boy. You've got a free hand. That's what we gave Polidor. You get him. But don't forget how Polidor finished up. If he wants you before you go to Washington, play ball. If he ever gets to Washington, go on playing it. From now all the Bellmaster and allied files are open to you. I've brought this one down to you—' he slid the file he had been holding across the floor to Kerslake, '—because I thought you might like to read it as a cautionary tale – a short one but illustrative of Bellmaster's methods. And I must add that it was done for us ... for our benefit. But it illustrates his methods.'

'Thank you, sir.' Kerslake picked up the file. The cover was endorsed *Very Reverend Albert Reginald Dalmat, MA*. He put it on his desk and asked, 'Is there a file on Lady Jean?'

'There is.'

'Could I ask how she got involved with Lord Bellmaster?'

'You may. She was Irish, as you know. Old title, but the family didn't have a bean between them. Damn great house in Galway and her father lived mostly – to put it picturesquely – on potatoes and poteen, and worshipped only one god, Equus caballus. Her mother had a little money he couldn't touch and she saw that Lady Jean was well educated and did a London season. After that she had to work and she got a job in the Foreign Office as a secretary. Bellmaster spotted her and took her up and made her his mistress. He found she was the material he needed and he completed her education the way he wanted it. But he never killed the mettle in her. In fact, sometimes I think he regretted his choice.' Quint paused and then with a little sigh went on, 'When she wanted to be she could be the most charming of women. She was also pure Eve, and I would lay odds against any normally endowed man resisting her if she had decided otherwise. Anyway, you read the file.' He stood up and looked out of the window, gave a little grunt as though he had seen something unpleasing and then turned and went to the door. Holding it open he looked over his shoulder and said with almost a compassionate note, 'You're a very long way from Barnstaple, my lad . . . *a very long way.*'

When he was gone Kerslake allowed himself a smile. The emphasized words carried the notes of nostalgia, but he knew that none was intended. It was a recognized way of Quint's to emphasize that a Birdcage man was a Birdcage man first, last and always. When you came in here there was no going back, no escape.

He put the Dalmat file on the desk before him and began to read it. Compared with most files it was brief. The Very Reverend Albert Reginald Dalmat, MA, had been a Canon Residentiary of a provincial diocese in the nineteen-fifties. Forty years old, married to the daughter of a bishop, he had been a modern, outspoken churchman far from shunning publicity, an activist in organizations opposed to the atom bomb, a great joiner of protest marches, a Christian socialist and an advocate of closer cultural and ideological relations with Russia. The world, he believed, need only be a few steps away from Paradise if the good will of all peoples could be awakened and set marching under the banner of universal peace. He was always ready to take a platform or to write his views for the popular press. In addition he was charming, good-looking and persuasive and an embarrassment to the establishment.

He was small fry but with the prospect of growing into a big fish rapidly. No note was in the file of where the need for a move against him had originated – but there would have been no file, Kerslake knew, unless it had been tacitly decided somewhere between Whitehall and more pious purlieus that he should be rusticated to some lesser Eden than the one he envisaged for the world's proletariat. Lord Bellmaster had been given the assignment and he had wasted little time or finesse over it. Dalmat – who democratically made no distinction between croft or castle – had been invited first of all to Conary Castle. Here he had met Lady Jean who had made it her business to give him all her sympathy for his views while not neglecting the most obvious show of admiration for him as a man as well as a crusading priest. A short sequence of letters to her from him on the file marked the progression from ready friendship to heart-felt and warm admiration. While he condemned flattery, on being in receipt of it he very soon convinced himself that in his case it was not unseemly since it so obviously sprang from so charming and virtuous a source. He was invited to spend a few days on the *Lion de Mer* during a cruise among the Western Isles where, as they watched the Aurora Borealis together, he first put an arm round Lady Jean's waist in a brotherly way. There was in the file a wickedly funny minute written in that lady's hand for Bellmaster who had broken the cruise to go off to Conary Castle on urgent business for a couple of days, so leaving them alone. The following night – seduced by moonlight, Bellmaster's wine, and the charms of Lady Jean – Dalmat had made the mistake of going to her suite for a nightcap and had found himself in bed with her. Full of remorse and mentally and spiritually flagellating himself he had left the yacht the next day. But there had been no escape for him. Penances aplenty might shrive his soul and restore him to blessedness, but the record of his temptation and fall was forever fixed in black and white on the film which a hidden cine-camera had taken.

The rest was child's play for Birdcage. The Very Reverend Albert Reginald Dalmat retired from a too-public life and accepted a living in a remote parish in Wales. Six stills taken from the camera film were in an envelope attached to the inside of the back cover of the folder. Kerslake looked at them briefly and then closed the file.

With a sudden touch of sentiment, remembering his meetings with Sarah Branton, he found it hard to believe that she could have been this woman's daughter. But undoubtedly she was and Lord Bellmaster her father.

He spent the rest of the day reading the files which had been released to him. The biggest and the most interesting was Lord Bellmaster's.

Within the next three or four days Farley read through Lady Jean's diary at intervals when he knew that he would be free of interruption from Sarah. She was happy and busy sorting out her clothes and making arrangements for their trip to England. Her father had replied to her letter in amicable terms, expressing his happiness about her intention of marrying and insisting that, of course, they must come and stay with him. Usually he kept the diary locked in his suitcase. Very quickly he found that he could read it quite unemotionally – almost as though it were a work of fiction with no power to intrude on his personal life and relationship with Sarah. It spread itself over a wide range of years and there were gaps in the record sometimes of months and once of a whole year ... the period, in fact, which covered Lady Jean's marriage to Lieutenant-Colonel Branton and the birth of Sarah. Through all its pages ran a continuous, almost love-hate relationship with Lord Bellmaster. It became clear to him that Lord Bellmaster had – maybe still did have – some confidential foreign interests, which he combined with his own private interests, that now and again – as in the entry about the death of the man Polidor – had involved the two of them in dangerous and lawless activities. In some odd way Farley found himself now and again being less shocked than almost incredulous of some of Lady Jean's record. She had been promiscuous and unprincipled almost to the point of – the only word he could find for himself was paganism. Now and again despite himself anger broke into his reading; anger that she should ever have seen fit to cache it away with even the remotest chance of Sarah's ever reading it.

Loving Sarah turned him to find some excuse for her mother and the only one that came his way – and it was apparent enough in Lady Jean's not unfrequent outbursts in the diary – was that Lord Bellmaster with a Svengali-like fascination had dominated and controlled her. The more he read, the more there arose in him an angry pity and compassion for Lady Jean and a clear, robust detestation of Lord Bellmaster. With every page he turned he hated the man's guts more and more. Having no conception of what he looked like more and more the little sketch made by Lady Jean of a satanic creature lolling in an armchair holding a cigar and a glass of port came into his mind. Tenuously at first, but more and more firmly as he read, he realized too that with the breakup of Lady Jean's marriage there could have been from

157

her and Lord Bellmaster and from Colonel Branton, too, though he was a lay and probably a helpless figure, subtle pressures put on Sarah to turn her towards the idea of life as a nun since none of them wanted her around to impede in the slightest way their freedom. Sarah had been a sacrificial figure.

There were times when he had put the diary aside and go for a walk to calm himself down. That the man was a murderer was quite clear, for a little further on in the entry where she had written that Bellmaster had finally made her an accomplice to murder she had briefly set out the facts of an arranged boating accident staged to cover the killing of a man called Polidor. Despite her loyalty, under duress or not he had gone on to cheat her over the girdle of Venus. In an entry a month later she had written that Bellmaster had taken the belt away to be revalued and for its insurance to be readjusted. That his nature would provoke him to do something, Farley knew. But just what eluded him. In many ways he was glad that they were going to drive leisurely to England. He would have plenty of time to think over things and sort them out. In the meantime he was absolutely determined still that Sarah should never read the diary.

Luckily for him she was so absorbed with her day-to-day life and the prospect of going to England, that the diary, which she had not missed from her desk seemed to have gone from her mind.

To his surprise, however, two days before they were to leave for England, as they lay in bed together in the early morning, she said to him idly, 'Have you got my mother's diary, darling? I was going to put it away in the safe before we went off.'

Casually he said, 'Yes, I've got it, my love. But I haven't got far with reading it.' He had in fact finished it.

'Do you find it amusing?'

'Very. I'll put it in the safe for you before we take off. Now, what are we going to do today? Shall we make up a picnic and I'll drive you out to Cape Saint Vincent?'

'Oh yes, I'd like that. Giorgio drove us there once and there was a terrific gale blowing and the Rolls got covered in salt sea spray. He was furious.'

'All right, we'll go.'

That evening before they went to bed he came into her room with the diary, got the keys from her bureau and locked the diary in the safe as she watched him from the bed. But when they left the villa the next morning it was in his suitcase, and he already was beginning to see what he probably, as a matter of policy and good form, would first have to do about it. Lord Bellmaster inhabited a world of which he knew little. He would have to have good sound advice from the most discreet source. Probably someone like the Branton family solicitor, or even Colonel Branton himself to begin with. But that he would have to decide after he had met the man. Lady Jean had married him, and although she had often written cutting things about him in the diary, she had obviously been very fond of him, but not to the point of ever considering being faithful to him.

As they drove up the Lisbon road, Sarah beside him full of happiness and high spirits, he decided to put the matter from his mind until they reached England. Whatever happened they had their whole future before them and the idea of buying a place in the Dordogne and running an hotel had become one of which they talked more and more.

Listening to her chattering away he was suddenly overwhelmed by the joyful fact of the enormous change which had come over himself and his life in a few short weeks. Not just himself either. They had both, it seemed, been reborn to a newer, brighter world against which bloody Lord Bellmaster was no more than the smallest of dark clouds lingering on the horizon of their bliss.

Lord Bellmaster at the sideboard, his back to Kerslake, smiled to himself. For the first time in the flat the young man had accepted the offer of a drink. Outside evening was shadowing the park and car lights moved in erratic chains of gold and silver.

'Soda or water, Kerslake?'

'Neat, please, sir.'

Over his shoulder as he poured whisky from the decanter Lord Bellmaster said, 'Good of you to come along, Kerslake. Nothing official about this. Just a casual chat ... personal stuff. I thought you might be able to fill me out on a few points.'

'Anything I can do to help you, sir, I will.'

'Decent of you.' Not, thought Bellmaster, that he was deceived by the slight change towards ... perhaps not affability but certainly mildness in Kerslake's manner. Quint would have talked to him. Oh, he knew his Quint. Probably mentioned Washington already.

He carried the glass to Kerslake and went on, 'Forgive me if I don't join you. Heavy lunch you know and I've got a big city dinner date tonight. Captains of industry and finance are like any other captains, drink eases the strains of high command. So you take your whisky neat, eh?'

Kerslake smiled. 'I'm Devon born, my lord, but my father and mother were both Scots.'

'Point taken. Now ...' He walked to the window and pulled the curtains to shut out the evening. 'You met Geddy, the solicitor, didn't you?'

'Yes, sir. Before I went to Portugal.'

Still standing, the little, engrained habit of psychological dominance so natural now that he never marked it himself, Bellmaster said, 'Just had a letter from him. Tells me that he's heard from Sarah Branton that she's going to get married. Did you know that?'

'Yes, sir. Mr Geddy informed Mr Quint.'

'Oh, did he?' He felt no surprise. 'So dear old Geddy still sings now and then for Birdcage. But who, once having been there, doesn't, I suppose you've been through my file there?'

'Yes, my lord. Mr Quint thought it would be helpful in view of certain ... well, possible developments which might occur in a few weeks' time.'

Lord Bellmaster laughed. Yes, he liked Kerslake. He knew just how far to go, handled himself well. Rough granite now being well polished by Birdcage. 'Delicately expressed. And to keep it that way, then you'll know that I have a more than friendly regard and concern for Miss Branton?'

'Yes, sir. I know that she is your daughter.'

'Yes, indeed she is. That's why I wanted to know something about this man Richard Farley. You've met him. Tell me about him.'

'He's a nice chap, sir. I liked him. I've naturally been into his background for other reasons than your present one. There's nothing against him whatsoever in ... well, sir, shall we say our terms.'

'Is he a Catholic?'

'No, sir.'

'Well, that can be sorted out. All right, give me all you've got, and your own personal impression of him.' Lord Bellmaster sat down in a deep armchair and lit himself a cigarette and listened, fingering his gold case, while Kerslake gave him all the details he had of Richard Farley's life and background. When he had finished Bellmaster asked, 'What's his nearest family? There must be some.'

'He did mention when he had dinner with me that he had a very old widowed aunt – no children – who lived somewhere in Wales.'

'You liked him?'

'Yes, sir.'

'Born loafer – or just not found a slot?'

'Not born. I think he let the family tragedy get to him too much. I should think personally that marriage and its responsibilities might be the answer. He's no fool and he comes from good stock. Perhaps I should add that Miss Branton clearly felt very warmly towards him.'

'Why shouldn't she? He saved her life. Still, what you tell me is very gratifying. I wouldn't want her to be mixed up with some loafer or ne'er-do-well. Well ...' Lord Bellmaster stood up. 'I'm grateful to you, Kerslake. I'm sure that in the not too distant future we shall find ourselves getting on very well together. Now—' he went to the mantelshelf and took two theatre tickets from it. Handing them to Kerslake, he said, 'Couple of theatre tickets for tomorrow night. Can't use them myself. Find yourself a pretty girl and have a night out.'

'That's very kind of you, my lord.'

'Nothing at all. And thank you again, dear fellow.'

Going down in the lift Kerslake looked at the tickets and saw that they were for the National Theatre. He would ordinarily have used them for he was fond of the theatre. But since they came from Lord Bellmaster he tore them up when he reached the street and like a good citizen put the scraps in a litter bin.

In his flat Lord Bellmaster sat thinking about Richard Farley. The chap sounded all right. Good Service family. Pretty bloody end they had had ... but there. Marriage would pull him together. Later he might be able to do something for him discreetly. Always ways of working it so that he need never know the true source of his good luck. But the real point was that the man was going to marry his daughter. Lady Jean had she been alive would probably have wanted Sarah to fly higher ... she would certainly have wanted a slap-up wedding. Saint Margaret's, Westminster. Pages, bridesmaids. No quiet family affair. Big reception with a sprinkling of royalty, home and foreign. He smiled. She had known how to manage that kind of thing. Well, that's what he wanted. She was his daughter and – for the girl's sake and out of sentiment for Lady Jean – that was what he would like for her. The only problem was how the hell to arrange it. The only open status he had was that of godfather. That allowed him to make her a handsome wedding present. Odd, how this business of giving her a grand wedding had grown in his mind since he had heard the news. Perhaps he was growing sentimental and soft with age. Well, as far as Sarah was concerned he could allow himself that indulgence. The trouble would be handling Colonel Branton. He might be stuffy about being only a front man and allowing things to be taken out of his hands. Would he though? These Service people liked pomp and ceremony. If he were a wealthy man he might well have settled for it himself. He would have to handle him carefully but in the end he knew that he could work it. A fat cheque would ease the bite of wounded pride. The only basic problem was the right approach. Go and see him and talk it over? Or write him a letter to give him time to think it over and adjust himself to the idea before they had a man-to-man talk about the practicalities and the *quid pro quo* for allowing him a surrogate but masked position as the real father? He wanted to do the big thing for his daughter. The American union had only thrown boys – a bloody handful, the two of them. He smiled fondly. Chips off the old block. But a girl was something else. Sarah was his girl. If the Boston millionairess had produced a filly he would not be thinking like this now – no, not true. He still would have wanted it for Lady Jean's sake. He had never truly loved anyone else. All right, there was self-interest too. This would be a good-will offering through Sarah to the gods that Lady Jean had not decided one day to reach out from the grave and put him in jeopardy. She must have thought long and hard about that. Being Irish and a gambler like her father she would have, her mind once made up, gambled on the wildest chance to get at him. Being Catholic, though, she had no doubt forgiven him for the sake of her immortal soul. Now, a letter or a personal visit to Branton?

He stared at the Russell Flint beauties at their toilet. One of them, though only distantly, reminded him of Lady Jean. A sudden tiredness took him. What a bore this bloody dinner was going to be. And this Washington business – did he really want it? Birdcage would never let up on him. They would be on his heels till death and then have someone watching the catafalque – he grinned – in case he had cheated again. What he should have done when he had taken her from the Foreign Office was to have married her and stuck to Conary and a quiet life. *Domus et placens uxor.*

He made up his mind. A letter first.

They drove up to Lisbon and on to Estoril and stayed two nights at the Hotel Globo, much to the joy of Melina and her husband Carlo. For Sarah it was the beginning of one of the happiest periods of her life. She spent a lot of time talking with Melina, who clearly liked Richard. It delighted her that she did for she took without any embarrassment a simple pleasure in other people liking him. Carlo liked him too, and the pair of them – after Carlo learned that he had once run a restaurant and now thought of finding a place in the Dordogne – spent their time discussing hotel practices and Carlo was proud to take Richard around the Globo and to go into all the details of its management.

163

Before they left Melina, alone with Sarah in her bedroom, said, 'You have found a good man. One can always tell when it is the right thing. And never must you have any feelings about leaving the convent. That was all a big mistake. Once, you know, just before your mother died and when it was all settled that you should one day become a religious I told her I thought it was not for you. A thing against your nature ... your true nature. You know what she said to me with that wicked smile of hers?'

'No.'

'She said, "Don't worry. My Sarah is like me. If she finds she doesn't like a thing, she doesn't put up with it."'

Just then Farley came in with a parcel under his arm. It was a new suit which he had bought at Sarah's urging to replace the shabby old thing he had had for years. Melina left them and Sarah made him put it on to please her.

'You look marvellous, darling. I know you don't care about clothes much, but Daddy's always been a one for being properly dressed. I suppose it was being Army and all that. Now take it off and I'll pack it away properly in your case, not just throwing things in as you do.'

'I've been doing it for years.'

'Well, from now on I do it.' She came across to him and kissed him. As she did so he remembered how his mother had always packed for him when he went off to school and always clucked at the state of his case when he brought it back. It was a memory which had come to him, too, in the villa just before they left so he had decided not to carry the diary in his case. He had wrapped it in newspaper and it now travelled in the car safely hidden under one of the back seats.

From Lisbon they motored without hurry to Biarritz and then Bordeaux and then inland to Périgueux where they stayed three days at a small hotel, got a list of properties from an estate agent and spent their time inspecting them. Three or four interested them and they decided that they would visit them again on their return and perhaps make a decision.

As they lay in bed on their last night in the Dordogne Sarah said, 'I like this way of travelling. With my mother it was such a business. Cases and trunks and complaints if the hotel or the service didn't please her.'

'No wayside picnics with a bottle of wine, a loaf and pâté?'

Sarah laughed. 'Sometimes we did but you should have seen! Folding chairs and a table, damask cloth and silver. It was always a *fête champêtre de luxe.* Wine from a cooler and Giorgio serving. Everything had to be absolutely right, particularly if Lord Bellmaster was with us. Daddy never minded so much for all the grandness.'

His arm round her, glad of the darkness in which they lay, Farley asked, 'What was Lord Bellmaster like?'

'Oh, I don't know ... I suppose even at that age knowing what he was to Mama I shouldn't have liked him. But I did. He was always charming to me. Far nicer really than Daddy usually was. Though there were times when *he* would change, and then he would be fun, far more fun than Lord Bellmaster. Isn't it funny ... now, after so many years away from the real world ... I seem to have come back understanding far more about it. I think Mama was always, deep down, unhappy ... what she showed other people was a part she had decided to play.'

'You mean unhappy because Lord Bellmaster didn't marry her?'

'Perhaps. But, you know, I think that though that was what she wanted, to be Lady Bellmaster, she didn't really love him. Though things went wrong between them – Melina told me an awful lot that I didn't know – I think she loved, really loved Daddy.'

'Sounds a proper mess. How did your father and Lord Bellmaster get on?'

'I didn't see them together very often. They were polite, I suppose. No more.'

'I can't understand why your father didn't kick him out.'

'Perhaps Mama wouldn't let him and he loved her so much he just accepted things. One thing Melina told me which I didn't know was about Giorgio. About the way he left. I was away at convent school then. The Rolls-Royce belonged to Lord

Bellmaster, you know. But Mama always had the use of it. One day his lordship told Giorgio that the Rolls was getting old and he was going to change it and buy something different. I don't know what, a Daimler or some splendid American car. Melina did say the name but I've forgotten. Anyway Giorgio exploded! He was washing the car at the time, at the villa and Melina and Carlo overheard it all from the servants' quarters. He told Lord Bellmaster that he had no wish, nor intention of driving anything else but a Rolls and if his lordship changed it for anything else but a Rolls then he would hand in his notice.' Sarah's body shook with laughter. 'They had a real shouting match, Melina said. And when Lord Bellmaster said the last thing he would buy would be a Rolls just for the convenience or something of a chauffeur Giorgio gave his notice which was bad enough but he then went on to tell Lord Bellmaster what he thought of him as a man. Then Mama came out and pleaded with them both and that made it worse, because she lost her temper and told them both what she thought of them ...' Sarah giggled. 'And Melina said she had to hang on to Carlo because he wanted to go out and join in because he didn't like Lord Bellmaster and he didn't like Giorgio. Weren't they all stupid? Just over a silly old car!'

'So what happened in the end?'

'Giorgio left that day. And Carlo became chauffeur and the new car was something or other. Not a Rolls anyway. But that wasn't the end. Oh dear.' She lay for a moment or two shaking with laughter, and then said, 'Do you know what? Two weeks after they had it poor Carlo, who wasn't as good as he thought, hit a tram in Lisbon, or somewhere, and smashed it up. And then ... then ...' She rolled towards him, her laughter muffled against the bare skin of his shoulder, unable to speak for the mirth in her, and in those few moments his love for her was boundless, a wordless all-encompassing joy.

'And then what?' he asked. 'Come on you can't have the joke all to yourself.'

She drew away from him and, calming, said, 'And then guess what? Lord Bellmaster replaced it with a Rolls. Isn't it a silly story? Such a lot of pettiness. But it's funny. I really must look some time and see whether Mama wrote about it in her diary.

Maybe she did one of her little drawings. I'll look and see when we get back to the villa.'

Later, lying awake in the dark while she slept, knowing there was no entry in the diary for the incident, he knew that he was never going to let her read the diary and wondered whether the sensible thing would not be to go off alone for an hour and burn it somewhere. Perhaps he should. Perhaps he would. She always slept late and breakfasted in bed. He could walk out tomorrow and do it in some quiet place. Then his mind hardened against it. Bellmaster ... it was time he did a little paying and he had to find a way to arrange it, though God knew how. He really wanted someone to counsel him; someone who would be discreet and understanding and give him good advice. Certainly not Colonel Branton. He was too involved and had been for too long far distant from Sarah. Eight years in a prison. Bellmaster had been partly responsible for that, and then, when Sarah was free, he had turned out also to be a cheat over the girdle of Venus. Perhaps Kerslake would be the man. Yes, Kerslake. A solicitor would stop him from doing anything silly. He would look him up in Cheltenham while they were staying with Colonel Branton.

From Périgueux they drove leisurely through Limoges and Orléans to Paris where they stayed for three days and enjoyed themselves.

It was a beautiful late May morning, the long racemes of the laburnums hanging golden against the cloudless sky, the lilacs down the driveway dwarf-pinnacled with wine-purple blooms, the house martins back and neating under the house eaves, the coat of his neighbour's mare in the paddock across the road as sleek and glossy as a polished chestnut. And on his study desk, unopened, the morning mail. Seldom for many years had any letter arriving for him merited being categorized as a harbinger of joy. Bills, bloody bills mostly.

Colonel Branton sat down and quickly leafed through the five envelopes. He was in a good mood for no reason that he could readily isolate unless it was the season of the year. He was off soon to motor to the Wye for a day's fishing, half of which he would spend with the wealthy, tax-fiddling, aspirant country gentlemen who kept the wheels of industry and the cash registers of finance turning and clicking. Had to say, though, that some of them were good chaps . . . not many, but some.

Five letters. He recognized two of them as bills on their first delivery to him. He tore them up unopened and put them in the waste-paper basket. He opened a third, an uncommercial envelope, and found – canny tradesman to use a good plain envelope – that it was a final demand bill subscribed politely but firmly asking for a quick settlement. He stuck it on a spike next to the reading lamp. The fourth letter, with a foreign stamp, he turned over once or twice, trying to place the writing. Then failing, opened it and found that it was from Sarah in Paris. Pleasure moved gently in him. It was short but affectionate. She and the Farley man would be in England in a few days' time. They would telephone him on arrival. Well, no problem about that. She was his daughter, damned if he was going to regard her as anything else and they would stay with him. Push the boat out, too. Why not? Celebrate now and tighten the old belt later. Wouldn't be the first or the last time.

The other letter, in an expensive plain envelope, had his name and address written in a vaguely familiar handwriting. Postmark no help, only a blurry, typical post office mess as though the machine or the man suffered from the palsy. What this country damned well needed was . . . well, what was the good of even saying it?

He opened the letter and a glance at the deckle-edged note-paper with its embossed address enlightened him. Our dear old double-dealing friend Bellmaster. He put the letter down and lit a cigarette. Beautiful day outside. Rain earlier in the week. The river should be just right. He'd like to take Bellmaster along and shove him in with a weight round his neck. Wonder if this Farley man fished? Probably did. He'd take him over for a day. That's how you got to know people. Big fish on, heavy river, and one look at the way he handled it would tell you more in a few moments than a thousand personality tests. In the saddle the same . . . Feeling good, he stubbed out the cigarette and began gently to whistle to himself as he read the letter. The whistling died after a few moments.

The letter read:

My dear Branton,
I heard recently from Geddy the very happy news that dear Sarah is
to be married to this Richard Farley man who saved her life in
Portugal. He told me that he is apparently a very decent sort of
fellow – good Service family and all that – though he hasn't done
much with his life so far. But that can easily be remedied when the
time comes with a word here and there. Naturally, as her godfather,
I am as delighted for Sarah's sake as you must be. Our dear Lady
Jean if alive might perhaps have wished for her to fly somewhat
higher in her choice, but these days that doesn't go for much with
titles and honours being dished out two a penny to any Tom, Dick or
Harry who can play a guitar or in other affairs has been promised a
quid pro quo!
Still, I thought that if you were likely to be in London soon you
might care to drop by and we could have a chat to see what we could
agree between us about rolling out the red carpet.
Yours sincerely,
Bellmaster

The mild euphoria raised by the beautiful May day and the
prospect of some successful fishing died in Branton. With an
oath he pushed the letter from him. The bloody man! How well
he knew this kind of approach. And how well he could read his
mind. In so many ways it ran parallel to the line Lady Jean
would have taken over the wedding. A bloody great fuss over it.
Saint Margaret's, Westminster ... Everything out of his hands.
Not even a passing query as to what Sarah might be wanting.
Oh, no – Bellmaster, Bellmaster; what Bellmaster wanted was
the important thing. Well, he was damned if he should have his
way. Sarah was the one to choose.

A phrase from the letter ran blood-red through his mind
'... *a very decent sort of fellow – good Service family and all*
that – though he hasn't done much with his life so far'. That
might be Farley but it was also himself, and Bellmaster had
fixed it that way. Well, over his dead body would he agree to
anything that Sarah herself did not want. By God, he had not
been a good father to her one way and another, but it was never
too late to start. She should have what she wanted, and only that.

At that moment his wife put her head round the door and

said, 'Oh, you're still here. I thought I hadn't heard the car go. Darling, on your way through Cheltenham I wondered if you would do something for me?'

The rage which had been rising in him burst free and he almost shouted, 'On my way through Cheltenham I'm not doing anything for anybody, unless some jay-walking civilian steps in front of me and then I'll run the bugger down! And on the river if some half-arsed sod of a Birmingham gent begins to tell me about his new Jaguar when he should be watching his line, I'll push the ostentatious crap-hound in and watch him drown. And if—'

His wife suddenly laughed. 'Oh, darling, I love you when you get like that! You've been very peaky lately. It's nice to see you back in form ... full of fire. Can you keep it up until we get to bed tonight?'

Grinning, rage suddenly gone, he said fondly. 'You're a vulgar bitch. But I like you. Now clear out otherwise I won't wait until bedtime.'

'Yes, love. It's a parcel waiting for me at our jewellers. I told them you'd call.' She made a quick kissing-mouth at him and withdrew laughing.

Calm now, smooth from his outburst, he picked up the letter. How nice to be Bellmaster, he thought. How nice it was going to be too, ditching the bastard over this wedding thing. If he knew Sarah she would want something quiet. He had danced a puppet to his strings for years. But no more. No bloody more.

chapter eight

Sarah lay in bed reading. It was their second night in her father's house and because they both wished to observe the proprieties they had separate bedrooms. Her father and his wife had made them both warmly welcome. Casting back through her memory she found it hard to see now in her father the man who had been so distant and self-contained during her girlhood. There was about him a tenderness and, well, happiness she supposed, which she could not remember before. She liked the wife, too. Generous, a great chatterer, busy and efficient and so clearly very much in love with her father.

It pleased her that both of them had readily taken to Richard and he to them. She had looked forward with some trepidation to their meeting. Dreaded it somewhat. But all her fears had been dissipated within a few hours. Neither of them had said a word about the convent or of the way Richard had come into her life. It was just as though she had returned from a long absence to find a familiar life waiting into whose rhythms and patterns she had been immediately gathered. Made welcome. That was how it was. And Richard, too, she saw, had quickly felt at home here.

Farley came in, wearing pyjamas and dressing gown, to say goodnight to her. He sat on the edge of the bed and kissed her, then made a face and said, 'We're being very proper, aren't we?'

'And so we should, my love. It's not that they would mind whichever way it was. But I think it's the right thing.'

'I agree with you. He's a nice bloke, isn't he? Bit outspoken at times—' he laughed, 'particularly to her. But she doesn't seem to mind. She's all right, though. Must have been quite an eyeful when she was younger.'

'She's not his real wife. Did you know that?'

'Yes. He told me. If that's the way they want it, what does it matter?'

'She wants to take me to Cheltenham tomorrow to do some shopping.' She paused, took his hand and caressed his hard brown fingers. 'She's thinking about wedding clothes, hers, and perhaps mine. They haven't said so directly, but I think they would like us to be married while we're over here – and from this house. What do you think?'

'That it's a first-class idea. But we'll have to sort it out. You're a Catholic and I'm not. So it's either a Catholic church or a Registrar's office.'

'I don't care what it is. Well, yes, perhaps I do. I don't think a church ... not after everything ... Well, you know.'

'Of course I do. Well, we'll sort it out. I could go and see your solicitor and he could give me the form.'

'Then you could drive us to Cheltenham tomorrow and go and see him.'

'Not tomorrow. Your father's driving me over to the Wye for a day's fishing.'

'Bother. Anyway, in that case, we could have your car and she could drive me into Cheltenham. Is that all right?'

'Yes, of course.'

'Good.' She sat up in bed impulsively and put her arms around him, her face buried against his neck, and said, 'Oh, Richard, every now and again it hits me hard. All that's happened. That I should be so happy.'

He smoothed her cheek. 'You've got a lot of happiness due to you. And I'm going to see that you get it.'

The next morning Farley went into the study to see Colonel Branton, who was dealing with his post before they went off to the Wye. Under his arm Farley carried Lady Jean's diary, which was wrapped around with newspaper and held by rubber bands.

Branton tapped the letters on his desk and said, 'Dealing with the daily torment. Bills ... bills.' He nodded out of the window. 'We're going to have a good day if the fish cooperate. Not too much sun. I phoned just now for the river condition. Just about right. What's that you're hugging to your manly bosom?'

'A present for Sarah. Her birthday is coming up fairly soon.'

'My God, so it is! Early June. Thank you for reminding me.'

'I wasn't doing that, sir. I've had it hidden in the car, but they're both going off in it shopping and I didn't want Sarah to find it by accident. I wondered if you could put it in your safe for me?'

'Of course, my boy. The key's in that old tobacco tin on the bookshelf over there. Don't bother with security very much. Nothing in it worth a damn. It's one of Chubb's museum pieces. Used to belong to my grandfather where – scandal had it – he kept a very fine collection of early pornographic books. If he did then I think my father must have burnt 'em. He was a splendid man but very much *mens sana in corpore sano*. I must tell Dolly about the birthday. We must do something about it. Have a few people in.'

'That would be nice. Sarah hasn't had a lot of company lately.' Farley broke off momentarily, and then said, 'Sorry, sir. I didn't mean anything by that.'

'Then you should have. I blame myself to some extent. One of these times – since you're going to be family – we'll have a chat about it over a bottle of Croft's 1955. One of a very few survivors from my father's cellar.'

'I'll look forward to it, sir.'

Farley got the key of the safe and locked his parcel away.

As it happened, they discussed the bottle of Croft's and other things that evening. They drove to the Wye and had a day's fishing in perfect conditions. Before lunch they had taken a salmon each, both fish hens, Branton's a ten-pounder and Farley's a twelve-pounder. Branton recognized at once with a great deal of pleasure, that Farley was a very good fisherman. He threw a good line, knew how to mend and work it and all the while the fly was in the water there was no let up in his concentration. He played his fish without fuss and with authority and he tailed it by hand, confidently and without hurry. After lunch the Colonel lost a big fish and Farley took another twelve-pounder. Farley drove the Colonel home since he had celebrated with the picnic gin at lunch, so great was his pleasure in his future son-in-law.

Half an hour after their return Dolly telephoned Branton from Cheltenham to say that, after a successful afternoon's shopping, they had decided to have an early dinner in Cheltenham and then they were going to the theatre as a treat for Sarah. She was sure that the two of them were perfectly capable of looking after their own evening meal. Which they were. They made a fry-up of eggs and bacon and sausages which they ate with a bottle of an anonymous Châteauneuf-du-Pape, and then retired to the study to deal with the already decanted Croft's 1955 – Colonel Branton in the best of humours and Farley mellow, but in far better command of himself than his father-in-law to be.

After his first glass of port, Colonel Branton leaned back in his armchair and was silent for a while. Outside the light was going, a blackbird sang joyfully matching the joy which he carried in his own heart. Farley was a good, sound chap and he thoroughly approved of him. He had not missed the fact that he had gone very easy on the gin bottle at lunch, guessing that someone should stay sober to drive home. Damn considerate of him.

The port in him making any preamble unnecessary, he asked, 'You think you can make a do of this Dordogne hotel thing, Richard?'

'We'll try. If not in the Dordogne, somewhere else. Sarah's keen on it. She'll make a good shot at it. We'll both do our utmost. Must do. I've kicked around for too many years. It's time I settled myself to a steady job.'

'You will, you will. Both of you. Wish I were your age and could have another crack of the whip. By God, I'd do things differently. You never know, do you? Just one bad decision and you're stuck for life on the wrong side of the fence. Few things I got to tell you though. Now's the time when we're alone here with the whole place to ourselves.' He pushed the port decanter across the small table between them for Farley to help himself, and laughed. 'Not a father-in-law lecture or anything like that. Fact just the opposite as you'll hear. There I was, you know, good soldier, everything ahead of me. Nothing to stop me. Or so I thought. All the lights showing green. Know what I did?' He raised his glass and drank, watching Farley's face. Nice chap, pity to make him uncomfortable but damned if he was going to have any hidden nonsense between them. There had been enough of that in the past. Very deliberately he repeated, 'Know what I did?'

'No sir, I couldn't possibly imagine.'

'By God, that's true. Nor could I at the time. Well, I'll tell you. I tried to do the decent thing. Whether you tell Sarah about this is your business. I certainly shan't. But you ought to know. You must have heard a lot from her about her mother, Lady Jean?'

'Yes, I have.'

'Marvellous woman but tricky Irish with it. I'd known and loved her for years. She was a wild one, mind you. But I worshipped her. For me she could do no wrong though she did do wrong, one way and another, most of her life. Not talking out

174

of line, you know, Richard. *De mortuis nil nisi bonum.* But that doesn't apply now because you're going to marry her daughter...' He paused, cleared his throat and then went on slowly, 'You're going to marry her daughter but not mine, Richard. No, not mine and you ought to know it, and what you do about telling Sarah will be your affair absolutely.' He laughed drily. 'Bit of a facer, eh? But there it is, you're entitled to the truth. Only decent that you should know.'

Farley was silent for a while, and then said quietly, 'I think, sir, it would be better if I just sat and listened except I have to say one thing. I don't care a damn whose daughter Sarah is. I love her and I'm going to marry her.'

'Bully for you. Just what I knew you'd say. Well, I'll give it to you penny plain. Lady Jean tells me one day that she is four months gone with child and the father wouldn't marry her, though she would have liked him to ... for considerations I may say other than love. So I married her and (I'm ashamed to say it now) I agreed to accept certain, well, what shall we call them?' he questioned suddenly savagely. 'Considerations, sweeteners, promises of sure and pretty fast promotion from the other man. And don't think he wasn't in a position to make all his promises good. He was but once we were married he conveniently forgot or made excuses for not fulfilling the one promise which really meant anything to me. Promotion in due course. In fact, I've learnt since that he threw his weight in the other direction. Nice chap, eh? And bloody stupid fool me. Except that I loved her and wanted her. But even that went. It had to.' He refilled his glass to the brim and raised it with a very careful hand to his lips. A trickle of purple wine ran down his chin and he wiped it away with the back of his hand.

Farley looked away from him out of the window. The stars were showing. Two moths were beating at the uncurtained window. He knew, because he had known it before in his life with other men, that there was nothing to be done when the moment came for an outpouring of self-pity. You just sat and listened. Nothing was asked from you but that. The man talking was finding his own comfort.

'Yes, that went. She never stopped being his mistress.' Branton laughed suddenly. 'Skeletons rattling in the old family cupboard tonight, aren't there? But I was damned if you should start your marriage without the truth. Oh, we kept up appearances, and all that. Right up to the time she died.'

'Who persuaded Sarah that the life of a nun was for her?' He did not have to ask who Lady Jean's lover had been. He already knew. That Sarah was also Lord Bellmaster's daughter made no difference to him, nor would he ever tell her. Of Bellmaster himself he rigidly allowed himself no thoughts. The time would come for that.

'I don't know. It was six of one and half-a-dozen of the other. One of Jean's sisters had been a nun. You know the Irish, one to the Army, one to the Church, and one to stay at home and plough the bogs. Sarah seemed taken with it, so I didn't object. Jean was for it. In her way she was religious. Don't ask me how a woman sorts that out with her conscience. Don't ask me now why I ever loved her ... and, damn it, still do.' He laughed, his manner changing to a surprising mildness and almost apathy. 'You'll think me pretty maudlin. But I just had to get it off my chest. Damned embarrassing for you. I apologize. But – and you must bear with me over this – there's more to come. When Lord Bellmaster – did I say that was the chap's bloody name?'

'No, sir. But I'd already guessed it must be. Sarah's talked about his always being around her mother.'

'He's a right royal bastard. Full of money and power and ambition and God knows what else besides. Thing is, the settlement she thinks she's getting from me comes from him. I could never have afforded it, and why he wanted to make it is his business. Perhaps he had a touch of the guilts. If he did it must have been for the first time in his life. He'll probably keep it going. I don't know.'

Farley lit a cigarette and as he dropped the matchstick into the table ash-tray, he said quietly, 'You may not know, sir. But I do. We don't take a penny of his money. You can just write to us and say things have gone tight financially and you'd had to stop it.'

'Sounds good, yes. But Bellmaster might have other ideas. Just being done in the eye makes him pretty determined to get his own way.'

'I don't care what he wants. I can handle your Lord Bellmaster. And I'm going to.'

'What do you mean by that?'

'I'd rather not say, sir. Sarah may be his daughter. But she's going to be my wife.'

'You've got something in mind?'

'Only Sarah's happiness. And I can handle Lord Bellmaster.'

'Well, don't do anything stupid. I'm sorry I had to saddle you with all this. But you had to know there was no point in not getting it off my chest as soon as possible.'

'I'm glad you told me.'

Lying in bed that night, sleep far from him, Farley slowly came to a decision about what he should do. It was not a decision which pleased him. He would have preferred a face-to-face approach to Lord Bellmaster but he very soon saw this was out of the question. It would achieve little and still leave him with his main decision to make. The man had wrecked Lady Jean's life, Sarah's almost, and certainly Colonel Branton's. He had heard him come stumbling up the stairs long after everyone else was abed. It was curious, he found, that he could . . . what? . . . dislike, despise or condemn Lord Bellmaster so much. A man he had never even seen. He made himself so far as question what his action would have been if he had never met Sarah and had come across the diary purely by chance. Would he have decided then that something must be done to bring the man to justice? Probably not. The situation was too hypothetical to allow a ready answer. The simple fact was that he was involved personally and emotionally because of Sarah, and it was only on that basis that he could make any decision. But he was not going to be damned fool enough to risk wrecking Sarah's and his life by doing anything without proper advice. Lord Bellmaster had twice committed murder and twice involved Lady Jean. Years ago, maybe, but that did not absolve Bellmaster. Time did not automatically create an amnesty. He was uncomfortable about it. He freely admitted that to himself. He was not going to feel good about it.

He could call it his duty ... any high-sounding, righteous word to support his action. But underneath he knew that there lurked his own primitive personal feeling towards a man he had never seen. One thing he knew for certain, however, was that he would not move a step without legal advice. And for that he had only one acceptable source. Kerslake, or his employer Geddy. They were the Branton's family solicitors. They had to be his choice and he would be quite happy to abide by their decision because it would be completely impartial, a matter of law and justice, not sentiment.

The following afternoon Sarah and Dolly were going out to tea locally with friends, and Colonel Branton, feeling a little off colour from the previous evening's port, retired to his study for a quiet sleep. Before he settled down into his armchair he unlocked his safe and took from it a faded leather jewel case in which was a small diamond necklace that had belonged to his mother. With the case open in his hand he stood by the safe. Worth quite a bit, he thought. What should it be? Sarah's birthday or wedding gift? Whichever it was it needed cleaning. Well, Richard was going to Cheltenham and he could take it in to their jeweller's place and ask them to do it. He had thought of it over lunch, but with Sarah there had not been able to ask Richard to take it for him. Leaving the safe door open he walked out of the house and round to the stable block to find Richard. He gave him the necklace and asked him to take it to the jeweller's, saying, 'You can look at it. Used to belong to my mother. Can't make up my mind whether to give it to Sarah for a birthday or wedding gift. No hurry anyway.'

Going back to his study he saw the open safe door and went over to close it. His eyes were caught by the rubber-banded newspaper-wrapped parcel – Sarah's birthday present – which Richard had put there. Damned odd sort of wrapping for a birthday present. Well, perhaps he was going to make a better job of it before the day. From outside he heard the sound of Richard's car going down the drive. Not feeling too bright, for on top of his hangover he had taken two stiff gins before lunch and some white wine with it, he felt the heavy prick of sleep in his eyes. Getting old, he thought. Can't take it the way he had years ago. Drink and dance all night and be on parade sparking with life at six in the morning. To be twenty-one again. *Annus mirabilis*. All life before you. Damned good job he had not known then how it was going to turn out. He laughed to himself, and then picked up the newspaper parcel. Odd sort of wrapping for a present. Wonder what he was giving her? Damned bad form to take a peep. Part of the wrapping had been worn and partly torn along one of the sides of the parcel. Without tearing the paper further, he eased it back to show what looked like the spine of a book. Old one of some kind ... worn blue suede. Would not have thought old books were Sarah's cup of tea. Two words of the title in tarnished goldleaf caught his eyes, *Catharine of Genoa*. Religious stuff. Ah well, maybe Sarah was still a little way that inclined. Odd, though ...? He put the parcel back in the safe and locked the door. Sleep. Two hours' sleep and he would be as right as rain. Thank God the women were going out and wouldn't be chattering about the house. Nice though the way they got on. Dolly was quite perked up and looked years younger. God – he slumped into the armchair – the wedding-talk that was going on! And that reminded him. Have to do something about Bellmaster's letter. Well, that was one disappointment in store for him. From the way they had been talking it was pretty obvious that Sarah and Richard wanted a quiet affair. Bad luck, Bellmaster ...

He put his feet up on a stool and stretched himself out comfortably. Nice the way Richard had handled his fish. Learnt from his father he had said. Bloody awful way he and his wife had gone. Damned wogs ... He'd tried to teach Jean to fish once. Hopeless ... everything in a tangle and she'd sworn like a trooper. Old memories and pictures of her floated through his mind. Coming into her room when she was dressing to go out for the evening, bending over and kissing the side of her neck, her hands coming back to touch his face .. affectionate as you liked when she wanted to be. Long, slender fingers beginning to unfasten the little gold chain with its medallion which she wore always unless she was going to go out *décolletée*. He dropped into quick sleep and then woke himself almost at once by snoring.

From the past, sliding through the labyrinth of memories, he heard her voice ... *Oh, this stupid catch. Darling, undo my Catharine for me...* Odd that ... Catharine. Yes, of course, Catharine of Genoa. Her favourite saint. Funny, where had he seen that name recently? He sighed ... Pity he had lost that fish. Must have been lightly hooked.

Geddy, emerging from the depth of a legal document he had been reading, was betrayed into a moment or two of stupidity as he automatically answered his telephone which had rung.

He said, 'Will you please repeat that?'

The girl at his reception desk said, 'Yes, sir. There's a Mr Farley here wanting to know if Mr Kerslake could see him for a few minutes.'

'Kerslake?'

'Yes, sir. You said—'

'Oh, yes. I know. Ah ... Yes, well, bring Mr Farley up to me.'

In the short time while he waited for Farley to be brought up he sat rubbing his chin, a little annoyed with himself that he had even momentarily stumbled. Years ago he would never have been caught off his guard. Dear, dear ... And only a few days ago he had met Branton and heard that Sarah and Farley were staying with him. Going to be married. Well, that was a nice romantic conclusion. Hero marries the beautiful princess he has saved from drowning. He would have to go carefully about Kerslake. Should write him off from the firm now. Yes, that would be the best thing. Better ring Quint about it.

Farley was shown in and they went through the affabilities of first meeting and when Farley was seated and said that he had no wish for a cup of tea, Geddy explained. 'I'm sorry our Mr Kerslake isn't here at the moment. He's in London dealing with some business for one of our clients. Perhaps I can help you. But first let me say how very happy I was to hear the news about Miss Branton and yourself. A most felicitous and romantic development.'

'Thank you, sir.'

'Mr Kerslake will be sorry to miss you. But I am sure that you understand I am fully cognizant of all Miss Branton's affairs.'

'I'm sure you are, sir. But it's not really about her that I've come. I'm very much in need of advice and I felt that Mr Kerslake would be able to help me.'

'Would you rather talk to him than to me?'

'Oh, no. I didn't mean that. In fact as it's turned out I'd rather talk to you because you must have known the Branton family a very long time.'

Geddy smiled. Nice man. Seemed solid and sensible. Kerslake had liked him, and he saw why. He said, 'I've known the family ever since I was a boy. And my father before that handled their affairs. I'm at your disposal, Mr Farley.'

'You know Lord Bellmaster, too, I presume, sir?'

'Yes, I do. In fact we've acted for him in one or two small affairs.'

'Do you like him?'

Caught unawares Geddy covered himself with a dry laugh and shaking his head said, 'Oh come, Mr Farley. That's not the kind of question you ask a solicitor.'

'Maybe not. But for my part I hate his guts.'

'I see . . .' Instinct told him that every step from now on must be taken warily. Something was eating into Farley and it would be the easiest thing in the world for himself – elderly, solid, respectable Cheltenham solicitor – to say or do the wrong thing until he was on much firmer ground. Unless he were very mistaken, noting the grimness of Farley's face, this could very well be a case of. Take care of the sense and the sounds will take care of themselves. And why not? Lord Bellmaster's and Birdcage's worlds were all pure Alice in Wonderland except that the executions and the blood were real. Gently, he suggested, 'You may not be alone in that feeling for him, Mr Farley. Men in high positions naturally attract animosity. Sometimes deserved and sometimes not. But one thing you must understand – if it's in your mind, of course – is that I cannot discuss one of my client's affairs with you.'

'I know that, Mr Geddy. I'm not here to discuss anything. I'm here to give you certain facts and then I would like your advice on what course I should take. And I think it's only fair to you to make my position clear first.'

'I've no quarrel with that, Mr Farley.'

'Good.' Farley smiled unexpectedly. 'I'm sorry if I sound a bit grim and worked up so I think it's better if I get some obvious things out of the way. I mean things that you would obviously think upset or anger me. I know from Colonel Branton that Sarah is Lord Bellmaster's daughter by Lady Jean. I know that Colonel Branton's marriage was one of convenience, arranged by Lord Bellmaster in return for a generous payment to the Colonel. And I know that Lady Jean never ceased being Lord Bellmaster's mistress until the time she died.'

Geddy nodded. 'That's all quite true. And I think since you're going to marry Sarah that you should know. May I ask if Sarah knows about her father . . . her true father?'

'No. Do you think she should?'

'Did it make any difference to your feelings for her when you learned this fact?'

'Not a damned bit of difference.'

'Then you must know that she will feel the same way. Though I would advise you in telling her to choose your time and place carefully. When and where are your responsibility. I give no advice about that.'

'It's a little more complicated than that, Mr Geddy. It's not just a question of learning who her real father is, but of what he is.'

'I don't follow you. He's Lord Bellmaster, a public figure and a wealthy man.'

'He's more than that. He's a murderer twice over if not more. And he trapped Lady Jean into being an accomplice.'

Geddy looked for some moments directly at Farley and then slowly rose and went to the window. He knew his own agitation of mind, but more than that he had a dark sense of a gathering of events somewhere on the near horizon which when they broke into positive movement might – unless he was capable of the utmost caution and skill – sweep him away in their vortex. Since the night in a Positano hotel room there had been no true turning back to the placidity of provincial life. The outward show and movements were there but true peace of mind had never been his. All he cherished now was his own known image in this city and in his profession. There could be no question of putting that in jeopardy.

He turned and said evenly, 'That's a very, very serious accusation to make against any man, Mr Farley, as you know. I presume that you can substantiate it?'

'I most certainly can.'

Geddy hesitated for a moment. That he was here and not at a police station was, maybe, an act of the gods. If it were then he must use such grace as had now been given him to protect himself for a while until he could take advice from Birdcage. The simple exposure of the fact that Kerslake had never been on his staff could lead ... well, God knew where it might lead. Nevertheless the first step was clear. He was a respectable solicitor and must act as such, and pick his way delicately through the hazards that undoubtedly lay ahead.

He went to his desk and sat down. 'Before we go into this allegation, Mr Farley, and before you say any more to me about it, I must ask you a few questions.'

'Ask what you like, Mr Geddy.'

'These facts which you have about Lord Bellmaster, are they so far as you are aware, known to anybody else?'

'As far as I know, not to another living soul in the world.'

'Why did you come to me and not go straight to the police?'

'Because I wanted a solicitor's advice first. It's hardly the kind of thing I could spell out to some duty sergeant at a police station. Besides, in a way, it's a family affair, and the family solicitor seemed the right man.'

'Quite so. All right—' Geddy let his tone become brisk, 'I've had some strange things happen in this office. But I think you've topped them all. What I would like you to do is to start at the beginning and go very clearly and with the utmost factuality through the whole thing. I shan't say a word until you have finished. I just want the whole matter quite clearly laid out before me. So ...' Feeling more comfortable he smiled briefly. 'The floor is yours.'

Farley told him the facts, and he listened as he had promised without interruption and was glad that he had to make none because his own private thoughts had freedom to run without bar as the story emerged. Some things he knew at once he would have to do and he refused to look into their consequences and their hazards to himself and ... the knowledge gained ground with him all the time he listened ... undoubtedly to Farley. One hazard to himself which he saw clearly was that he would have to tell Quint at Birdcage everything before he could even pretend to give Farley any advice on the action he should take. And listening too, he was resolute in not contemplating the action which Birdcage would take. They would be delighted, he knew, to get Lord Bellmaster at last and would accept this gift from the blue without a thought of the irony of its receipt from such a naïve and unexpected quarter. He might not be able to do much for Farley but as far as possible he must protect as many others as he could, including himself. Misery and self-disgust would come later and he knew that he would learn to live with them.

When Farley had finished, he said, 'Now let me ask you some questions, Mr Farley. Are you sure that Sarah has never read this diary?'

'Absolutely sure. She doesn't even know I've got it with me.'

'And Colonel Branton?'

'No. He knows nothing about it. But it is in his safe at this moment. Wrapped up. I said it was a birthday present I was keeping for Sarah.'

'I see. And you say that Lady Jean writes specific accounts of how Polidor and Matherson were killed?'

'In detail. The one in French and the other in plain English.' Farley stirred impatiently. 'But what am I to do about it, Mr Geddy? That's the point.'

'It certainly is the point. And my answer is simple. For the moment you do nothing about it. You keep the whole thing to yourself and you don't let the diary leave that safe. When is Sarah's birthday, by the way?'

'June the third.'

'Ah, yes, I knew it was June some time. Well now – you go back to Branton's and wait until you hear from me. It won't be long. Please don't say you've been to see me. Sometimes a slip of the tongue brings awkward questions. I shall have to talk this over with someone in authority, you realize that?'

'Yes, of course.'

'But it will be in the strictest confidence. Then I'll let you know what is to be done.' Geddy stood up and, fiddling with a ruler on his desk, he said, 'You realize what this will mean to Lord Bellmaster, I'm sure?'

'Yes, I do, sir. And if you're going to ask me if it had been anyone else but him would I have acted the same way – the answer is that I don't know. But in his case I haven't any doubts. The men he killed mean nothing to me, they may even have deserved it. But the lives he ruined ... Lady Jean's, Colonel Branton's and almost Sarah's – well, all that means something to me. I hate his guts but I can tell you that I would be a damned sight happier if Lady Jean had burnt the diary before she died. But she didn't and that's why I'm here.'

When Farley had gone Geddy went to his cupboard and poured himself a neat whisky and sat at his desk sipping it, and trying to sort out his thoughts. He had to let Birdcage know. There was no avoiding that. And once they knew he would be in their hands. There was no avoiding that either. And not only he, but Farley, too, would be in their hands. And then God alone knew what would be decided. Warboys and Quint would never look a gift horse in the mouth. One thing was as clear as sunlight. They would never bring any public charge against Lord Bellmaster. They would have him exactly where they had always wanted him – singing and dancing for them until the end of his days, the rest of his life a penance for his past treachery to them. And very useful he would prove to them in his new role. But to have that power over him would only be possible if Richard Farley were not living and wanting to know what he should do about Lord Bellmaster. Like so many of the people whose corruption Bellmaster had engineered – he among them – Farley would become victim in his turn. There was no hope for him.

He finished his whisky and left the office. A few streets away, knowing he was prepared to live with his own shame for the rest of his life, he stepped into a public call box and dialled Quint's ex-directory office number.

*

Stretched out on the shabby armchair, his feet up on the broad window seat, Quint was relaxed and contented. Close by Big Ben began to strike five, and the street below was alive with a growing confusion of movement from home-going workers; ants moving with little thought but for their own affairs. Euphoria moved through him like the first touch of long-needed alcohol after a day of stress. Not alcohol, no – elixir, the balm of Gilead, the joy that came from the warm and only too rare smile of slow-working Fate.

Watching him Kerslake sensed the rare mood which held him. He had walked in and sat down without a word and he knew that his part was to wait equally silently for his first words. When they came his understanding, faltering only for a few seconds, moved into tandem with Quint's.

Quint took a deep, leisurely breath, and the sound came clear and untouched by any hint of wheeze or asthma, the satisfaction in him working like ephedrine.

He said, 'We've got Bellmaster. The gods of chance have delivered him. Nothing to do with us. It happens that way but so rarely. You go looking for something that's hidden and its lying out in the open, waiting to be picked up. Kicking around the place, disregarded. Do you think you merit blame for missing it? Then don't. She probably just shoved it on a bookshelf meaning to have a look at it sometime. But all her thoughts were on the Venus girdle. Why not? A woman in love wanting to reward her saviour and lover. A limp-bound blue suede-covered book entitled *Dialogues of the Soul and Body* by Catharine of Genoa. Stir the memory at all?'

'No, sir.'

'She never even got round to reading it. Which pleases me for her sake. But Farley did and was so shocked that he kept it from her – and still will – and brought it to England because he wanted to consult you about it. But when he went today to Geddy's office it was Geddy he saw. He telephoned an hour ago. He made a strong plea for Farley. You know what for, of course?'

'Yes, sir.' Kerslake felt the words come thickly from him. He knew what must follow but for the moment shut it from his mind.

'I had to say no to him. Inevitable. The Fates are on our side not Farley's. We can't have Bellmaster going off as *our* man in Washington, and Farley wondering why nothing has been done about him. I gather he can be a very forceful type and moreover has a strong personal feeling against Bellmaster. He could spoil everything. He has to be the one and only scapegoat. Ironical, because he wanted to finish Bellmaster – there's a full report coming down to you in a short while. This is only a friendly chat. Polidor and Matherson – clear proof. But Bellmaster will go unharmed in body or reputation to dance for as long as he lives at the end of our string. Or to use an exact metaphor the canary will be singing in the birdcage once more.' Quint dropped his feet from the window ledge and swung round to face Kerslake squarely. 'You knew your moment had to come. It's a bit early. If anyone else could do it I would give you the charity of a little more time. But only you, in the circumstances, can handle this. Respectable solicitor giving advice to a client. When you've read the full report let me have your formula. He's on his own. Nobody about him knows anything of what is going on. The world is full of unsolved mysteries. Try to be too clever and you open margins for error. Keep it simple. You'll have all our cover. Make sure that he tells no one he is going to see you. He'll cooperate because he's after Bellmaster's blood. We'll cover your break from Geddy's employment afterwards without any fuss. I don't have to tell you that. Birdcage looks after its own. The sooner it's done the better – and with discretion use Geddy as much as you want.'

Quint heaved himself slowly out of the chair and walked to the door.

Kerslake said, 'Will you be here for a while, sir?'

Quint nodded. 'Yes. I shan't leave until you've read the report and come to me with your programme.'

Left alone Kerslake walked to the window and stared out. The evening was clear and warm. The newly returned swallows and swifts were hawking over the lake. They would be doing that over Barnstaple too. That morning he had had a letter from Margaret saying that she was engaged to be married. Tom Bickerstaff, a car salesman. He had played rugby and drunk many an after-match pint with him. What would have been their reaction if they could know that he now stood watching office lovers meet by the lake and briefly walk with arms around one another before they parted to catch their trains, waiting to turn his mind to the planning of his first killing? What did he feel? Nothing. That was the best way to deal with it. Nothing. Instinct told him that this was not the dangerous moment. That was to come. And once that moment had passed he would be Birdcage completely ... like Warboys, like Quint, like all the others. That damned diary. It had probably been on the bookshelf, staring him in the face all the time. *Dialogues of the Soul and Body*. Lady Jean had had a sense of humour ... or irony? Well, the one thing he could not allow himself was that kind of dialogue.

There was a knock on the door and his secretary, Joan, came in. She put a sealed quarto envelope on his desk and said, 'Mr Quint said you were waiting for this.'

'Thank you, Joan.'

'Lovely evening, isn't it?'

'Perfect.'

She smiled. 'Makes you feel you want to do something ... well, extra special for fun.'

He smiled back. He knew she fancied him. The love life of Birdcage people tended to stay parochial and was encouraged. He said pleasantly, 'I've got a bundle of work otherwise I might suggest we do it together.'

'Pity. That would have been nice. Some other time, perhaps?'

'Why not?'

When she was gone he sat down and opened the envelope. Geddy's report over the telephone was long and minutely detailed. At some time he must, he guessed, have broken off and reversed the charges – unless he had had a pocket full of small change. He read slowly and carefully, without emotion. Emotion over his work had been an early casualty when he had come to Birdcage.

chapter nine

They had gone to bed late after having motored that day to the Welsh border, taking Dolly with them for the outing, to visit Farley's aged aunt. When Farley had gone in to say good-night to Sarah he had stayed with her and they had made love. Now they lay together quietly talking to one another.

'I liked your aunt so much, Richard.'

'She's pretty ancient, isn't she?'

'But so young really – in spirit, I mean. And what a lovely house, looking right down over the river. And those acres of rhododendron shrubberies. I've never seen such an enchanting place.'

'I doubt whether she finds it enchanting to keep up. The place is big enough for a regiment.' He ran a hand down the side of her cheek slowly and she moved and bit one of his fingers gently. 'She did say something to me about selling up and going to live with an old school friend of hers in Shrewsbury. Very sensible too, I should think.' He was silent for a while and then, wondering how she would take it, he went on. 'As a matter of fact she made a suggestion to me. You really liked the place didn't you?'

'Oh, of course I did!'

'Well, when you were walking ahead with Dolly, I told her about buying a place for an hotel in the Dordogne and she said what on earth did we want to go there for?'

'Well, why do we?'

'I thought you were all set on it?'

Sarah laughed quietly. 'Not if she said the same thing to you as she did to me when I was freshening myself up in her room before lunch.'

'What was that?'

'You must know. She told me and she told you separately so that we could both think it over and then . . . and then like now.'

'You mean about letting me have it cheaply so that we could turn it into an hotel?'

'Yes, darling. Wasn't she a cunning old dear?'

'You mean you'd like to do that? Change your mind about living abroad . . . about the Dordogne?'

'Why not? It's an ideal place. Plenty of rooms and parking space. Fishing in the river . . . two tennis courts—'

'Full of weeds. And a hell of a lot to be spent to bring it into shape.'

'But not too far away from Daddy and Dolly. And it's England. We've both been away too long. Oh, love – I really could be happy there. It said something to me right away. And after all it is a kind of family house, yours and . . . well, that will make it mine as well.'

He raised himself on one elbow and looked down at her and grinned. 'You two cooked it up between you, didn't you?'

'Of course not!'

'Of course yes. She told you before lunch but me after lunch.'

'Does it matter, darling?'

'Not in the slightest. I think it's a first-class idea.'

Later, lying in his own bed, knowing that sleep was still far from him, thinking about his aunt's Shropshire house and the things they could do with it, he was suddenly aware of the change which had come over his life in the last very few weeks. From somebody who had been content to be a nobody without destination he had become somebody who knew where he was going. Not a cloud on the horizon . . . well, yes, perhaps the Bellmaster one. But really that was out of his hands now. Old Geddy would take official advice and he would abide by it. Since talking to Geddy he had had moments when he could have wished the diary had not existed, moments when he knew that the strength of his feelings against Bellmaster before seeing Geddy had begun to change. It was all old history and he felt uncomfortable in his own mind at the strength of his . . . what? Vindictiveness? Something like that. Nothing could bring back the dead. Revenging himself on Bellmaster could never alter the fact that Sarah had passed eight years in a convent or that Lady Jean had been his creature. And come to think of that – why had she been? She had been a woman of character and self-will. She had gone along with Bellmaster surely not entirely unwillingly. Poor old Branton was the one who had come off worst. But would he have been any better off, any happier if he had never married her? He could not see it. Like him he did but there was no denying the obvious innate features of his character. He would have been happier to have married someone like Dolly right from the start. When Geddy telephoned him (he had made it clear that he, himself, should not call him) he would tell him that he now did not care to make a fuss about the Bellmaster business any more. No good, though, was it? Once you started something and it became official then everything was out of your hands. What a mix-up. He should have put the diary on the fire and burnt it.

Funny thing, too. Right from the start with Geddy he had begun to have the feeling that the old boy was wishing him anywhere than in his office. Well, he could see that. Bellman was his client from time to time. Not a nice thing to have to handle.

To stop himself thinking about it any more he switched on his bedside light and picked up a book. But before his eyes could comprehend the print he knew quite suddenly and certainly that he had done wrong and that there was now no changing the course of whatever events would come. As old Branton would have said with his Latin tags – *hominis est errare*.

Kerslake, having made an appointment with Geddy, drove down to his house in the Cotswolds the following morning. The meeting place had been Geddy's suggestion.

They sat now in Geddy's study, a pleasant book-lined room. On the mantelshelf a glass-domed display case full of brightly coloured tropical birds was flanked either side by silver-framed photographs of relations and one – the features clearly recognizable – of Geddy as a schoolboy in Eton jacket and a straw boater. The electric fire was burning against an unseasonal nip in the air and they sat before it either side of a low scallop-edged table on which Geddy's housekeeper had put the coffee tray.

Coffee pot poised to pour, Geddy hesitated and said, 'It's a bit late in the morning. Perhaps you would prefer sherry, Mr Kerslake?'

'No, thank you. Coffee's fine.' He watched Geddy pour and saw there was no shake to his hand. An old, wise bird who knew how to control himself even though he had now to be far from happy.

'I asked you here because the less you are seen at the office the wiser, I think.'

'I understand. Anyway, after tomorrow you won't be troubled with me again.'

Geddy made a wry face and said, 'Not by you, no. But troubled still nevertheless. Is it absolutely essential?'

'You know it is, Mr Geddy. We don't like it at Birdcage any more than you do but it is essential. Anyway, your involvement will be absolutely minimal.'

Geddy shook his head. 'Comforting words but not true. A human being is going to be killed – there is nothing minimal about that.'

'You've handled it before I understand, during the War.'

Geddy smiled unexpectedly. 'Oh, yes. I was trapped into it. But the young woman did happen to be fair game and since it was wartime it was open season. But don't worry, Mr Kerslake, I shall do everything asked of me. It's curious ... I think I was falling in love with her. She was very Italian in her looks. She lay there in the morning with her dark hair over the pillow and the bloom on her cheeks had a dusky peach flush. I couldn't believe she was dead. It was a long time ago and I have to confess that the memory only rarely troubles me.'

'There will be no trouble about this. If even the edge of it begins to show Birdcage will cover it no matter with whom – the police, the politicians or the press. The world is full of unsolved mysteries.'

'Your confidence warms and comforts me. Nothing is impossible for Birdcage and its high priests look after their altar servers and acolytes. And, far from being cynical, I even think a very valid, almost ethical, case could be argued for its existence in the world today. Given the death – for that is what it has become – of the holy spirit in man, then he is left to defend and succour his own by using the weapons, or more effective ones that his enemies turn against him. Sometimes at night you must have taken comfort from that.'

'Of course.'

'May I jump a few preliminaries and ask you whether it is to be at your hand?'

'Yes, it is.' Although Geddy was being tiresome he was patient with him because he understood him and sympathized with him, though such understanding could make no difference.

'For the first time?'

'Yes, Mr Geddy, for the first time,' Kerslake said, his tone, he knew, reaching near to curtness for he preferred to preserve a near immunity at the moment to the thought of the coming moment which would bind him to Quint and the others for the rest of his life. He went on, looking down at his untouched coffee cup, a thin film, as the liquid cooled, now formed on the top, wrinkled like a relief map, 'And now, shall we just confine ourselves, sir, to the exact details of the matter in hand?'

'By all means. "I'll be judge, I'll be jury," said cunning old Birdcage, "I'll try the whole cause and condemn Farley to death." Lewis Carroll wouldn't forgive me. But there because I treasure my own place and skin I am entirely at your service.'

Vaguely, knowing that dimly Lewis Carroll meant something to him somewhere . . . school perhaps . . . Kerslake considered the possibility of unreliability in Geddy but quickly dismissed it. The man had too much to lose to try any kicking over the traces.

He said, 'I would like you, while I'm here, to give Mr Farley a call. Briefly you are to say that so far you have not done anything about approaching the police or any authority, nor spoken to anyone about this matter. Your reason is that, while you don't doubt his word it has occurred to you that you must satisfy yourself first that the diary exists. It's a precaution any sensible solicitor would take to avoid going to the police with a hare-brained story. He'll understand that, won't he?'

'Of course he will. And my professional pride makes me add, it had not escaped me that I should have to do just that. Mr Farley is a sensible man and will, I'm sure, cooperate.'

'Also, that you think it advisable not to meet in your office but at some spot in the neighbourhood, reasonably secluded but unremarkable like a beauty spot or the car park of a country pub or hotel. I would suggest, in fact I would personally wish it to be tomorrow, say in the afternoon. There is no virtue in delaying things unnecessarily.'

'None at all.'

'Also that he is to say nothing to anyone of this appointment. And again if, say, Miss Branton or anyone else should show curiosity about his receiving a telephone call and ask who had made it he should say frankly that it was from you saying that you had heard about his coming marriage with Miss Branton, that you gave them your congratulations and if you could be of help legally and so on you would be very willing to oblige them. Or however you would put that.'

Geddy smiled. 'I would put it something like that. And where would you like this meeting to be?'

'I leave that to you, sir.'

'Very good. Are you fond of scenic views? For I presume that it is you who will be meeting him?'

'I don't care about the view as long as the place is reasonably secluded. And, yes, I shall be meeting him.'

'And I presume that this will not be a noisy business or involve any activity likely to attract attention?'

'Neither. I shall be sitting alongside him in his car having explained why I have come instead of you. The sound will be no more than a loud hiss and death charitably almost instantaneous.'

'Ah . . . let us be glad of a little touch of charity.'

Unexpectedly stung by the sarcasm Kerslake said, 'I happen to have liked what I saw of Farley. I think when you did your first elimination you were in a somewhat similar position.'

'Almost. Except that I thought I was merely drugging the girl so that I could search her luggage. However, I did not mean to upset you. I have a great understanding of your position and shall be as fully guilty as you will be. I'll ring and see if Mr Farley is in.'

Geddy went to his desk and telephoned. As he waited for a reply he fiddled gently with a small bronze Taiwan temple horse which he used as a paperweight. As luck would have it – since Dolly and Sarah were out and Colonel Branton had gone to London – Farley answered the telephone. His talk with Farley lasted only a little more than five minutes, and the meeting was fixed for half past three the next day. Rising from his desk Geddy went to one of his bookshelves and took down a Royal Ordnance large-scale map to show Kerslake the rendezvous which had been picked.

Opening it he found the spot and explained to Kerslake, 'Above Painswick here, there is a beauty spot called the Beacon. Most lovely views from the top. A golf course runs up most of the southerly slope. The club house is just here, at the bottom of the Beacon. Just beyond the club house is a cemetery with a wide strip of grass parking space along its front. This bit here ... which gives a view across the far valley. More important, you are screened at the back by the cemetery wall and its shrubs and trees. Lovers and picnic parties favour it. But at this time of year there should not be, at the most, more than three or four cars there.'

'Thank you, Mr Geddy.'

'You won't expect me to say that the pleasure is mine. Where will you be staying the night?'

'I haven't decided yet.'

'Well, I would suggest somewhere around Stroud. You would only have a few miles to motor. There are plenty of hotels in the district.'

'I'll do that and drive by the spot on my way there today.' Kerslake stood up and, refraining from any gesture to shake hands, said, 'I am obliged to you, Mr Geddy.'

Geddy shrugged his shoulders, then turned to the door to show Kerslake out. That night Kerslake stayed at an hotel on the Common above Stroud. He lay in bed awake for some time seeing in his mind the long stretch of grass verge outside the cemetery which he had visited. Barnstaple, as Quint had once said, was a long way away. The car he had driven up from London had false number plates, its true origin long obscured by Birdcage. While using it he had worn wash-leather gloves and would do so up to the last moment and also when he went to sit in Farley's car. He had telephoned Quint that evening and arranged a meeting place close to the M4 motorway where a Birdcage car would pick him up. Five minutes after they left his car and were speeding down the motorway a timed device would set it on fire. In the Birdcage underground shooting gallery he had sat beside the dummy mock-up of Farley and three times had taken from his pocket the miniature weapon, the latest in a long line of Birdcage sophisticated accessories, its bulk almost obscured in his hand – and from two inches had fired it with less sound than a heavy sigh – into the left-hand higher portion of the dummy's skull, the trajectory slanting upwards.

Farley would die almost instantaneously, unaware that death was taking him. Quint had stood by and nodded approvingly. But both of them knew that this was only the shadow of the reality to come. Neither of them marked with open words that in that coming future finger-pressure would rest the fruition or otherwise of Kerslake's long apprenticeship.

Many a man and woman in Birdcage had come to this point before him and, in the few seconds before moving to take action, had discovered the real truth of their own natures. Ruefully he thought that Geddy had been lucky. Oh, Lord forgive me for I knew not what I was doing.

Kerslake put out his bedside light, turned on his side, and thought of his secretary Joan. To escape the true turn his thoughts wished to take, he escaped into a slowly increasing erotic comfort of imagination and finally slept.

At three o'clock the following afternoon Farley went out to his car which was parked in the drive. He had already put the newspaper-wrapped diary safely in his car before lunch. Colonel Branton was away in London still so there had been no problem in taking it from the safe.

As he was about to get into the car Sarah came round the corner of the house wearing gardening gloves and carrying a small trug with a weeding trowel and fork in it.

She came up to him and said, 'Richard? I didn't know you were going out.'

'Yes, love. I've got a little business to deal with.'

'Oh, could I come too? I could easily do my gardening chore later.'

Smiling Farley said, 'No, you can't come, Sarah.'

'Oh, why not?'

He leaned forward and kissed her lightly on the cheek. 'Because I don't want you with me. And don't frown. Among other things it happens that in a few days it will be the birthday of someone I love and it's customary to mark such days with a gift.'

Sarah laughed. 'Well, yes, of course that is rather special. Would you like me to make a few suggestions?'

'I think I can get by on my own. So why don't you buzz off and join Dolly and give the herbaceous border hell between the two of you?'

Sarah kissed him and as he got into the car said, 'Drive carefully, darling.'

'I will.'

As she stood watching the car go down the drive, feeling her love for him a warmth inside her, Dolly came up behind her and said, 'Where's he off to?'

'To buy me a birthday present.'

'Did you make a few suggestions?'

'No. I like surprises.'

Dolly nodded. 'So do I. But I don't often get them. Your father never varies. Birthdays mean either Chanel or Arpège. And every trip to London a box of chocolates, very expensive, and always hard-centred – which he likes and I don't much. All right let's go and attack this bastard of a border. Used to be two permanent gardeners here—' she chuckled, 'so we're up to strength for today anyway.'

As Lord Bellmaster came down the steps from the entrance of his St James's Street club, where he had been looking out for Colonel Branton's taxi, Branton had the strong, almost euphoric feeling that the gods were with him. Even if they should decide eventually to turn away from him it wouldn't matter a damn. But there was no reason why a man shouldn't give thanks for a chance to keep his own hide intact. From his own club the previous evening he had telephoned Bellmaster and suggested that they might meet to talk over Sarah's wedding arrangements. Since they were both engaged for lunch Branton had suggested that he drop by Bellmaster's club and pick him up and they could go on to the flat and talk. The day was Thursday and he had picked it deliberately, knowing from long experience that this was the weekly day off of Bellmaster's manservant. No help from the gods there. But Bellmaster might easily have been lunching at home and then, he, Branton, would have had to face the hall porter and cover his real identity. He was going to kill the man, but he saw no reason why – if it could be avoided – he should jeopardize his own life. He would have faced that risk, minimally covering it by wearing a false moustache and saying he was a reporter from *The Times*, could his Lordship spare him a few moments to comment on . . . well whatever came into his head. Bellmaster was publicity-hungry enough to fall for that. But the gods had been good, and with luck now the hall porter would scarcely register him as he came in with Lord Bellmaster.

Bellmaster dropped into the taxi seat alongside him, his big face mildly glowing with lunch and port and an aura of Havana aroma about him from the cigar he still smoked.

'Good of you to pick me up, Branton. Damn long time no see. You're looking well. Both of us getting older though, what?'

'True, my lord . . . there comes a time when we begin to feel our years. More's the pity about some things. *Volo, non valeo* begins to creep up.'

Bellmaster laughed. 'That kind of visit to town was it?'

'Among other things. But chiefly I wanted to talk to you.'

'Well . . . I've got most of the afternoon free. Got to see the PM at five though.'

'Well, this won't take long.'

The taxi picked its way westwards as they talked to one another. When they reached Claremount Mansions Lord Bellmaster insisted on paying off the taxi and they went into the hallway together. The porter was in his little office cubicle and half-rose saying, 'Good afternoon, my lord.'

' 'Afternoon, Banks. I'll do the lift.'

'Thank you, my lord.'

Branton kept his face turned away from the porter as he stood on the far side of Bellmaster. They went up in the lift. At the flat Lord Bellmaster opened the door with his key, saying, 'Rogers' day off. So we've got the place to ourselves.'

Going in Branton kept his hands in his overcoat pockets, knowing too that he was going to touch nothing in the flat with bare hands. No coffee, no drink, and gloves on before he left. Over his absolute resolve to kill the man, he could sense the slow run of excitement in himself ... not from fear – he did not care what might happen to himself, though he was not going to be foolish enough to give any hostages to fortune. Life was good still, but he had had a long run and if things went wrong for him well he would have settled Bellmaster's hash. Wiped out the score. The odd bullet or mortar bomb at Anzio and a dozen other places could have wiped him out years ago. Risk was part of his profession. But unnecessary risk was for fools.

He sat down in a chair by the fireplace and eyed the mounted salmon on the wall while Lord Bellmaster went into his bathroom to wash his hands. Nice fish. Conary water was good. Pity if he were never to handle another big springer, but he had had his share. Feeling the bulk of the gun in his pocket he knew his hand would be steady ... as steady as the resolve in him. Handy little pistol which he had picked up in Italy during the war, a Walther 'Manhurin', only six rounds left in the nine-round magazine, two should be enough. Couple of backfires from a passing car. He took off his gloves and laid them on his knees. He rested his elbows on the chair arms and gently clasped his hands. No tremble. Why should there be? He would take whatever the gods sent him but he would take Bellmaster first.

Lord Bellmaster came back and settled on the settee by the window. Branton was offered a drink which he declined and said that he would keep his coat on ... thought he had a bit of a chill coming on.

Lord Bellmaster nodded. The sunlight through the window touched his head and the scalp showed palely through the thin white hair. He smiled warmly. 'Well, it is good to see you again. You look in pretty good trim too.' He patted his stomach. 'Trouble with me these days is that I don't get enough exercise. Haven't had a day's hunting since I don't know when. Bedroom antics not the same thing, eh?'

Branton said, 'Heard a rumour in the club that you might be getting something pretty big. Give you a chance to try some of the Maryland fences.'

'Rumours, dear chap. Westminster is full of them.' He reached into his waistcoat pocket for his gold cigarette case and motioned it towards Branton.

'No, thanks.' As the other lit his cigarette, Branton thought of Lady Jean and knew, as he had known ever since he had finished reading her diary which young Farley had left in his safe, that he was going to do in a very few minutes nothing to revenge her or the men she and Bellmaster had eliminated. He wanted to even the score for himself, the career he could have had and the promotion he could have won for himself without either of them. Selfish, he supposed, but satisfying.

Bellmaster said, 'Well ... you got my letter. I gather he's a good sort of chap, and Sarah's charming. No harm in pushing the boat out for them.'

'I suppose not.' He could give him that little bit of charity to die with. All he wanted now was a short while to sit here and look at him, knowing what he was going to do. 'But you know my finances. I can't match up to that form.'

'We can arrange that quietly. You can always say you're splurging a small nest egg you'd been cherishing for such a day. All I want is an affair that Lady Jean would have wanted and, without offence, of course, she is my daughter.'

It was on the tip of his tongue to say *I wonder?* But he held back, and said, 'Of course.'

'And it's her big day. Any girl would want a real slap-up affair.'

'I suppose that's so.' Without touching the arms of the chair Branton stood up and walked towards the window. 'But I think I ought to warn you that you could have trouble with Farley.'

'Oh, nonsense. If Sarah wants it he'll agree. Damn bad form if he doesn't!' From momentary indignation Bellmaster's voice turned to a humorous one. 'If Sarah's in the slightest like her mother he'll be putty in her hands.'

Branton nodded. Outside the park was looking lovely, flowers, trees in new leaf. 'Would be so normally. But there's one small problem. When they came to stay he asked me if he could put a parcel in my old Chubb for safe-keeping. Said it was a birthday present for Sarah that's on—'

An edge to his voice, Bellmaster said, 'I know when it is as well as you do, Branton. But what on earth are you driving at, man?'

'This parcel. Badly wrapped, you know. Just some old news-paper and a couple of rubber bands. A few days later I happened to go to the safe for something I wanted. Bit off form of me, I suppose but I took a look at it.' Deliberately enjoying himself and moving back now that he could get the full benefit of Lord Bell-master's face ... odd he had not noticed how much he was developing dewlaps ... he spun out the tension. 'Fact, I undid it. Ever heard of a book called *Dialogues of the Soul and Body* ... by some Saint or other?'

'No, I haven't.' Bellmaster rose and went restlessly to stand with his back to the fireplace.

'Oh ... well it could have been you had. You spent more time with Lady Jean than I ever did. It's just a spoof title. Inside it turned out to be a diary she'd written over the years. Very interesting reading too. I spent damn near a whole day at it while they were away in Shropshire visiting some aunt of Farley's. Damn funny in places ... outspoken too. Also plenty of her little drawings. You remember how good she was at that. Got you and me, I must say, off to a tee at times.' Enjoying himself, seeing the colour of good living fade from Bellmaster's cheeks, he was in no hurry to finish. 'My God, she didn't pull any punches when she took against people. You remember that squirt Archie Cardington who was in the King's Troop—'

'Branton!'

'Yes, my lord?'

'Don't think I'm a fool. Say what you've come to say. You don't care a damn about the wedding and neither do I at the moment.'

'No, I suppose not. Well, the fact is she was very indiscreet. I must say you pushed her into doing some pretty dirty things at times—'

'Jean never needed any pushing. She was what she was!'

'Aye, more's your misfortune. She should have had the good sense not to record it all.'

'All?'

Branton smiled. 'Yes, all, my lord. She gave very full details, the pages on which they occur were marked by slips of paper, by Farley I presume, of the murders of two men called Polidor and

Matherson. There's also a fair amount of stuff about various contacts of yours during and after the War with different foreign agents ... I mean secret agents. Particularly one Cuban called Monteverde and another—'

'All right, Branton. You don't have to spell it out to me. Was the diary at home when you left?'

'Yes.'

'And Farley hasn't mentioned a word of it to you?'

'No.'

'Can he be bought?'

The edge of breakdown was in Bellmaster's voice, a tremble of anger and alarm ... or perhaps, Branton felt, the first stir of a whimper. Gravely, he said, 'If he can then I'm no judge of a man, my lord.'

'Any man can be bought.'

'Not this one, my lord.'

Bellmaster suddenly tipped his chin up, his lips pouting with sudden anger. 'You're bloody well enjoying yourself, aren't you?'

Branton nodded. Never, he felt, had he been so much at ease and contentment with himself. Slowly Bellmaster was crumbling before his eyes. He said, almost with kindness in his voice, 'Yes, my lord. I am. That I think I can claim as my due. But I came here to do you a kindness ... something which you would never do for yourself.'

'Look, Branton, and I don't care what it costs me but we've got to get together on this. There's just got to be a way of arranging this with Farley.'

Branton smiled. 'There's only one way, my lord. Farley would never do anything for you. He's not that kind. But I can. And I must say it will give me the greatest pleasure in the world, even though it is a kindness you don't merit from me. Something which will *rasa* the old *tabula* between us.'

He took the Walther from his pocket and fired. The noise was louder than he had expected. The bullet travelled at an incline through Lord Bellmaster's left eye and out of the back of his head and on through the Alfred Munnings painting on the wall. Bellmaster fell heavily backwards and he stayed standing over him, untouched by the smashed face. He had seen plenty of those before.

Branton said calmly, 'Sic transit your gloria bloody mundi,' then he turned and picked up his gloves. He went down in the lift, hat in his left hand, and as he passed the porter's box he raised the hat as though to put it on and obscured his face.

Some way down the road he caught a taxi, glanced at his watch to see what time he had in hand to get his train from Paddington and, finding he had plenty, he told the man to take him to Harrods. This was a special day. He would treat dear old Dolly to something better than a box of chocolates. Something in the lingerie line. When he got to Harrods it was three o'clock.

At half past three Kerslake sat in his car outside the cemetery. At the other end of the grass strip, well away from him, was the only other parked car. It had arrived after him and a woman had got out with a dog, locked her car, and gone off for a walk on the Beacon. At twenty-five minutes to four a car came down the road from the golf club house and as it neared him Kerslake recognized Farley driving. He put out a gloved hand and waved to him. Farley reversed his car to park on the grass a couple of yards from him.

Kerslake got out and walked over to the car. As he got in Farley gave him a smile and said, 'Nice to see you again. Sorry I'm a bit late but to be frank I got a bit lost around the lanes coming over.'

'That's all right. I've been enjoying the view and the sunshine.' Kerslake smiled and gave a half chuckle. 'Well, you've come up with something, haven't you?' He was the young and up-and-coming junior partner. In the past he had quite enjoyed playing the part. He would play it today, too, but with a difference for it would be the last time he could claim the role. Still wearing his gloves, he settled his briefcase on his knees.

Farley made a wry face. 'Well, I wish I hadn't. I wish now I'd never seen the damned thing. Or just burned it and said nothing. But there it is. God knows what's going to happen about it.'

'Well, that won't be your responsibility. Or ours. Did you have this diary while I was down there?' From a professional and personal point of view he was in no mood to hurry things.

'Yes, though I didn't know it then. It was kicking around Sarah's room on her desk or in a bookshelf, I think. It came with the Venus belt thing she got from her mother's old maid. Thank God she didn't read it and now won't get the chance.'

'She might ask about it. No matter what happens you should have a good story to tell her.'

'Don't worry. I'll think up something. At the moment her head's full of birthday, wedding and starting an hotel over here.'

'An hotel, where?' Let it flow, Kerslake told himself. You are a friendly junior in Geddy, Parsons and Rank. A magpie flew across the grass and settled on the eighteenth green. One for sorrow.

'Oh, over in Shropshire. Not certain yet. It's a marvellous place. Lovely grounds and a bit of river, and not far from a main holiday route. Sarah's mad about it.' He grinned. 'She's even started to draft the brochure and to think about things like curtains.'

'Well, if it does come off I wish you every success.' That his words sounded genuine gave him no surprise. Words were harlots, they did what you wanted them to do.

'Thank you.'

'You've got the diary with you, of course?'

'It's on the back seat there.' Farley screwed round and got the newspaper-wrapped diary. Holding it on his lap, he went on, 'What on earth are you going to do about it?'

Kerslake smiled. 'Well, nothing locally. I rather fancy that Mr Geddy will take it to the Home Office. He's got a few contacts there. You can hardly go trotting into a local police station with it, can you?'

'Well, that's what I thought. That's why I went to Mr Geddy. He's a dry old stick, isn't he? But I liked him.'

'Yes, he's all right.' A solitary golfer hit an approach shot to the last hole and as it landed the magpie flew away. The last words from Quint had been *play the part and don't think about the curtain scene.* Easy to say. 'Well, I'd better have a look at it.' He smiled. 'Not that we ever doubted your word, of course, that it existed. But you'd be surprised what some people try to get away with.'

'I can imagine.' Farley slipped off the rubber bands and took the diary from its newspaper. He said, 'This is not exactly the moment to admire them but I must say some of Lady Jean's drawings are wickedly funny. I've marked three places with paper slips. Once you've read the entries you'll know why my hair stood on end.'

Kerslake took the limp-bound volume in his gloved hands, rested it on his knees and then took off his gloves. From now on he touched no part of the car until he put his gloves on and left Farley. Taking his time he read the first entry in which, after Lady Jean had written that Bellmaster had made her an accomplice to the murder of Polidor, she went on to describe exactly how it had happened.

As he finished reading it and began to turn to the next marked entry Farley said to him, 'Pretty story, isn't it? But it's clear that in the kind of world they moved in . . . all this intelligence business . . . it was no more than par for the course. God, one reads about that kind of thing in books and it's just like a fairy story for adults. Doesn't touch you. But it happens. We all know that. What kind of people must they be? Makes your guts turn over. The Matherson thing was almost as primitive.'

Kerslake made no answer. He turned the pages to the next paper-slip marked entry, and found for a moment or two that he was just looking at the words written in the fine renaissance script without comprehending them. The little pen-and-ink drawing in the margin stood out boldly. It showed two stags locked in a rutting battle while a hind watched from the background. The stags had human faces, one, Lord Bellmaster's, clearly recognizable. The other was a face unknown to him but, he guessed, that of Matherson. The female in the background sported a woman's face which he recognized from the painting on the stairs at the Villa Lobita, as Lady Jean's. What kind of people could they be, Farley had asked. Well, his kind. Quint's kind. Just people – doing a dirty job which the world as it was made necessary. Birdcage gave you a sophisticated initial lecture on the validity of its ethics when you entered . . . so bloody convincing too. A crusade against evil until you took the field and found you were using the

Devil's own weapons with not a tithe of his honesty of purpose.

Control coming back to him, marshalled with a flick of self-anger, he read the diary entry.

It read.

Belly knew, of course, what Matty was after and afterwards was quite frank about it. He left Conary in the afternoon saying that he was driving south to get the late afternoon London train from Inverness. So that night for the first time I was alone with Matty. Such a dear, but in his way as deep as B. Not so good at handling his drink though. He left my room about three o'clock. At least he died with pleasant memories, falling down three flights of the tower stone steps and breaking his skull. I didn't hear a sound being fast asleep. My maid woke me at seven with the news.

B. phoned at eight to say that he had had trouble on the road and missed the train, but would take the morning one, and then asked how things had been? I said there was nothing I could tell him he did not know already and he laughed and said something about when love put stars in a man's eyes he should watch the way he walked. He told me when I met him two days later how he had come back and waited for Matherson to leave my room. There were a dozen ways he knew of getting into Conary without being seen. Matty was cremated at Golders Green. Over dinner afterwards B. gave me the emerald necklace which I sold later. I've hated emeralds ever since.

Kerslake closed the diary, saying, 'I don't think I want to read any more.'

'I don't blame you. He could twist her round his little finger once she'd kept her mouth shut about Polidor. You know ... sometimes I can't believe it. I've looked at Sarah and – you may find this hard to believe – been glad that she became a nun. If she'd been left free with that lot God knows what might have happened to her. The man is a bloody vulture. He'll deserve all he's going to get. Only one thing worries me, that's if there's going to be a lot of publicity when it all comes out. After all, it's Sarah's mother. Jesus, I feel quite sick about it. I don't want anything to muck up our relationship.'

'I'm sure she will understand. Let's face it, you only did what was clearly your duty.' Kerslake opened his briefcase and slipped the diary into it. 'We can only hand it now over to the right people and they will do the rest. They may be able to keep your name out of it.'

'That suits me. I just want to have it from me and forget it all. It's your baby now.'

'Quite so.' Keeping the briefcase on his knees Kerslake pulled on his left-hand glove slowly and then slipped his right hand into his coat pocket. What had to be done was as evil as anything which Bellmaster had ever done, no matter the official cover which Birdcage gave to its own. He was no better, not anywhere near as good, as the man who had come by night and slaughtered his father's fancy pigeons. Bellmaster had clearly relished every twist and turn and dark device which he used to further his ambitions and greed. He envied him that peace of mind ... or was it a mild madness, a detached semi-godlike conviction of the right to claim a different and justifiable set of ethics? He felt the metal of his weapon begin to warm against the palm of his hand, and distantly, it seemed, heard Farley saying, '... if this hotel thing in Shropshire comes through. And I don't see why it won't – well, it would be handy if your firm could take charge of all the legal details.'

'We'd be very glad to.'

Hand in his pocket he heard, without really comprehending, Farley talking on. 'Be a marvellous place for bringing up kids, too ... Have to watch the river, of course, until they can swim. I remember some fool of a man with a small toddler down at Mombasa once, took his eyes off him while he had a nap and—'

At three o'clock a Bellmaster tap print-out from the communications room was brought to Quint. Normally there were only two a day. One in the morning and the last at five-thirty. Any report in the interim meant that it was urgent and could merit immediate attention.

Alone he read it through. It read like a stage play excerpt, stripped of all directions or indications of mood or movements, but the lines of dialogue carried the name of the character speaking. He read fast, his eyes jumping ahead, taking in what was coming as the present word-images flowed into his consciousness.

BRANTON . . . Fact, I undid it. Ever heard of a book called
Dialogues of the Soul and Body *. . . by some Saint or other?*
BELLMASTER No, I haven't. . . .

Quint read on and as he did so reached out and lifted his telephone mouthpiece from its rest and above the words in his mind
caught the faint purring of the waiting instrument.

BELLMASTER Any man can be bought.
BRANTON Not this one, my lord.

He read on seeing the two men and the Russell Flint painting on
the wall which carried the bugging device that – so much had
they wanted Bellmaster – was manned twenty-four hours a day.

BELLMASTER Look, Branton – and I don't care what it costs me –
but we've got to get together on this. There's just got to be a way of
arranging this with Farley.
BRANTON There's only one way, my lord. Farley would never do
anything for you. He's not that kind. But I can . . .

His eyes jumped to the end of the speech, to read: (Sound of
shot. Smallish calibre. Considerable pause. Then—) *Sic transit*
your *gloria* bloody *mundi.*

Quint pulled the telephone to him and began to dial Geddy's
office number in Cheltenham. It was five minutes past three. At
half past three Kerslake was meeting Farley near Painswick. Say
twenty minutes for their talk – that made ten minutes to four
the deadline. That meant fifty-five minutes to put Geddy in the
picture and get him moving off to Painswick. Probably have to
walk some way to his car . . . Christ, it was going to be tight!
Cheltenham to Painswick – how far? He knew the area well.
Eight . . . ten miles? Could be done. But Geddy was no racing
driver. And Kerslake with Farley? Perhaps additional grace there
if, as he suspected, Kerslake would be slow to come to the point.
Not sure about Kerslake. He had a cynical bet with Warboys (they
always did with a new man. Fiver each in the kitty) that Kerslake
would never make it. Something Devonshire dumpling soft in him
he fancied. Let's hope so. Though, God knows, you could never
tell. Well, if he could not stop it then they would have to drop the

heavy fire curtain on the final scene. That would let Branton off the hook. Once he had made this call he would get someone round there to take over and start the cover-up. Suicide? No trouble. Geddy, Geddy, come on. *News has just come over the radio that Lord Bellmaster has committed suicide. Heard it on the car radio and as I happened to be in Stroud* ... Geddy would have no trouble with that one – *I thought I'd come up and tell you. No point in besmirching the man now that he is dead. Better just to destroy the diary.* And Geddy could take charge of it and send it on. Could be other stuff in it ...

He heard the click of Geddy's private telephone being lifted and his dry voice, saying, 'Geddy here.'

Farley was saying, '... and when it's all fixed up you must come and be our guest.'

'I'll look forward to it. What's in the river – salmon?'

'Salmon and sea trout. It's probably poached to hell at the moment. My aunt's no fisherwoman ...'

Sitting listening to him, part of him touched by the enthusiasm Farley was showing, part of his mind thinking of his own boyhood river, the Taw, Kerslake knew that he could not do it. What did it matter if he didn't? Only a comparatively few at Birdcage were ever selected for this kind of role and near half of them never made it. No blame came to them. Some just left, knowing that they could always be recalled, and some stayed on. There was plenty of other work. But if you wanted to get anywhere near the top you had to be blood-baptized. Quint's phrase. The metal against his palm was now quite warm against the sweat of his skin. How much did he want to end up near the top? Quint would release him, he knew. They never blocked that. He let the weapon fall free from his hand and wiped his damp palm dry against the lining of the pocket.

Farley said, 'I've wasted a hell of a lot of time over the years. But now I've got something worth while to live for and I'm going really to get my head down.' He smiled. 'Big brave words, eh? You were lucky to know you always wanted to be a solicitor and get a good partnership.'

'Oh, yes,' Kerslake said. 'I always knew what I wanted.' His hand closed round the metal of the weapon. The woman who had taken the dog for a walk had just come back and was coaxing it into the car. Unbidden, his secretary Joan came into his thoughts. When he returned by just looking at him she would know – yes or no. In a little while all the staff knew whether you had made it or not. Some of the girls preferred the ones who had.

The woman with the dog drove off. Farley was still talking and the clock in the fascia board almost read ten minutes to four.

chapter ten

It was nearly eight o'clock in the evening and the daylight still lingered. Quint stood at the window of Kerslake's room. The evening sky had the colour of a dirty duck's egg. Behind him he heard Kerslake light one of his very rare cigarettes. There had been no need to ask him the vital question. They had just looked at one another and he had seen what he had seen before in many young men's eyes. The thing that could not be kept out but the thing which only men like himself could recognize. Kerslake had tapped the blue suede diary on the desk and said, 'There it is.'

'Good.' That had been his only word as he went to the window. But now, without turning, he said, 'There may be stuff we can still use. I'll get it vetted.' His eyes watched a pelican by the lake raise itself high and flap its great wings. Above the trees he saw the lights burning in the windows of the Foreign Office. Bellmaster's death would not make too much stir there. They were used to death and disaster. Adventurers, cut-throats, the defence of the Empire. No empire now, but defence still needed and people to sacrifice themselves for the greatest good of the greatest number. Almost to himself but for the benefit of Kerslake, who had to be feeling in need of some comfort, however threadbare, he said, 'We shan't touch Branton. But, who knows, even at his age he might have future uses. You must listen to the tape some time. He was really enjoying himself. And he will more when they bring in a verdict of suicide. However, for all that in a way the final victory was Bellmaster's. He escaped.' He turned to face Kerslake. 'How do you feel?'

'Bloody.'

'One way or the other they all have after the first time. Rather different in your case, though. You'd still be waiting to learn the truth about yourself. I tried to get that fool Geddy to you in time, but he couldn't make it. You could have come back not knowing what you know about yourself now. A little interregnum to keep final self-knowledge still in the future. Well, there's no point in going too deeply into things tonight. You know now which side of the fence you stand. We'll have a cosy chat about it tomorrow or some time. I suggest you take yourself off, find some good company . . . be content to let tomorrow take care of itself.'

'I think I will.'

'Good.'

Moving by Kerslake, Quint touched him sympathetically on the shoulder and said, 'The river still flows under the town bridge at Barnstaple. Whatever we do and whatever we are the sun rises and the sun sets over a world which God made and man has mis-shapen.'

Quint gone, Kerslake sat on at his desk and knew that he was not the same man as the Kerslake who had last sat there. The Kerslake who sat now was crippled by self-discovery. The door opened and his secretary Joan came in. She closed the door gently and stood with her back to it looking at him, her face still. They looked at one another for a few moments and then he said, 'Does it show?'

She nodded. 'Always for a time. No matter which way it has been.'

'And which way has it been?'

She moved to him and sat on the corner of his desk, the new familiarity unremarkable either to him or to her, he knew.

'Your way.'

'Are you happy or sorry?'

'Neither. I leave my emotions at my flat each morning.'

He stood up and touched the side of her face with the back of his hand gently. 'Perhaps we could go there and then you could tell me.'

'I'd like that.' She took his hand and kissed its palm.

He brushed her brow with his lips as she did it and then, with a dry laugh, said, 'You're going to think this a curious question. But can I take a bath there?'

She stood up, but held on to his hand. 'Of course, but I think you should know that you are not the first one feeling as you do who has asked me that question.'

He smiled. 'We are all subject to the same emotional and occupational hazards here.'

Geddy sat in his study at the highly polished pedestal desk. His housekeeper had long retired to her room. Although he seldom drank after dinner he had now before him a silver tray on which rested a cut-glass decanter and glass. The wine which he had carefully decanted after dinner was a vintage *Château Margaux* which, after the first few sips, he realized was rapidly going over from its prime; but even so, through his body it was slowly spreading its benison and soothing the last, faint agitations of his mind. Glass in hand, he leaned back and stared at the Taiwan horse. In the old days, he thought, his father could have ridden his old bay cob from Cheltenham to Painswick almost as quickly as he had in his car that afternoon. Roadworks, traffic, old bangers crawling up Fiddler's Elbow and a great stream of impatient drivers behind baulked of any passing until the hilltop was reached.

And then when he had turned off on to the road to the golf club house Kerslake's car had come towards him. The road being narrow he had pulled over a little on to the grass verge. They had briefly stopped alongside one another and both had wound down their driving-seat windows. He had begun to speak, to explain why he had come, but Kerslake had cut him off fiercely, not demanding a reason for his presence, but ordering him to turn round and drive away. 'Just do as I say.' And then he had driven off. Well ... he sipped at the claret ... even after all these years the old Birdcage discipline had held. Whichever way it had been up there it was either too late to remedy it or unwise to rouse Farley's curiosity by his appearance. Geddy of Geddy, Parsons and Rank ... So he had turned and driven away. And still he knew nothing, had heard nothing and would take no steps to find out. Bad news could wait and good would keep. In between the coming of either a man could pray, except that he had long lost belief in prayer, though very content to go through its outward form in church. Life would never run short of tomorrows to give man the answers they sought today. Either Kerslake had lost his nerve and Farley was alive, or – since it did not strike him that Kerslake was likely to fail his first elimination assignment – he was dead. Black and white. There was no Tweedledee-ing out of it ... 'if it was so, it might be; and if it were so, it would be; but as it isn't, it ain't. That's logic.' Well ... not far from Birdcage logic, anyway.

He drank a little more wine, and stared at the photograph of himself as a boy in a boater on the mantelshelf. Boyhood, youth, and young manhood. And there it had stopped ... Oh, dear, the claret was making him a little fuddled. See Naples and die, they said. How true. That's exactly where he had died, all those years ago.

It was ten o'clock. Branton had had four large whiskies since dinner. Not that he had eaten much. Drink was the answer even though you knew you were going to stay sober. The door opened and Dolly came in. She flopped into the chair opposite him, reached out her hand for his glass and drained it.

'Easy, old girl.'

'More.'

He filled the glass from the bottle and stood up to fetch a clean glass for himself. Thank God for whisky. Did more than any parson could.

He said, 'How is she?'

'How would you think? How could any girl be? She's pole-axed with the injection the doctor gave her. But she's going to wake sometime and see it's daylight and that there's no Richard left in the world. Nothing left but life and living without him. What in God's name was it all about?'

'Don't ask me, old girl or Him. God says nothing. Perhaps He thinks it's wiser. We aren't grown-up enough to understand. I've seen the best chaps die. The good 'uns. While the bad 'uns walk through it. Unnatural selection, I call that. Time's the answer. Life, or whatever it is, like an everflowing stream. She'll get over it. In three or four years she'll find some nice chap. Human memory is no rock. It wears smooth fast.'

Dolly, tears in her eyes, looked up and moaned, 'Oh, God, Jimmy, I've forgotten to lock up those bloody hens.'

'Don't worry. I'll do it. You cut on up to bed. And take a couple of pills.' He stood beside her and held a hand comfortingly to her cheek for a moment before he went out.

As he walked down the drive to the chicken run he heard a vixen bark distantly. Young cubs about now, hungry bellies to be fed. The palest slip of the moon dying out of its last quarter showed briefly between clouds. Wrestling with the stiff catch on the wire-netting door to the fowl enclosure, he thought, I don't know, and I'm damned certain nobody else does. Nobody in the whole bloody world or anywhere else.

The vixen called again. The grass was wet from a sharp evening shower and the dampness soon soaked through his carpet slippers.

Peter Nieswand
The Underground Connection 90p

The tip-off came from the CIA in Riyadh. The PLO hit-men had pulled off a kidnap for five million dollars. Sources said they planned to 'spend' in London. There was nothing to go on – nothing except the mystery man Ziad, whose name cropped up all along the line. As London dozed in the June sunshine and Geneva prepared for another round of Middle East peace talks, the minutes ticked by to zero hour.

'The plotters are young, chilling pro-Palestinians; the avengers, workaday fuzz . . . the terrorist is on the streets' GUARDIAN

'Suspense, realism, cold-blooded horror . . . excellent'
EVENING NEWS

E. V. Thompson
Harvest of the Sun £1.25

A magnificent saga of passion and conflict in Africa a century ago . . . The ship was bound for Australia. Aboard, Josh Retallick and Miriam Thackeray, prisoners destined for the convict settlements – until their vessel was wrecked on the Skeleton Coast of South West Africa. Far from their Cornwall origins, the two strangers in a hostile land meet Bushmen and Hereros, foraging Boers and greedy traders in an alien world of ivory tusks and smuggled guns.

'A host of characters and adventures' MANCHESTER EVENING NEWS

Ashley Carter
Panama 95p

Philippe Jean Bunau-Varilla – by profession a skilled and ambitious engineer, by inclination a sensualist and womanizer. The strange and lovely Madelon enters his life. Unwanted wife, a ravishing beauty scarred by love, she comes to dominate Philippe's every moment . . . But he was destined to build a waterway between two mighty oceans, a project bedevilled by disease and disaster in a hostile land of vicious voodoo warriors.

Nicholas Monsarrat
The Master Mariner:
book 1 **Running Proud** £1.50

'He will not die: he will wander the wild waters until all the seas run dry . . .'

The flawed courage of one man imperilled Admiral Drake's masterstroke on the day the English fireships sailed against the Armada in the Calais Roads. That coward was Matthew Lawe, Drake's coxswain, cursed from that day to sail the seas for all time to purge his guilt – through centuries of wind, wave and warfare . . . with the doomed Hudson to the Arctic, to the sunbleached Main with Morgan the pirate, as clerk to Pepys at the Admiralty, with Cook to bloodstained Hawaii and with Nelson at Cape Trafalgar.

'A rich, rare and noble feast' THE TIMES

'The cruel sea and the valiant men who sailed on it through all the generations' DAILY MAIL

David Toulmin
Harvest Home 95p

These stories bring to vivid life the world of the Buchan farming folk of half a century ago. John Rettie, doctor to man and beast, whose pony brought him safely home sober or no . . . Maggie Lawrence who found a suicide deep in her well . . . Jotty McGillivray, the fiddle-playing blacksmith, and Souter Duthie, whose shop was the place for news and a blether and smoke thick enough to cut with a scythe . . .

'A born writer who recreates . . . the incredibly hard, rough life of farm workers in north-east Scotland . . . moving, tender, astonishing, funny and grim' SUNDAY TIMES

'A commemorative edifice to a way of life that was unique and has passed into history' ABERDEEN PRESS AND JOURNAL